The Gift at
SUGAR SAND INN

SUGAR SAND BEACH
BOOK 1

LEIGH DUNCAN

The Gift at Sugar Sand Inn
Sugar Sand Beach Series, Book #1

Copyright ©2021 by Leigh D. Duncan

This book is a work of fiction. The characters, events, and places portrayed in this book are products of the author's imagination and are either fictitious or are used fictitiously. Any similarity to real person, living or dead, is purely coincidental and not intended by the author.

Digital ISBN: 978-1-944258-24-5
Print ISBN: 978-1-944258-25-2
Gardenia Street Publishing

Published in the United States of America

Welcome to Sugar Sand Beach!

Escape to Sugar Sand Beach with Michelle Robinson and her best friends for a second chance at all life has to offer.

At forty-five, Michelle has a great life. A husband who loves her. Two children on the fast track to success. A beautiful home in the rolling hills of Virginia. And three of the best friends a girl could ever want.

But with the sudden death of Michelle's husband of twenty-five years, her life turns upside down.

Forced to sell their forever home and at odds with her children, Michelle faces a bleak future. Until an unexpected inheritance starts her on a path paved with bright possibilities.

Join Michelle, Reggie, Nina and Erin as they journey to Sugar Sand Beach where fresh opportunities for life, love and happiness are as limitless as the blue Florida skies.

One

Michelle

*L*ight played across Michelle Robertson's eyelids. Despite the thick drapes she'd chosen for their room-darkening features, a beam of bright sunlight streamed through a small gap in the panels. She must not have closed the curtains all the way last night. She batted at the glare that hit her square in the eyes. When that failed, she pulled the covers over her head. No luck. Not even the best Egyptian cotton sheets could block the sun.

With a resigned sigh, she rolled over. She might as well get up and face the day. But why bother? She glanced at the pillow that lay, smooth and undented, on the other side of the bed. Allen was gone—dead a year tomorrow. Her throat tightened. Tears filled her eyes.

She didn't bother to blink them away. Oh, how she missed that man. His laughter. His arm around her shoulders. His support. She wished he was here right now to tell her life was precious and not to waste a minute of it. But the man she'd loved since the first moment she'd seen him, the man she'd spent twenty-five years sleeping beside, the man she was supposed to grow old with had disappeared from her life in a blink of an eye. She gazed through her tears at the clock on the nightstand. Nine fifteen. She eased into a sitting position and groaned.

Maybe she shouldn't have had that second glass of wine last night. It always made her maudlin. Not that anyone cared. Or was even around to notice. These days, she padded about the big, two-story Colonial all by herself. Ashley and Aaron had been devastated by their father's sudden heart attack, of course. But at twenty-one, the twins were young and resilient. They couldn't relate to a grief so heavy it made getting out of bed a monumental chore. A week after the funeral, Michelle had encouraged them to get back to their normal lives, and, relieved, they'd both returned to the university. It was just as well. She didn't want them sitting around, worrying about their middle-aged mother who, after twenty-five years of marriage, suddenly found herself adrift. Without purpose.

Enough of that.

She grabbed the notebook and pen she'd left on the nightstand last night. The bereavement counselor down at the Y had suggested making a list as a way to anchor her day. Hers consisted of only three things: Dress. Brush teeth. Check mail.

She lifted the pen, tempted to scratch through that last item. Letters and envelopes spilled from the basket on the antique secretary by the front door. She'd let the mail accumulate for far too long. Just the thought of opening it all was enough to make her want to climb back under the covers. Instead, she gave herself a stern talking to. She was better than this. She didn't want to spend every day in a downward spiral that left her toddling off to bed in an alcohol-induced haze after midnight each night. That wasn't her life. That wasn't *her*. Allen had been gone nearly a year. It was high time she got her act together and faced life head-on.

Which she'd do...as soon as she had her morning coffee.

Or maybe after she got past an anniversary of the worst kind tomorrow.

Tossing another look at the rich Waverly print draped at the windows—okay, she did dearly love that print—she forced herself to her feet and headed for the dressing area. His and hers walk-in closets stood facing one another in the hallway that led to the master bath. She ignored the one on the left—she hadn't looked beyond the door to Allen's since the day she selected an appropriately dark suit for his funeral, and she wasn't about to start now. Not if she was going to get her life back in order, she wouldn't.

She turned to the right. A faint trace of her favorite perfume greeted her as her feet sank into the plush carpet inside her own large and well-appointed dressing area. On one side, perfectly creased slacks hung in precise order, light to dark, summer to winter. Opposite them stretched a long row of blouses and dresses in a variety of prints and hues. One look at the rainbow of colors made her head swim enough that she clung to the high-backed chair in front of the mirror.

Baby steps, she told herself. She'd allowed herself a year to mourn, but it was time to start living again. Still, she wouldn't rush, wouldn't push. She'd take it one small step at a time, like all the books said she should. Today, she'd promised not to lounge around in her pajamas until bedtime, and she wouldn't. She grabbed a set of gray flannel from a stack at the back of the closet. Sweat pants counted as clothes, didn't they?

Two hours and three cups of coffee later, she tossed the last envelope into the trash can and placed the final bill on a deceptively short pile. She shoved her fingers through hair that hadn't seen the inside of a salon in so long, the straight strands of her chin-length bob tickled her shoulders. How had things gotten so out of hand?

She plucked a thin sheet from the top of the stack and frowned. Paramedics had tried to revive Allen all the way to the hospital, where the cardiac team had pulled out all the stops. Their efforts had been futile. Her husband's doctor swore Allen was gone before his head struck the Oriental carpet in his office. So why had the hospital and doctors held her responsible for thousands of dollars in medical bills for procedures and drugs that hadn't done one bit of good?

It just wasn't fair.

Then again, these days, not much was.

She shoved her hair behind her ears. Determined to look at the bright side, she tapped her fingers on the distressed kitchen table she'd transformed with chalk paint the year the twins had gone off to college. The year she'd thought adjusting to her newfound status as an empty-nester was the toughest change she'd have to make for a long time.

Leigh Duncan

The bright side. There had to be one, right?

The twins' college expenses were paid for. That was a plus. She and Allen had poured money into Virginia's state-run program starting the day Ashley and Aaron were born. Next May, her son and daughter would graduate from the University of Virginia debt-free. Which, according to the whispered conversations among her friends, was a rarity these days.

Unfortunately, that just about wrapped it up for the good news. She tapped the checkbook. Medical bills had taken a huge bite out of Allen's life insurance policy. Funeral expenses had taken another chunk. What was left had barely covered the cost of running the house for a year. There was little more in the checking account than enough to pay another three months on the mortgage. Even with that, she'd have to squeeze every nickel until it squealed in order to pay for niceties like electricity, gas and, oh yeah, food.

She frowned at a midsection that pouched out a little more than it had a year ago. Why did carbs provide solace for grief? More to the point, why didn't fresh veggies do the same thing? She didn't know the answer, but after a year of damping her tears with donuts and cake, she could stand to lose ten pounds. Okay, to be honest, fifteen wouldn't hurt. Before Allen had

6

keeled over in the middle of a phone call, she'd overheard several of the girls at the gym talking about the benefits of fasting. At the time, she'd wondered why they didn't just call it The Starvation Diet. But hey. She'd give it a try. If it worked, both her body and her pocketbook would thank her.

Plus, it was high time she started thinking about her future. A future that included a j-o-b. She hadn't held one of those since she'd had the twins. Which meant she'd been out of the market for what? Nearly two dozen years? How on earth had so much time slipped past? Turning forty-five hadn't been nearly as traumatic for her as it had for some of her friends. But that was before. Before her husband died and left her to face an uncertain future. A future where youth was the name of the game. Or so Allen had said when he got laid off by the tech company he'd gone to work for straight out of college. She pinched her belly. She had to admit it, the extra fifteen pounds she'd packed on made her look like someone's grandma. She'd be much more apt to land a job once she lost them.

Which left the little matter of finding someone who'd hire a middle-aged woman with absolutely zero job experience. Oh, she could decorate circles around most interior designers.

Her casseroles and appetizers had starred at countless potlucks. Her Sunday brunches were the stuff people wrote home about. As the wife of a senior vice president of a large tech company, she'd thrown so many parties and organized so many charitable events, she was on a first-name basis with every caterer, florist and baker within a twenty-mile radius of their Fairfax, Virginia, home. Great skills, but she hardly thought they'd be among the requirements for an entry-level job answering phones or filing papers in a dull and dreary office.

Of course, she wouldn't be in the job market, wouldn't be facing such an uncertain future if Allen hadn't died. If he hadn't lost his job in a merger with another, bigger tech company over two years ago. At fifty, Allen hadn't been ready to throw in the towel. He'd loved his job. He'd planned to work well into his seventies, then enjoy the fruits of his labors throughout a long and quite comfortable retirement.

The layoff had sucked, big-time, but he'd been determined to bounce back by launching his own start-up company. To hear her husband tell it, his new business venture couldn't fail. He'd made success sound so simple and straightforward—so probable—that she'd had no choice but to agree with him. She'd supported him when he emptied their savings accounts and raided their retirement account in his effort to get the new company off the ground. When he'd asked her to co-sign the loan on the beautiful brick Colonial they'd purchased soon after the twins were born, she hadn't so much as raised an eyebrow. She'd simply assumed—as he had—that Allen would pay back the money once his new business landed its first big contract. He swore he'd do exactly that, too.

Only things hadn't quite turned out that way.

There'd been no warning, no sign. Neither of them had suspected that her strong, strapping husband, a man who played racquetball twice a week and ran four miles the other days rain or shine, would succumb to a cardiac event while sitting at his desk and talking on the phone.

She shook her head. Nope. She hadn't seen that coming.

She lifted the cover of the checkbook, stole another glimpse of the balance and swallowed. Three months. She had enough of the insurance money left to last three months. And then what? She wouldn't kid herself. She had no idea what entry-level positions paid these days, but she was pretty sure the salary wouldn't cover her mortgage and living expenses. That left her with two choices. She could stick her head in the sand

and pretend everything was Pollyanna perfect. Or she could face facts.

Either way, she was going to lose the house. No doubt about it. In three months, give or take, the bank would almost certainly foreclose. When that happened, she could kiss what little equity she had goodbye. Or she could sell now and walk away with…something.

She drummed her fingers on the table. As if she was seeing it for the first time, she glanced through the big bay window to the yard, where roses and azaleas ran riot. Her body wasn't the only thing she'd let go this year. The yard cried out for attention, too.

She hauled her gaze back inside and, for the first time in a long time, gave her home a critical look. In the living room, the soapstone top on the fireplace mantel that once graced a room in the long-since demolished National Hotel was in great shape, but Aaron had gouged a long scratch on one leg of the wooden side while dribbling his soccer ball one spring. To fix it the right way, she'd have to refinish the entire unit. The housekeeper came, regular as clockwork, every Tuesday morning. In between her visits, empty takeout containers sprouted atop the kitchen counters like clover in the spring. The sink leaked. On the other side of French doors, leaves and algae floated in the once-pristine backyard pool. Ugh. The whole house needed a good sprucing.

She grabbed a pen and paper and began jotting down a list of problems she'd have to address before she called a real estate agent. By the time she finished, she'd filled three pages, and long shadows stretched from the weeping willow and the oak trees that lined the backyard. Just looking at the list was exhausting. She rubbed her forehead, where a headache threatened.

She pushed herself away from the table. She'd accomplished enough for one day. She'd tackle the first item on her list tomorrow. She'd start her diet then, too. For now, though, a coffee cake in the kitchen called her name. She paused. She really ought to toss the carb-laden treat into the garbage and get a head start on starving herself. But she'd paid good money for the cake, and in her precarious financial position, who knew when she'd be able to afford to splurge again? She wouldn't let it go to waste.

Although a tiny part of her said that wasn't the *waist* she should worry about, she tossed the dregs of her coffee into the sink. Opening the box from her favorite bakery, she inhaled the scent of cream-cheese filling and sugary white icing.

She cut a good-size hunk of the heavenly dessert and sat down at the round table in the cozy kitchen nook.

Tomorrow. She'd start her new diet and tackle that list tomorrow. The day after at the latest.

Two

Erin

E rin Bradshaw struggled to keep her smile in place as she exchanged firm hand-shakes with Joe Caruci. Her fingers closed over the bills the construction foreman from New York slipped into her palm. She widened her smile a smidge. Tipping her was the least Joe could do. He and his wife had been royal pains from the moment they stepped from a gas-guzzling rental car onto Marathon Key's white, sandy beach an hour behind schedule. Ordinarily, Erin would have chalked them up as no-shows and been long gone, but she'd wanted to get out on the water one more time. Besides, the couple had paid in advance for her guide services. So she'd stuck around, but she soon wished she hadn't.

Despite a serious case of frayed nerves—caused, no doubt, by her clients' constant complaints—Erin thanked Joe for the tip. She even managed a smile for Joe's wife, Barbara. Tucking the money into the pocket of her shorts, she forced herself to sound cheerful and upbeat as she offered the couple a bright, "I hope you enjoyed the tour. Come back and see me again next year."

But not if I see you first.

She'd taken at least a thousand customers on kayak tours through the maze of canals that ran between the thick patches of red mangroves in the Keys. Most people exclaimed about the natural beauty, the plentiful wildlife, the quiet. Not these two. The first words out of the mouths of the paunchy Joe and his bleached-blond trophy wife when they arrived at the launching spot had been, "Oh, my gawd, the humidity!" and "I'm hawt." Still, Erin had tried to make her last tour of the season a good one.

It should have been.

The morning had dawned clear and bright, with only the barest wisps of clouds in a perfectly blue sky. With temperatures at a balmy eighty-two, a light breeze kept the mosquitoes and no-see-ums at bay. Despite getting a late start, they saw a pair of bottle-nosed dolphins working the shallows in search of a midmorning snack. The efforts of the big mammals drew the attention of pelicans, which took turns diving into the waves, hoping for a leftover or two. A short paddle had taken her clients to the mangroves, where overhead branches and leaves created a shady canopy. Intent on giving her customers their money's worth, Erin had paddled slowly past a rookery of herons and pointed out ibis standing stilt-like in the clear water.

Too bad Joe and Barb hadn't seen any of it. They'd spent most of the trip complaining and bickering over which one of them had thought paddling through mangrove tunnels was a great idea. According to them, it wasn't. Whenever Erin slowed to a stop, each of them whipped out their cell phones. But instead of snapping blurry pictures of the wildlife, they'd competed to see which of them could talk the loudest. Erin doubted the pair had even noticed the roseate spoonbills and osprey they'd paid so handsomely to see. As for the manatees, Erin had been all but certain Barbara was going to capsize—her cell phone glued to her ear—when one of the gentle giants had surfaced five feet off her bow. The woman's scream had frightened an entire flock of egrets into flight.

Now, while Joe and Barbara headed for their rental car, Erin peeked at the bills she'd slipped into her pocket. Her eyes narrowed. Two fives.

That's it?

While her clients had stood idly by drinking coffee from their non-recyclable cups, she'd single-handedly hauled their kayaks down off the boat trailer and put them in the water. She'd strapped the couple into life preservers, settled them into their boats and taken them to all her best spots…and they'd tipped her a measly ten bucks? She shook her head. They should be ashamed of themselves.

Or maybe it was her fault. She couldn't deny that her patience had worn thin. And not just with these particular tourists but with others as well. As a matter of fact, her whole way of life didn't thrill her as much as it once had.

She shook her head. Was she getting old? At forty-five, she'd spent the last twenty years shuttling back and forth between Seward, Alaska, and the Florida Keys. The money she made as an eco-tour guide at opposite ends of the country paid for month long trips to exotic locations like Kenya, French Polynesia and the Yucatan. Though she didn't regret a minute of her nomadic lifestyle, lately, in the quiet moments, she'd begun to wonder what it'd feel like to put down roots somewhere.

She chuckled. Wait till Chelle found out the woman who prided herself on having a rootless existence was thinking about settling down. Her best friend would laugh out loud.

Except, well, she hadn't heard Chelle laugh in a long time. Not since her husband of twenty-five years had worked himself into a fatal heart attack last year.

Crap.

Erin glanced at the date on the waterproof watch strapped to her wrist. Tomorrow was the anniversary of Allen's death. She'd nearly let it slip by without so much as a phone call. She adjusted her sunglasses and stared out over the crystal-clear water. She might not know where she was headed next week, but she knew one thing—she needed to work harder at being a better friend.

And what about the others? She stretched, rolling a sudden tension from her shoulders. Nina hadn't returned her last phone call, but that wasn't unusual. A line cook in a restaurant with a much-coveted Michelin star, she worked days and nights on end without a break. As for Reggie, her sister had her own special problems. She'd touch base with both of them before she packed.

But she would pack because tonight was *the* night. As she did every year at about this time, she'd drive up to Islamorada before dusk and feast on fresh seafood at her favorite little seafood dive. The place was strictly BYOB, and though she wasn't much of a drinker, she'd bring along a nice pinot. Back at the cottage, she'd polish off the bottle before throwing a dart at the world map she'd pinned to the closet door of her cottage. Wherever the dart landed, that's where she'd spend the next six weeks until it was time to head north to Alaska.

She tightened her ponytail.

For the first time in as long as she could remember, the thought of planning another trip, slinging her duffle over one shoulder and heading out to points unknown sounded an awful lot more like work than fun.

Three

Nina

Nina Gray inhaled the scent of the fragrant red pepper sauce that played a starring role in the head chef's signature dishes. *Heaven.* To be sure she'd nailed the recipe, she swirled a bit of stale bread through the thick topping and tasted. The flavor of blackened bell peppers exploded on her tongue. Roasted almonds and hazelnuts added just the right amount of crunch, while hearty sourdough bread crumbs lent texture and balance. She took a plastic lid from the stack over her station. After writing today's date and her initials on the cover, she started to close the container. Motion at her elbow stalled her movements.

"Nina, isn't it?" The man in the white chef's coat didn't wait for an answer. He brandished a small spoon. "A taste?"

Chad.

She'd been wondering how long it would take the new guy to meddle with her station. Tomas, the previous sous chef at Arlington's famed Cafe Chez Jacques, had respected his team. The kitchen's second-in-command had rarely interfered with the line cooks while they worked, only offering a bit of advice here or a teaching moment there. This new guy, though, he was a piece of work. In his first week on the job, he'd already reduced the pastry chef to tears...twice. He'd accused several assistants of waste and had spent an entire day instructing the grill cook in the steps he needed to follow in order to achieve the perfect char-broil. *As if.* Charlie had manned the grill for longer than she'd worked at the ever-popular restaurant.

It had only been a matter of time before Chad sauntered down the aisle to the saucier's station. Today it looked like it was her turn. Great. *Not.* She stiffened.

"Yes, chef." Her back ramrod straight, Nina slid the container toward him. Silently, she dared the new sous chef to find anything wrong with the dish. She'd been the head saucier for over a year now. Her work had been flawless. Even the head chef said so.

"Needs more salt."

Before she could object, much less stop him, the man grabbed a ramekin full of Himalayan and dumped out enough pink crystals for two entire batches of sauce. Nina stifled a groan. Did the guy have any idea that he'd just ruined the topping for tonight's swordfish? Swiping a piece of bread through the sauce that had taken hours to prepare, she offered it to Chad.

"Taste, chef?"

Chad popped the crumb into his mouth and chewed. "Brighter." He frowned. "But it needs… something."

How about less salt? Ya think?

Nina rolled her lips between her front teeth and bit down, hard. She'd gone toe-to-toe with an self-important chef once before. She wouldn't make the same mistake a second time.

Chad snapped his fingers. "More texture. That's what it needs. Fix this." He shoved the bowl aside.

"Yes, chef." Nina nodded as if what the man had said made a lick of sense. Stirring in more crushed nuts and bread crumbs would throw the depth of flavors, the delicate balance of bitter and sweet completely out of whack.

"Well, what are you waiting for? Carry on, Nina."

"Yes, chef." Watching Chad head for his next target, Nina traded raised eyebrows with Charlie. They both knew there was only one way to fix the mess Chad had created. She'd have to start over. She sighed, thinking of the time she'd spend assembling the mise en place, charring another batch of peppers, toasting more almonds and hazelnuts, and putting the fresh sauce through the food processor. Thank goodness, she'd finished her other tasks for the day and had intended to take the evening off. She'd have just enough time to create a fresh batch before the dinner rush.

Intending to dump the ruined sauce once Chad was out of sight, she pushed it to the back of her station. "Taking my break," she called to no one in particular. Jacques, the head chef, would stay in his office for another hour or so, and their new sous chef hadn't figured out yet that scheduling breaks was part of his job description.

"Heaven save me from baby chefs," she muttered as she removed her apron.

She grabbed a bottle of water from the fridge and headed outside. As the door swung closed behind her, traffic sounds replaced the clatter of pots and pans and the usual chaos of the busy kitchen. The rich smells of meat on the grill, simmering tomatoes and onions were instantly smothered by the faint stench that rose from the dumpster at the far end of the alley. As far as places to relax and chill went, she'd known better. But after dealing with young Chad, she couldn't afford to be choosy. She twisted the cap on the water bottle and downed half of the cold liquid in deep swallows before sinking onto an empty vegetable crate.

The back door of the kitchen swung open, and Charlie joined her. At six-two, the muscular black man cut an imposing figure, even with a hair net poking out of his shirt pocket. She swallowed a laugh. That was another of the useless changes Chad had instituted in his short reign. Charlie's polished head was as smooth rolled fondant.

She tipped the plastic bottle in his direction. "Young Chad found better things to do than teach you how to finish a steak with butter?"

"Chef called him into the office. Something about a problem with next week's schedule."

She nodded. "I wondered how long that would take." As second-in-command of the busy kitchen, Chad made out the weekly work schedule as part of his job responsibilities. His first attempt had been a disaster of overlapping shifts and gaps. It sounded like his second one wasn't much better. "He's young, still wet behind the ears. Chef will straighten him out." She could only hope.

"I don't know. He thinks he knows every-thing. Has a lot of newfangled ideas he picked up in culinary school. My money says he won't last the month." Charlie pulled up another crate and lowered his considerable bulk onto it.

"I wouldn't count on it." Nina shook her head. "I heard he's related to one of the owners. A nephew or something."

"You don't say." Charlie grunted. "Him and me ain't ever gonna be best buds. If you know what I mean."

"I hear ya." Charlie had presence, and Chad had been on his case from the moment they met. Nina refused to believe it was personal—Charlie was as nice as they came. She thought it was far more likely that Chad saw the man as his competition. After all, Charlie had been the senior member of their staff. In a perfect world, the position of sous chef would have been his. But she'd learned long ago that nothing was perfect in the restaurant business. She stretched.

"You ever wonder if we're getting too old for

all this?" Cooking was a young person's game. At forty-five, only the head chef had more years on her.

Charlie pulled the hair net from his pocket and twirled it around his finger. "Doesn't matter. I'm a long way from retirement. I got mouths to feed, a mortgage to pay."

"You ever want more than just being a line cook?" Even seated, she had to look up at the taller man. "Maybe run your own kitchen?"

The big man shook his head. "Not gonna happen. My cousin and me, we talked about opening up a little barbecue joint. Nothing fancy. Just ribs and pulled pork. Maybe some chicken. Things never worked out. Now that the kids are getting older, the wife's lookin' at colleges. She says it's gonna take every dime I got and more to get 'em through. So, nah. Long as I can cook good food in a place that 'ppreciates my skills, I'm happy." He stood. "I'll give this youngster a few weeks to settle in, but if things don't get better between him and me, well, there's lots of other places I can work."

"You got that right." In busy Arlington, openings for grill cooks were as plentiful as cherry blossoms around the Tidal Basin.

"How about yourself? You angling for a job as head chef one day?"

"Not anymore. There was a time…" Her voice trailed off. She'd been on the fast track once. Fifteen years ago, though, a single mistake had derailed her career. If she'd known how long it would take to climb out of the hole she'd dug for herself that night, she might have found an entirely new line of work. She cleared her throat. She'd really wanted to run her own kitchen. Truth be told, she still did. But she'd faced facts. Opening a restaurant took a boatload of money. Since she only had to fend for Mr. Pibbs and herself, she had a healthy savings account. But she didn't have near enough to open her own place.

Charlie slipped the hair net over his bald head. "I'm heading back in. You?"

Nina hefted the bottle. Water sloshed against the sides. "In a bit. I came in early. Thanks to Chad, it'll be another late night." Not that she had anything better to do with her time. Single and, okay, she'd admit it, a bit of a workaholic, she answered only to herself and Mr. Pibbs. The tabby never complained about her long hours. He was perfectly content with curling up at her side while she slept, as long as he got his tuna and kibbles.

She downed another slug of water. Her phone buzzed. She slipped it from the pocket of her chef's pants. The number in the display put a smile on her face.

"Hey Erin," she said, glad to hear from one of her best friends. "Where are you?" Erin spent summers jetting about the globe. She could just as easily be calling from the Antarctic as New Zealand. Assuming Antarctica even had cell phone service, that is.

"Headed home. My flight gets in around noon tomorrow."

"Oh? Your folks okay?" Erin had been born and raised in Fairfax, but her parents had relocated to West Virginia when her father retired.

"They're good. But tomorrow's the anniversary of Allen's death. I thought Chelle could use some company. You in?"

"Absolutely." Nina thought furiously. Taking the day off meant she'd have to work even later tonight, but it'd be worth it to be there for her friend. "I'll have to hustle to get things done here at the restaurant." In addition to the red pepper sauce, she was running low on the spicy andouille cream Chef Josh used in the Friday special. She'd make a fresh batch before she left for the night. Her two assistants could handle the rest for one day. "You want to call Reggie?"

"Hmmm. Would you mind? Last time I

visited the folks, she was kinda distant. I probably did something to upset her, but I'm not sure what."

"She hasn't mentioned anything to me. But sure. I'll give her a call."

She, Michelle and Erin had been best buds since the first day of kindergarten. Erin's younger sister had evened out the group when they'd all returned home for their first summer break from college. Over the next twenty-plus years, they'd turned to one another for dating advice, supported one another through failed relationships and divorces, celebrated victories and milestones. Though they rarely got together more than once or twice a year these days, each of them knew they could count on the others to drop everything in times of trouble. Like they had last year when Allen passed so unexpectedly. For the next month, they'd taken turns making sure someone stayed at Michelle's side day and night.

"Let's meet at Chelle's around two," Erin suggested. "I'll bring the wine. Can we count on you for a cheese plate?"

Nina laughed. "I think I can do better than a few crackers and some cheddar." She pictured a beautiful charcuterie board, filled with the perfect blend of sharp and mild, savory and sweet.

"Good. We'll Uber someplace fun for dinner."

"There's a new gastropub near City Hall downtown," Nina suggested. She'd been dying to check out the place.

"Works for me. Bring an overnight bag in case Chelle needs us all to stay over."

Nina grinned. She hadn't taken a full day off in nearly a year. It'd be great to have a girls' night out with her friends.

Erin's voice dropped. "Do you know how she's doing?"

"I saw her last month. Regina and I took her to dinner at The Grill." Known for mouthwatering burgers and the best cheesecake this side of New York City, the restaurant was a Fairfax institution. "She's hanging in there, but you could tell it's been tough." She could only imagine. She shook her head. She had no idea what it must be like to lose someone after twenty-five years of marriage, and the way her life was going, she never would. Most chefs worked long hours, usually showing up at the restaurant by midmorning and working into the wee hours. That kind of life didn't mesh well with a home and family. The one time she'd been tempted to give it a try, she'd ended up getting burned so badly, the smoke from that failed relationship still haunted her.

"Okay, well, I'll wear my raincoat in case there's waterworks."

"Ha ha. I see what you did there." She pitched her empty water bottle into a nearby recycling bin. She'd been away from her station long enough. "Look. I gotta run. See you tomorrow."

"Yeah. Tomorrow."

When the screen went black, Nina sent Regina a quick text and rose. Twisting back and forth, she worked a few kinks out of her back and smoothed a hand over her chef's jacket. Having delayed the inevitable as long as possible, she slipped inside. She stopped only long enough to wash her hands before she headed to the cooler, where she filled a basket with red bell peppers. It was going to be a long night. The sooner she got started on it, the sooner she'd head home to Mr. Pibbs.

Four

Reggie

*Y*our HGC levels haven't changed. I'm sorry, Mrs. Frank."

Not. Pregnant. Reggie's head pounded. Her vision tunneled. Surprisingly dry-eyed, she sat on the edge of the bed and fought nausea. "So I'm not pregnant?" she asked, just in case she'd misunderstood. In case—this time—the nurse had gotten it wrong.

"No. I'm afraid not. Dr. Thomas would like to see you in the office in two weeks to discuss options. Hang on, okay? I'll connect you with the appointment desk."

A soft moan escaped her lips.

"Mrs. Frank?"

"Yes?" she asked dully.

"Can I connect you with the appointment desk?"

"No." She punched the End Call button.

She couldn't. Not yet. She needed time. To mourn the baby who never was. To gather her resources. To pray for strength. Maybe tomorrow, she'd be ready to try again. Or next week. Or next month. But not today. Besides, what was the rush? She'd have to wait six weeks before they could start the process over again anyway. The shots. The mood swings. The endless waiting. All in hopes of hearing the voice on the other end of the line say the magic words, "Your HGC levels are up. Congratulations. You're pregnant."

So far, that hadn't happened. Not the first time and, apparently, not the fifth. The next attempt would be her sixth.

If there was a next time. Sam had sworn he was done with it all. The expense. The regimentation. The constant pressure.

He'd change his mind, though, wouldn't he? He knew how important having a baby was to her. To them.

But what if he didn't change his mind? Would they try for a surrogate? She shook her head. She'd heard too many horror stories of couples who'd gone that route only to have the birth mother back out at the last minute. She couldn't, wouldn't risk it. No, another round of IVF was the only answer, the only way she'd ever end up with a baby of her own in her arms.

She'd simply have to convince Sam to give it one more try.

She rose on shaky legs, went into the bathroom and splashed cold water on her face. Poor Sam. He worked so hard. A few months ago, the senior partners had handed him his first big case. His "big break," he'd called it. It must be a bear—he'd certainly grown as grumpy as one. Of course, working far past closing every day of the week and going into the office on weekends, too—that would wear anyone down. Tonight, though, knowing the test results would be in, he'd promised to be home by seven.

She brightened a bit at the thought of them spending a rare evening together. Between his long hours and her schedule at the plant nursery, most days they rarely caught more than a glimpse of each other. But tonight would be different. Tonight, they'd have each other all to themselves. In honor of the occasion, she'd fix his favorite pork roast. Make those tiny potatoes and carrots he liked, too. If she didn't waste time, she could even bake an apple pie for dessert. It'd be like old times—the two of them sitting down to eat together, swapping stories about their day, looking forward to the future. Somehow, she'd manage to tell him that this round of IVF hadn't worked, that they'd have to try again.

The thought triggered a fresh onslaught of tears. She brushed them away. She didn't have time for those now. There'd be plenty of time for crying later. When she shed tears of joy while she held their baby in her arms.

By six thirty, the mouthwatering smell of roasted pork wafted in the air of the two-bedroom apartment on the outskirts of Fairfax. Reggie studied the table in the cozy breakfast nook that served as their dining room. The good china had been a wedding present from his family. She normally reserved it for holidays and birthdays, but tonight it sparkled atop a floral print tablecloth. Spotless glassware and silverware gleamed at the two place settings. Candles flickered on either side of a low arrangement of pink roses and white hydrangea. She frowned. Something wasn't quite…

She snuffed out the candles. Dinner by candlelight on a weeknight was a bit over the top. Removing the pair of tapers and their short, squat candlesticks, she returned them to their usual place on the bookshelf.

On the other side the kitchen counter, a timer dinged. She rushed to the oven and peered inside. A tiny bit of sauce bubbled through a slit in the perfectly golden crust. Removing the apple pie from the oven, she placed it on a cooling rack. Her tummy growled as the scent of cinnamon mingled with the roast. The good smells triggered a smile, her first since the call from the doctor's office this morning.

Sipping water, she made a special note to thank Nina. Her friend preached that good food was a key to a happy marriage and had insisted on giving her several cooking lessons. She'd needed them. She certainly hadn't picked up any pointers from her mother. Edwina's idea of "cooking" involved rooting around in the freezer and sticking whatever she found in the microwave. And Erin wasn't much better. In all of her thirty-five years, Reggie'd never once seen her older sister actually cook something from scratch. Not that she saw Erin much to begin with. Between the ten-year gap in their ages and Erin's tendency to disappear for months at a time, they'd never so much as baked cookies together.

So, yeah, she owed Nina big-time for the lessons. They'd truly been a blessing. Without them, she'd probably still be serving burnt chicken and underdone vegetables for dinner each night.

A key rattled in the front-door lock. Regina took a deep breath. *Show time.* Mustering her courage, she smoothed a hand down the front of the tunic she wore over black leggings and made sure everything was ready for her husband. She smiled dreamily. She'd gotten lost in Sam's dark eyes the moment they met at a college mixer her senior year at UVA. Six months after graduation, she'd walked down the aisle in front of their family and friends, and he'd promised to make her every dream come true.

The truth was, she didn't ask for much. She certainly didn't need to drive the latest model car. Her gracefully aging pickup truck was actually perfect for delivering twenty-pound bags of mulch or a dozen flats of sod to customers. While many of their friends and co-workers had traded in their small apartments for houses with big yards, she didn't mind at all living in the cramped apartment close to the Metro station.

No, all she wanted, all she'd ever asked for was a baby. And if they needed a little help making one, that wasn't too much to ask, was it? Even if that help came with a jaw-dropping price tag attached?

Okay, so the money they could have spent on new cars and fancy houses had gone instead to pay for uncomfortable and expensive infertility tests and treatments. It wasn't going to stay this way forever. Once they had a baby of their own, they'd start saving for a house. Between her work in landscape design and Sam's salary from one of the largest legal firms in Washington, they'd have no trouble catching up with the rest of their friends.

But first, they needed a baby.

Wiping her hands on a kitchen towel, she hurried into the living room prepared to convince the man of her dreams they needed to give it one more try.

"Hi, honey!" she called, crossing the short distance between the kitchen and the front door. "How was work?"

Sam set his briefcase by the door. His shoulders hunched, he hung his coat on the rack by the door. Turning, he asked, "What's that smell?"

The question stopped her in her tracks. Not so much the question as the tone. Sam sounded... irritated. Had she burned something? She sniffed the air for something besides the aroma of the good dinner she'd fixed. Nothing. "I made a pork roast and those little potatoes you like so much."

"You didn't go to work today?" He issued the words like an accusation.

"I, um…" She'd been so upset after the call from the doctor's office that she'd taken a sick day. Hoping to delay that conversation until after dinner, when they'd both relaxed over a glass of wine and a good meal, she hedged. "The sod for the Ferguson place won't come in until next week." The family had hired the nursery to landscape one of the hundreds of mini-mansions that were springing up on what was once cow pastures around Fairfax. "When it gets here, I'll put in a couple of long days. I'll more than make up the hours. The good news is, there's apple pie for dessert. Homemade."

She'd expected that little piece of news to brighten her husband's day—he loved apple pie more than he loved his beloved Washington Nats. But Sam only grunted and headed down the short hallway toward their bedroom.

"Want me to pour you a glass of wine while you change?" she called to his retreating back.

"Nope." The door to the bedroom closed.

Reggie stuck her hands into the pockets of her tunic. Although her husband normally swapped his coat and tie for jeans as soon as he stepped inside the apartment, he used to take a moment, however brief, to give her a quick squeeze or a peck on the cheek. But not tonight. Come to think of it, it had been a while since he'd pulled her to him. She brushed a rogue hair from her eyes. When had Sam stopped kissing her hello when he arrived home? Or swinging her into a quick embrace? It wasn't like she'd expected the passion of their early days to last forever, but they'd only been married five years. *Sheesh!* If their ardor had cooled this much already, what would their love life look like in another five years? Or ten?

Not that she could blame Sam. The IVF treatments had put them both through a special kind of hell. For the past two years, she'd been at the mercy of the hormones her doctors pumped into her each cycle. And Sam, well, her poor husband never knew what he'd come home to at night—a whirling dervish or a basket case.

But not much longer. They'd give it one last try. That's all. She'd get pregnant this time, for sure. And then, then they could go back to being the couple they'd been before all the temperature checks and the doctor appointments and the schedules had driven the passion right out of them.

She glanced down the hall. The bedroom door remained closed. Shrugging, she headed to the kitchen to check on dinner. On the stove, the green beans looked a little dry, so she added a bit more water to the pan. The roast had rested long enough. Certain Sam would join her any minute, she took her best carving knife from its rack and cut the meat into the wafer-thin slices he preferred. She stole a quick peek at the potatoes and carrots in the warming oven. Were they getting overdone? She checked the timer and wondered what was taking Sam so long.

She exhaled slowly when she heard the click of a doorknob and a soft squeak. *Finally.* She'd been afraid the potatoes would get mushy if they delayed dinner much longer. She turned toward the living room, and there stood Sam. Dressed in jeans and a polo, he looked as handsome as he had on the day they met. The few gray flecks in his otherwise jet-black hair gave him a distinguished look. A few lines around his eyes told her he was tired, but the week was winding down.

She smiled. Maybe they'd both take Saturday off. Do something fun. Go to a craft fair in one of the quaint little towns nearby. Pack a picnic lunch and go for a drive in the country. Or, if he was too tired after the long week, there was always baseball. The Nationals were sure to be on a field somewhere. She'd make popcorn and they could cozy up on the couch together and watch the game.

"Ready to eat?" she asked. Thinking of the fun they'd have this weekend, she grabbed a pair of potholders and took the pan of potatoes from the oven. It didn't matter what they did, as long as they spent some time together.

"I've changed my mind. I'm going to have that drink, after all." He crossed to the nook that served as their liquor cabinet, where he poured a generous splash of bourbon into cut glass. He downed it in one gulp, poured another.

Lowering the pan onto a metal trivet, she quirked an eyebrow as unease sifted through her midsection. Sam didn't drink much. Had something gone wrong at work? "Is everything all right?"

"No. Not really." He downed the second glass and propped one shoulder against the wall as if he needed the support. "We need to talk."

"Ooookay." *This can't be good.* Shoving the potholders aside, she flattened her palms on the counter and braced herself. "Did things go south with that big case you've been working so hard on?"

Had he been fired? Her heart sank, and she took a moment to give herself a mental pep talk. Sam was smart, sharp. Some other big law firm would snap him up in a heartbeat, and they'd pick up where they left off then. In the meantime, she'd be supportive, encouraging. Why, she wouldn't even mention the next round of IVF treatments.

They could put those on hold for a few months. It wasn't like he'd be out of work forever.

"It's not the job," Sam said. "Well, it is, kind of. My case is going great. Better than expected, actually."

"That's good news. I'm glad to hear it." Relief whispered through her chest. Of course, she'd have been there for him if he'd lost his job, but she'd really had her heart set on starting the next round of IVF as soon as possible. She studied him. Despite two shots of bourbon, his jaw remained clenched, his shoulders stiff. Work might be going well, but something was definitely bothering him. What else was there?

"Did you get the results?"

"What?" The question had come out of the blue, and she blinked. There'd been a time when he wouldn't have to ask. That first round, they'd waited by the phone together, all optimism and high hopes. Later, he'd held her in his arms while she cried. The second time, he'd cautioned her not to get her hopes up, but the news had still crushed her spirits. Sam had been on an out-of-town business trip when the call came in about the third round. But they'd spoken on the phone that evening and been sad together. By the fourth round, he'd gotten his big assignment and was working more than ever. She understood. In the demanding private sector, a young up-and-coming attorney faced tremendous pressure. So she'd taken the call, left him a note and gone straight to bed.

"I did," she said slowly. "It didn't work." She gave herself points for not breaking down completely.

Sam nodded. Just nodded. He didn't sweep her into his arms, didn't offer words of comfort. Just a cold, distant nod. Followed by a whispered, "Well, at least that's over."

She sucked in a breath so hard her chest hurt. She had to have heard him wrong. "I'm sorry? What did you say?"

"We agreed. This was the last time." The finality in his voice turned her insides cold.

"It doesn't have to be. We can try again. Dr. Thomas wants us to come in, talk about the next steps, another round of IVF." Her words came in a rush, her voice taking on that pleading tone she hated. She fell silent, wishing Sam would say the words she wanted to hear. That of course they'd try again. That he wanted a baby every bit as much as she did. That he'd do whatever it took to make it happen.

Instead, he simply stood there, still as a stone while he looked at her like she'd sprouted two heads or something. She ran a hand through her curls, just in case he was right. Nope.

"No more appointments. No more treatments. It's over."

"But I—"

"No." His empty glass struck the counter in front of her with a thunk.

"Is it the money? 'Cause if it's the money, I can ask my parents to help." Now that her dad had retired, her folks probably couldn't cover the entire cost, but she knew how much they wanted a grandchild. They'd pitch in as much as they could.

"It's not the money."

She drew in a shaky breath. She'd been afraid of this. The hormones and other drugs had wreaked havoc with her moods, turning her into a shrew one day, sending her on a crying jag the next. Sam had to be as tired of the ups and downs as much as she was. "I can do better. You'll see. Now that we've been through the cycle a few times, I know what to expect. I'll deal with it better." As a matter of fact, she had done exactly that with this last round. Why, she'd been practically euphoric throughout the entire cycle. If he'd been home more, he would've noticed.

"It's not the money, Regina. Or the endless doctor appointments. Or any of the rest of it."

Sam pulled himself away from the wall. "I'm done with all of it."

"You don't want a baby anymore?" She stared at him in disbelief while sharp tears stung her eyes.

"Don't be ridiculous," Sam sneered. "But I'm done with all of this." He swept a hand through the air.

Used to Sam's constant put-downs, she ignored the jab while she followed his gesture. Did he mean their apartment? Their furniture? *What?*

"Do I have to spell it out for you?" Sam heaved a long-suffering sigh. "You. I'm talking about you and me. All of it. Us. I'm done with us."

The air whooshed out of her lungs in such a rush, she felt light-headed and woozy. She grabbed the edges of the counter. The hard, cold tile steadied her. She swallowed. "You want a separation?"

"A divorce," he said. The scathing tone of Sam's voice fell flat. "Admit it, Regina. It's been over between us for a long time." He cleared his throat. "You know it as well as I do. We aren't in love with each other anymore. We've just been going through the motions, each of us afraid to move on with our lives. I, for one, don't want to live like that anymore."

"You can't be serious." Her head swam. "We promised we'd always be together. Love. Honor. Cherish. Till death do us part." She grabbed the potholders from the counter. The thick cloth bunched in her hands. Sure, they'd hit a rough patch—couples did that, didn't they? That didn't mean they gave up on each other.

"I understand the last few months have been tough," she conceded. Spring was always her busiest time at the nursery, and heaven knew they needed the money, but for the sake of her marriage, she'd cut back on her hours. And Sam, he could do the same thing. After all, he'd been working so much overtime, for such a long time. And it had paid off—he'd said the case was going well. "We've hardly seen each other since you landed this big case. You've been going in earlier, staying later, working weekends. Let's—"

"Fine!" His voice rose as anger tightened Sam's features. "You want to blame it all on me? Go ahead. Make it all my fault. That doesn't change things. The fact is, I don't love you anymore, Regina. There. That's as plain as I can say it—I don't love you."

Her stomach flipped. She tasted bile. Not sure she wanted to know the answer, she asked, "Is there someone else?"

"No."

She stared at him for a long moment, trying and failing to convince herself the flicker of guilt in Sam's green eyes was a figment of her imagination.

He heaved in a breath. "I'm leaving."

"You can't leave. I made dinner!" Her gaze swept the kitchen. She'd spent the entire afternoon fixing all his favorites, and he was going to leave all of it—leave her—behind? "Everything's ready. Let's eat. We'll talk." If she could just get him to sit down and talk about it, he'd tell her this had all been a big misunderstanding.

But Sam only turned and walked into their bedroom. He returned a scant few seconds later carrying a suit bag and the carry-on he used for business trips. "I'll send for the rest of my things this weekend."

"The rest of…?" That didn't sound like this was something that would blow over in a day or two. Cold spread from the center of her chest, filling her with a numbing calmness. "Where will you go? What if I need to reach you?"

"The firm has an apartment near the office. I'll stay there for the time being. You have my cell phone in case of an emergency." He scanned the small apartment they'd called home for the past five years. "I'll pay the rent through the end of the lease. Our attorneys can work out the rest of the details."

Attorneys. Lease. Her knees went weak. "Sam, I..." Her mouth closed. She had no idea what to say.

Apparently, he did. "Goodbye," he said.

The door closed behind him. She crossed to the window. Staring down, she waited until Sam stepped onto the walkway below. A car waited at the curb for him, its motor running. He slung his bags in the back and climbed in behind them. In seconds, the vehicle disappeared around a corner.

Reggie's heart sank. On leaden feet, she walked to the apartment door and threw the deadbolt with shaking hands. Sensing her knees were about to buckle, she sank onto the couch.

How had things gone so wrong so fast?

Five

Michelle

Snip.

"Oops."

Michelle stared at the long stem lying atop the thin layer of mulch at her feet. At least a dozen buds sprouted along the green twig. She probably shouldn't have cut that one. She eyed the rest of the bush. It, along with the half-dozen others clustered around the front door, looked leggy and scraggly. The scattered blossoms smelled as delicious as she remembered, but the flowers were definitely paler than the rich, red velvet the plants used to produce. Should she leave them alone? For all she knew, this might be the wrong season for trimming altogether. The roses had been Allen's hobby, not hers. She could pack everything she knew about the flowers into a thimble and still have room left over. But something had to be done about them.

Who was going to take care of them if she didn't? Certainly not the people from the lawn service. When he was alive, Allen had put the fear of God into the workers, promising dire consequences if they so much as touched his darling babies. As for the twins, they knew the roses existed, but she doubted they spared more than a passing glance at their father's pride and joy. Aaron might break off a stem on his way out for a date. Ashley would occasionally pluck a blossom to put in a bud dish on the kitchen table. But as far as they knew, the roses pretty much took care of themselves.

They didn't, though. Not if the time Allen had spent on them was any indication. And without his tender loving ministrations this past year, they'd grown ragged and unloved. Which was not the first impression she wanted to make on potential buyers.

"Allen, if you're up there, let me know if I'm doing this right, okay?" she whispered. She wiped away a tear. It was only fitting that she'd chosen today, the anniversary of his passing, to take care of his precious flowers.

Sand crunched beneath tires as a car pulled to the curb somewhere close by. The sound of two people having a polite exchange drifted across the front lawn. She turned, expecting to learn that one of her neighbors had visitors. Unable to believe what she was seeing, she shaded her eyes against the bright afternoon sun.

"Erin?" she whispered. It couldn't be.

But the figure at the end of the flagstone walkway sure looked like her college roommate. The impression only deepened when the woman dressed in jeans and wearing a khaki jacket retrieved a duffle bag from the back seat of a silver sedan. The car door closed with a squeak and a thunk. The new arrival hoisted her bag onto one shoulder, turned, and headed toward her, a wide smile breaking across her face.

Michelle dropped the pruning shears onto the ground and tugged the work gloves from her hands. "Erin!" she called. "What are you doing here? Aren't you supposed to be on your way to Belize or Madagascar?"

"Surprise!" Erin dropped the duffle bag at her feet. She shoved a hank of shoulder-length, blond hair behind one ear and grinned. Dimples formed in her sun-darkened cheeks. "I was sure I threw that dart at India last night. My arm must've slipped 'cause the darn thing landed in Virginia. So here I am."

"Your aim's not that bad." Michelle folded

her arms across her chest. In the twenty-plus years since they'd graduated college, Erin had never once willingly spent her vacation in their hometown. Not even last year. Oh, she'd dropped everything and flown home the minute word reached her about Allen's death. And she'd stuck close to her side for the next two weeks. But once they'd put the funeral behind them and transferred all the accounts into Michelle's name, her friend had jetted off to Costa Rica. She'd stayed there until the tourist season opened up in Alaska. Michelle cocked her head. "No, seriously. What are you doing here?"

"What, can't a girl switch it up once in a while?" Erin swept the yard with an appraising look that landed squarely on Michelle. "Looks like I got here just in time. What on earth are you doing to those poor roses?"

"I was trying to shape them a little bit." She kicked the downed stem. "I'm not doing a very good job of it, I'm afraid. Allen used to make it look so easy." To her dismay, her lower lip trembled. Tears weren't far behind.

Erin didn't say a word. She simply stepped forward and pulled her into a hug. For a few long minutes, Michelle drank in the strength of the friend who'd flown a thousand miles to be with her on the anniversary of the worst day of her life. She half-expected Erin to end the embrace quickly. Instead, her friend simply held her, as steady and immovable as a rock, letting the tears flow until she'd composed herself.

"Sorry about that," she sniffed at last. "I guess I'm not handling much very well these days." She stepped away. Suddenly self-conscious, she blotted her tears on the hem of the old flannel shirt of Allen's she'd tugged on over shorts and a T-shirt that was definitely past its prime. She fingered the ragged ends of her hair. Erin had probably traveled all day to get here, yet she stood there looking as fresh as a daisy. While here she was, not wearing a drop of makeup, her windblown hair three days overdue for a shampoo.

"No one expects you to have it all together. Especially not today." Erin nodded. "Look, I've been on the road since four this morning, and I could really use a cup of coffee. Why don't we leave this for Regina to deal with and come inside with me?"

"Reggie?" Erin was the only one who called her younger sister by her full name. "Why would you say that? Reggie's not here."

"She will be, though. Her and Nina both." Erin slipped a thin phone from her back pocket and glanced at the display. "In about four hours.

That gives us plenty of time to get ready for a night on the town. But first, let's have that coffee and you can fill me in on what's been going on around here."

Michelle bit her lip while she fought off another onslaught of tears. Her children didn't understand why, a year after their father's death, their mother still couldn't get her act together. They'd relegated their dad to a cherished memory and moved on with their lives. But that was okay. Because her friends understood. Better still, they'd gather around her tonight, armed with shoulders to lean on and, she bet, purses filled with tissues.

She took a breath that barely shook. "Yes, let's. I have a lot to tell you."

Erin quirked an eyebrow. "Oh? Is there a hot new stud in your life?"

A righteous indignation stirred in Michelle's belly. It had only been a year, she started to protest. One look at the teasing grin that had slid across Erin's face, and her anger evaporated. "If there was, do you think I'd be out here doing yard work myself?" she shot back.

"That's my girl," Erin laughed. "Now, how about that coffee."

Michelle mashed the last few crumbs of coffee cake with her fork. She licked the bits from the tines and pushed the plate aside. "So that's it," she said. "That's where things stand." She'd expected to feel drained and empty after spending an hour bringing Erin up to speed on the depressing state of affairs in the Robinson household. But she didn't. If anything, confiding in her friend had been oddly cathartic. Rejuvenating, even. Unfortunately, though, the bottom line hadn't budged an inch. "Unless I sell the house within the next three months, the bank will foreclose. I'll lose whatever equity there is in it. Not that there's much."

Erin pushed away from the table. "I could use another cup. You?"

Michelle placed her hand over her cup.

"What about the money your parents left you?" Erin asked as slipped another pod into the Keurig on the counter.

Michelle shook her head. Both her adoptive parents had passed away nearly a decade earlier. As their only daughter, she'd inherited their estate. It hadn't been much—a modest house, some stocks. Probate costs and legal fees had eaten up half of that. What was left had gone into Allen's fledgling business, along with the rest of their money.

"Yikes. That hurts." Erin rose and scraped her uneaten cake into the trash. "What do the kids have to say about all this?"

"Nothing." She felt her face warm. "I haven't told them yet." When Erin's eyes widened, she rushed to explain. "I'm ashamed to admit it, but, well, I sort of put off digging into our finances until a couple of days ago. I'm just getting a handle on it all myself."

"You are planning on telling them, though. Aren't you?"

"I know I have to." That was one conversation she didn't want to have. She took a breath. "I thought they'd be home this weekend because—" She shrugged. "You know." She waited until Erin nodded before she continued. "But Aaron has a big project due, and Ashley had other plans. I probably won't see them until they come home for summer break the first week in June."

"You don't think you should tell them sooner?"

She sighed. "Probably. But it's the kind of thing that needs to be done face-to-face." She pretended to hold her cell phone to her ear. "Yes, I know we promised you could spend the summer after graduation in Europe. And Daddy said he'd buy you each a new car. But he's gone now, and there's no money. And, oh, by the way, I've put the only home you've ever known on the market." A fresh onslaught of tears welled. She blinked furiously.

Erin shrugged. "Aaron's a bright kid. He'll roll with it. It's Ashley you'll have to worry about. Daddy's Little Girl is gonna have a tough time. This is a pretty big pill for her to swallow. And you know how she gets."

Michelle laughed. Erin called it like she saw it, warts and all. And she wasn't wrong. Her redheaded daughter would likely throw a hissy-fit when she found out that the family finances no longer ran deep. She pressed her finger down over a stray crumb and flicked it onto her plate. From the moment she was born, and probably before that, Ashley had been nearly the opposite of her older-by-thirty-minutes twin. Where Aaron had been an easy baby, content as long as he was fed and changed at regular intervals, Ashley had been colicky and difficult. She'd been a handful in her early teens—acting out, running with a rough crowd—while Aaron had been content to spend most weekend nights playing Team Fortress and designing his own video games. Luckily, Ashley was every bit as smart as her brother. By the time she reached high school, she'd realized her gang was headed in a direction she didn't want to go, traded them in for a new group of friends, and buckled down. She hadn't lost the attitude that came with the red hair, though.

Where had all that red hair and fiery temper come from? Certainly not from Allen. He'd passed his jet-black hair on to his son. Ashley's coloring must have come from her side of the family. Not that she could prove it. She knew next to nothing about her biological parents. The people who'd adopted her, the ones she called "Mom" and "Dad," had only known their side of the story—how they'd gotten a call from an adoption agency in Florida and had been so excited, they'd caught the next available flight south without packing so much as a toothbrush. A few hours later, they'd taken one look at the pink cherub staring up at them from a bassinet in the social worker's office and fallen head over heels for the tiny newborn. Her adoption had sailed through without a hitch, but the names of her birth parents, along with any other information about them, had been sealed in accordance with Florida's adoption laws. She supposed she could have dug into it more, but even thinking of dredging up the past had always made her feel disloyal to the parents who'd saved her from the foster care system.

She drank the last of the cold coffee. Maybe one day, now that they were gone…

"Earth to Chelle. Where'd you go?"

She straightened. "Sorry. I was thinking about Ashley and how she was going to handle all this." She gestured toward the backyard and the pool that still sat under its winter cover.

Erin gathered the cups from the table and set them in the sink. She stretched. "I don't think I got more than an hour's sleep last night. It's starting to catch up with me. The others are going to be here around two. I might take a little lie-down before we start getting all gussied up to go out."

Michelle sighed. Much as she appreciated her friends, she really wasn't up for a night on the town. "You three ought to go without me. I'm afraid I won't be very good company. Besides, like I said, I can't afford much more than ramen these days."

"Oh, you're going out. Don't even try to weasel out of it. What are you going to do otherwise? Sit around here and mope? You just finished saying you were ready for a change."

True. At some point over the past hour while they talked, she'd said exactly that. But she still couldn't afford to blow a couple of hundred bucks.

Erin's fingers gave her shoulder a gentle squeeze. "Look. I hear you about the money. But my last client left me a tip like you wouldn't believe. I've got you covered."

Michelle sipped air. She refused to be treated like a charity case. "Only if you'll let me pay you back once I get on my feet again."

"Deal. Now that that's settled, where do you want me?"

"You know where the guest room is." She was reasonably certain the housekeeper had dusted and vacuumed the room earlier in the week.

With that, Erin headed for the front door, where she'd dropped her duffle in the entryway. Seconds later, Michelle heard the sound of footsteps as her friend climbed the stairs to the second floor. She rose from the table, loaded their dishes into the dishwasher and headed upstairs to her room. A shower and shampoo were definitely in order. She examined her fingers. Her nails were in pretty good shape, but a fresh coat of polish wouldn't hurt.

Six

Erin

"To Allen!"

Glasses clinked as the four women in Michelle's spacious family room raised another glass in tribute to their friend's late husband. Erin propped one elbow on the armrest of the sofa. For the past hour, she and the others had shared stories about the man Chelle had married over twenty-five years ago. Through it all, there'd been tears, but there'd been lots of laughter, too. She caught their host's eye over her wineglass. Her heart warmed when Chelle smiled. Getting the gang together today had been one of her better ideas.

Leaning over the coffee table, she used a perfectly toasted sourdough round to scoop up the last bit of Nina's special olive tapenade.

Salty goodness filled her mouth when she bit into the morsel. Not for the first time, she closed her eyes and let the feeling of bliss wash over her. Nina was an absolute magician. She deserved to run her own restaurant. She certainly shouldn't be playing third string in a kitchen that didn't respect her true talents.

Erin popped the last bit of the sourdough into her mouth. Savoring the taste, she assessed the damage they'd done to the enormous charcuterie board Nina had assembled after pulling container after container from cloth bags and placing them on Chelle's kitchen counter two hours earlier. The slivers of tangy blue cheese and the ripe, sweet figs had long since disappeared. So had that amazing cheese dip, the one laced with wine and roasted peppers. A handful of grapes, a few scraps of prosciutto, and some crackers were all that remained. Half-empty wineglasses littered the top of the coffee table. She retrieved hers.

Sinking into the cushions, she surveyed the faces of the three women who'd gathered in front of the fireplace. No doubt about it, Nina and Chelle were two of the best friends a girl could ever ask for. As for her sister, Regina wasn't half bad, either. Especially when she tossed out one-liners like confetti and kept them all in stitches.

Except tonight she seemed to be in some kind of snit. While she and Nina had done their best to bolster Chelle's spirits, Regina had looked up from her phone barely long enough to participate in the conversation. There'd been plenty of opportunities to throw out a few zingers, but she hadn't. Erin brushed a few crumbs from her lap. Something was up with her sister and, as usual, she didn't have a clue what it was. Maybe later, she'd ask one of the other girls.

She crossed one leg over the other, slipping her heel out of the stiletto to ease the uncomfortable pressure on her toes. When was the last time she'd really gotten dressed up? There'd been a time when slipping into a slinky dress and toddling around on high heels had been the norm. But those days were long gone. Life was pretty laid back in the Keys, where shorts and T-shirts ruled. In Alaska, things were a bit more rugged. If a girl like her had stepped into an outfit like this at camp, the guys would've laughed her all the way back to Fairfax.

Come to think of it, maybe she and Chelle and Nina ought to stop calling themselves girls and face up to reality. Reggie might be ten years younger, but those ten years would pass in the blink of an eye, while the rest of them had celebrated their forty-fifth birthdays this year.

She supposed that put them squarely in middle age, although to look at the group, not one of them looked a day over thirty.

Well, except maybe Chelle. The year since Allen's death had draped itself over her like a moth-eaten fur coat. Until this year, Chelle had followed a regimen of spa treatments and mani/pedis with an almost religious fanaticism. Now, her hair cried out for a decent cut, she'd bitten her nails to the quick, and Erin would bet a month's pay her friend hadn't had a facial in the last six months.

She supposed that was to be expected when a woman lost her husband. Not that she would even pretend to know what that felt like. She'd tried marriage once and quickly found out it was like slipping her arms into straitjacket. She couldn't wait to get out of it. As for Rob, he'd liked being married well enough. Just not to her. They'd agreed to an amicable divorce practically before the ink had dried on their marriage certificate. She'd been on her own ever since. She couldn't think of one good reason to change that.

But Chelle had been cut from a different piece of cloth. The girl was a throwback to the forties. If majoring in Home Ec had been a possibility at UVA, she'd have jumped at the chance. It wasn't, so she'd settled for the next best thing—a career in design. She'd been a junior when she'd fallen head-over-heels for her TA. Allen, who'd been working on his master's in engineering, often told folks that meeting Michelle had been the only good thing that came out of the business math course he taught as part of his work-study program. Erin had given their relationship a year, two at the most. She'd been wrong about that. Chelle and Allen had married not long after graduation, and they'd built a good life for themselves. She'd taken to being a stay-at-home mom like a duck took to water, and it had certainly paid off. Aaron and Ashley were good kids. A little self-centered, maybe, but wasn't that typical of young people these days?

Yeah, her friend had had the perfect life. And then Allen had up and died on her. And she'd discovered their perfect life wasn't so perfect after all.

Anger burned in Erin's stomach whenever she thought how badly Allen had handled things. She didn't like to think ill of the dead, but seriously? He couldn't have done better? Sure, getting laid off hadn't been Allen's fault. Mergers, like random bad acts, happened. When they did, the new managers were more apt as not to weed out the older, more experienced workers and replace them with youngsters who'd do the same job at half the pay. It sucked. But that's the way it happened. So, no, she didn't blame Allen for that.

She did, however, blame him for what came next. Burning through their savings and retirement funds? Mortgaging their house? What had he been thinking? Not that he was 100 percent to blame. Chelle should never have gone along with his inane plan. But done was done. Now her friend had to make the best of it.

The upshot was, Erin had no idea how a woman was supposed to cope after losing her partner of twenty-five years. Though she'd never walked a mile in her friend's shoes—and would never dream of trying to cram her own size nines into Chelle's perfect size sixes—she supposed it was only natural that the woman had let herself go a bit. No matter. She'd stick around long enough to get her bestie back on track. Okay, so they'd splurge on calorie-laden dishes tonight, but starting tomorrow, she'd clean out the cupboards, toss every highly processed, sugary-sweet, carb-enriched snack right in the trash where it belonged. Then she'd cajole her friend into pulling on her athletic shoes and hitting the bricks for an early morning run. They'd head out along the bike path that ran through the subdivision, where mature trees blocked the sun and gentle hills added a bit of challenge.

She eyed her friend. Okay, the way they were slinging back wine, maybe they'd make than an afternoon run.

"How about you, Erin? You always have the best stories to tell. You deal with any crazy tourists this year?"

"When are they not crazy?" she asked when Nina turned the conversation in her direction. They'd spent the past two hours scarfing down appetizers and working their slow way through a couple of bottles of very good wine. "Let me think." She skipped over her latest adventure with the tourists from New York and dredged up a memory from earlier this spring. "I had this one client who showed up with a fly rod. Said he'd always dreamed of catching a tarpon on the fly. I tried to explain that tarpon are big, strong fish and maybe trying to land one from a kayak wasn't the best idea, but he was insistent. And, you know, the customer is always right."

She checked to see if the others were following. Regina and Nina nodded—they'd dealt with stubborn customers a time or two. At Chelle's encouraging smile, she continued.

"I'd spotted some smaller tarpon during our tour the day before, so I got elected to see if we could put him on one. Now, tarpon—they call 'em the Silver Kings 'cause they're all silver and shiny—

they're real skittish and one of the most challenging fish to land. So I'm thinking if he's real, real lucky, he'll latch onto a two- or three-footer. Any fish that size would be a challenge in a kayak, but a tarpon, that'd really give the client a run for his money. This guy, though, he's clearly got something bigger in mind. He reaches into his bag and pulls out this monster-size fly." She held her hands a good eight inches apart. "It's a real beauty, too. Iridescent feathers and googly eyes. And of course, what happens? He casts that fly right in front of a fish on the first try. But is it one of the little ones I was hoping for?" She shook her head. "No such luck. Nah, he hooks a fish that had to be five feet if it was an inch. That's 150 pounds of pure muscle. Pure… unhappy…muscle. The instant that fish felt the hook, it took off for deeper water like a shot. And since the client wouldn't let go of the rod, it pulled him and his kayak along for the ride."

While Nina clamped one hand over her mouth, her eyes wide, Regina and Chelle giggled.

"Well, I couldn't very well let a paying customer get towed out to sea. That sort of thing is bad for business." She grinned. "So I'm paddling for all I'm worth and yelling at him to cut the line. But no. He won't do it. And we're getting farther and farther from shore. At last, that King, he jumps clear out of the water. He shakes his massive head from side to side and finally, finally, we see the fly sail out of his mouth and land in the water. It was impressive, I tell you. I'm still a good twenty yards, so I paddle on out to where he's sitting, calmly reeling in his line. And I'm like, 'Dude, that fish was too big. Why didn't you cut the line?' And he just looks at me and says, 'What? And waste a perfectly good fly?'"

When the others laughed, she finished up quickly. "I'll spare you all the details, but we were 500 yards off shore by then, and it took us the better part of an hour to paddle back in. Every time I think of it, my muscles burn. I was utterly exhausted by the time we got to the ramp. That's when he tells me, since he didn't actually land a tarpon, I owed him another try. Yeah, like that was gonna happen." She glanced around the room.

"What did you do?" Reggie asked.

"I didn't have to do a thing. That was pure karma," she answered, savoring the memory. "He was so irritated about the tarpon, he didn't pay attention to what he was doing, and the next thing I knew—sploosh!—over he went. Him, his kayak and all his gear." She shook her head.

"Never did find that fancy fly he was so proud of."

"Oh! Oh! Oh!" Nina hooted, holding her side and laughing. Her sister had tears running down both cheeks. Even Chelle had cracked up.

Reggie grabbed a napkin and blotted her eyes. "Too funny!"

"I'm going to have to redo my makeup." Michelle swiped her damp cheeks.

"Makeup!" Nina hooted. "I have to pee." She dashed into the bathroom while the rest gave in to another round of squeals and laughter. Moments later, the toilet flushed and water ran in the sink.

"Erin, you always have the best stories," Nina said, rubbing lotion on her hands as she walked into the room.

"A day rarely goes by without one of my clients pulling some kind of craziness." When she'd first started working as a guide, she'd laughed at their antics. Lately, she hadn't found them nearly as funny. "They keep me on my toes," she admitted.

Nina lifted the nearly empty wooden platter from the coffee table. "I'll run this into the kitchen. Anyone want anything?" When no one did, she headed for the back of the house.

The room fell silent when Nina walked out of

the room. This would be a perfect time for Regina to add to the conversation, Erin thought, and aimed a pointed look at her sister. When the younger woman only stared at the phone in her hand, she cleared her throat. "Expecting an important phone call, Regina?" she asked dryly.

Regina tore her eyes away from the screen long enough to give her a confused look. "What?"

Erin let both eyebrows rise. "You've been checking your phone every two minutes ever since you got here. Must be something awfully important. Unless…" She paused for effect. "Unless you're sexting with Sam?"

"Sex—" Regina sputtered. "Not hardly! I'm— I'm checking on my work schedule for next week."

Gotcha. Erin grinned when her sister's cheeks turned a lovely shade of pink. Regina never had been a good liar. Her sister hadn't been watching for a business call any more than she'd been trading sexy one-liners with her husband. She watched as her sister gave an exaggerated sigh before sliding the device into her purse. Not that she intended to let the matter drop. She leaned forward, questions about who, what, and why forming on her tongue. Before she had a chance to ask, Nina spoke on her way back from the kitchen.

"Oh, I do love this place!" she said striding into the room. "I have to admit it. I get jealous every time I walk into your kitchen, Michelle. You must love working in there."

"I have," Michelle murmured, her face turning pale beneath her makeup. She glanced toward the airy room that looked out over the shady backyard. "I've fixed a lot of good meals and baked a lot of cakes in there," she said, a wistful note creeping into her voice.

Knowing that her friend's days of preparing family feasts in the roomy kitchen were drawing to a close, Erin straightened.

"I bet you have," Regina piped in, once again misreading the signals. "You know, I've been working on those McMansions out west of town. I just don't understand why they clear-cut all that farmland. You'd think they'd leave at least a few trees. We're planting saplings around all the new houses like crazy, but it'll take twenty years or more for things to get big enough to enjoy. You're so lucky! This neighborhood is full of forty- and-fifty-year-old trees. And your azaleas. Oh, they're gorgeous. A little overgrown right now, but still. If I had a place like this with a big backyard and plenty of room, I'd never leave."

"You should try cooking on that thing they

call a stove in my place." Nina rented a tiny studio apartment near the beltway. "I wish I had appliances like yours." She nodded at Michelle. "I'd cook day and night."

Regina stretched her arms wide along the back of the sofa. "This is the perfect place for entertaining. And you've done such a great job with it. Everything looks like it was always meant to be here, you know? My apartment's a mishmash of cast-off furniture and tag sale finds. Plus, it's so small, we'd have to sit in each other's laps if we met there."

Michelle gazed about the room, her face growing paler by the second. "Yes, um." She clamped one hand over her mouth. Her eyes filled with tears. "Excuse me a minute, okay?" She stood abruptly and left the room.

Nina watched her go, then turned to face Erin. "I didn't mean to upset her."

"Was it something I said?" Regina asked.

Yes.

"She'll be all right," Erin soothed. "Just give her a minute."

Nina's eyes watered. "Is it too much for her, having us here today?"

"No. It's…" She trailed off, unable to break Michelle's confidence. "She'll tell you when she's ready."

Nina sucked in a breath. "She's not sick or anything, is she?"

"No, nothing like that." Erin shook her head. When Nina remained doubtful and Regina's eyes grew round, she held up her hands. "Trust me. She's fine." She paused. A new topic of conversation was definitely called for. "What time are our reservations?" She looked to Nina for the answer. Between her years in some of the best kitchens in the area and her reputation as a fine cook in her own right, the cook had connections at practically every restaurant in the area. Tonight, she'd snagged them a table at a trendy new hot spot.

"Seven." Nina bent to gather up napkins and plates. "We have a half hour before we need to leave." She glanced at Regina. "You're going to call an Uber, right?"

Clearly relieved to have a reason for using her phone, Regina retrieved it from her bag. She glanced at the screen before saying, "Right. I'll give them another ten minutes before I call." On a weekday night, it'd take less than a half hour to make the drive across town.

"Okay, then. Why don't we clean up this mess and take a few minutes to freshen up," Erin suggested. "I know I could use it."

Regina sent a doubtful look over one shoulder to the stairs Chelle had climbed moments earlier. "You're sure she's okay?"

Erin felt her heart melt a little. Her sister really did care. "I'm sure," she said softly. "Just give her a few. If she's not out in ten minutes, I'll check on her."

Regina stood, gathered up the wineglasses and trailed Nina into the kitchen while Erin stared after both of them. As much as she wanted to confide in their friends, this wasn't her story to tell.

Seven

Reggie

*M*usic poured from speakers that hung among the white pipes crisscrossing the black ceiling. The sound bounced off the black slate flooring and texturized walls done in a pale gray. According to their waiter, the twenty-foot octopus a local artist had painted on one wall had been featured in the *Washington Post's* recent write-up.

Personally, Reggie thought a mollusk was a poor décor choice for a restaurant this far inland, but what did she know. She rubbed her forehead. Not only did the incessant beat of the music prevent all but the most determined efforts at conversation, it was giving her a headache. Which was soooo not what she needed. She'd already run afoul of Erin once tonight.

She refused to do it again. No matter how much her head—or her heart—hurt.

Beneath the cluster of industrial-style drop lights hanging over their table, she studied the remains of their meal. She had to admit, dinner had been pretty good. They'd ordered every single appetizer and small plate except for the—*ewww*—okra. The waiter had placed the dishes in the center of the table, where they proceeded to divvy them up. One succulent shrimp on a tiny bed of spicy, cheesy grits for each of them. A small serving of crispy fried Brussels sprouts drizzled with a balsamic sauce Nina had called "riveting." The mushroom caps filled with smoked salmon and cream cheese had been far tastier than she'd expected. But the star of the show had definitely been the corn relish. She could have devoured an entire bowl of that. She wouldn't have passed up a second helping of the melt-in-your-mouth bone marrow, either. Not that it or steak tartare were her usual fare. She'd probably be a vegetarian, maybe even a vegan, if it weren't for Sam. He'd always been more of a meat-and-potatoes kind of guy. Though she might not have to worry about that now. She sniffed and gave the phone in her lap a surreptitious glance. Nope. He hadn't called or texted. Not tonight. Not once in the three days since he'd packed his bags and walked out of their apartment. Much as she hated to admit it, she was beginning to think he'd really meant it when he said he was done with her, with them.

She averted her eyes quickly and froze when her gaze landed on two distinguished-looking men bearing down on their table. "Heads up, gals. We may have company," she said just before the pair slowed to a stop across from her. They took up positions on either side of Michelle and Erin.

"Good evening, ladies. I'm Rob," said the taller of the two. "This is my friend Jim. We couldn't help but notice you enjoying yourselves this evening. What brings four such beautiful women out tonight?"

Beside her, Nina straightened. "Guys, you're interrupting our dinner," she pointed out.

Rob pulled a long face. He clutched at his chest. "Oh, you wound me. We're just talking here." He leaned closer to Erin. "Where are you gals from?"

Regina smiled to herself as her sister appeared to simper at the unexpected attention. She'd seen Erin in action before. The men should have taken Nina's hint. They were about to get their heads handed to them on a platter.

"More or less," Erin said, her accent thickening into that of a Southern belle. "My friends"—she waved a languid hand toward the rest of the group—"live right here in Fairfax. How about you boys?"

Rob must have thought he'd struck pay dirt because his chest puffed out beneath his white shirt. "Jim and me, we're partners at Latham, Jones and Latham."

"In the District," added Jim.

Despite the attractively throaty timbre of Jim's voice, Erin arched one brow and shot a look at Nina. Were they supposed to be impressed? Law firms were a dime a dozen in downtown DC.

Nina flipped her long, straight hair over one shoulder. "Really?" she said, feigning interest. "Regina's husband is at Shorter and Grominsky. Maybe you know him? Sam Frank?"

The mention of Sam's prestigious firm earned her a respectful glance from Rob. "Can't say as I've had the pleasure." Interest sparked in his dark eyes, but he must have thought better of the idea of poaching another attorney's wife. His gaze lowered to Erin.

"How about you, um…?" Clearly angling for a name, he let the question dangle.

"Erin. I'm in town visiting my friends."

"Oh, and where's home?"

"Wherever the wind blows." Erin adopted a mysterious tone.

"Sounds interesting." Rob traded a smug look with his wingman, who'd proven himself an equal-opportunity voyeur and was busy chatting up both Michelle and Nina. At Jim's subtle nod, Rob sent a pointed glance toward the serving station along the far wall. "Let us buy your table a round of drinks. We'll have the waiter bring over a couple of chairs and join you."

"I don't think so, Rob," Erin dropped all trace of her Southern accent.

"No?" His gaze circled the table, lingering a moment on each of the women. "You don't mind, do you, girls?" He beckoned a server.

Across the busy restaurant, their waiter took a step toward their table before he spotted Erin's raised palm. The man executed an about-face that would have made a drill sergeant proud and returned to the station, where he wisely busied himself folding napkins.

Meanwhile, Jim grabbed a chair from the empty table next door. As he wedged it into position on the corner, his smile widened. "Four beautiful women out on the town. This must be some kind of occasion. What are we celebrating?"

"The anniversary of my husband's death,"

Michelle said, calmly lobbing a bomb into the middle of whatever the two men had in mind.

Jim was the first to recover. "I'm so sorry for your loss," he said after stumbling a bit. "Has he, um, has it been long?"

"A year today," Nina put in. She cupped her hand protectively over Michelle's.

"So you can see why we'd rather be alone," Erin added.

"But thank you for your interest." Reggie held up her wineglass in a mock toast. "It's been…interesting." Making it clear with her tone and her posture that whatever Jim and Ron were selling, no one at this table was buying.

To their credit, both Jim and Ron straightened. Without blinking an eye, Jim removed the chair he'd borrowed from the other table and returned it to its rightful place. He tipped his head toward them. "Michelle, Nina. I'm sorry we intruded on your evening."

Ron studied Erin for a long moment before, with a nearly imperceptible sigh, he stepped away. "Erin. Regina. Another time, perhaps."

The two men sidled closer to one another. Jim slung an arm around Ron's shoulders and steered him toward the exit. Watching them go, Regina exhaled slowly. Across from her, Erin leaned forward. "Are they gone yet?"

Regina nodded as the two men ambled through the door. "They're gone."

Erin fanned herself. "Well, that was fun."

"Gotta give them points for courage," Nina added. "Not many men would be brave enough to approach a table of four women."

"Four beautiful women," Regina said, echoing Ron's tone.

Michelle picked up her water glass and drank deeply. When she'd drained it, she set it down and grinned. "Well, girls. We still have it."

Regina felt the laughter build within her. It had been so long since Sam had paid her a compliment, she'd almost forgotten what it felt like to capture the roving eye of a good-looking man. And no doubt about it, Ron and Jim had been good-looking. Their personalities might have strayed over the line from smooth to oily, but so what. She swirled the last few drops of wine in her goblet and lifted it. "To us," she said.

Glasses clinked as the rest of the women joined her with whatever beverage they had at hand.

As if by magic, their waiter appeared at the end of the table. A concerned frown crossed the face that had remained stoic throughout the evening. "Is everything all right here?"

"Fine," Nina assured him. She cocked her head. "Please relay our thanks to Chef Paul. Dinner was amazing."

"Wonderful," Michelle chimed in. "The marrow was sheer perfection."

After Erin and Regina added their compliments, the waiter bowed slightly. "I'll convey your compliments. He'll appreciate them, I'm sure." He waited a beat. "Would you like to see the dessert menu?"

"Oh, by all means, bring it on," Nina said.

"And coffee all around," Erin added.

"Make mine a decaf," Regina murmured. The last thing she needed was a caffeine buzz keeping her up all night. She'd been having enough trouble sleeping lately as it was.

In seconds, the efficient waiter returned with a short stack of miniature chalkboards, which he handed out around the table. "Take a moment to look over these while I get your coffee."

"Hold on. We'll make this quick and save you an extra trip. I'm having the pumpkin ravioli with cinnamon sauce," Nina announced. "How about the rest of you?"

"That's far too adventurous for me," Erin declared. "I'll stick with the chocolate lava cake."

"Make mine tiramisu." Michelle handed the miniature chalkboard with today's dessert selections written on it back to the waiter.

"Regina?" Nina bumped her elbow.

"Yeah. Right." She skimmed down the short list of offerings. "Lavender crème brûlée?" She shrugged. She'd prefer plain old vanilla, but it'd be hard to go wrong with the creamy pudding.

"Thank you. I'll get those out to you right away."

"Hold up." Reggie held out her hand as she glanced around the restaurant. The crowd had thinned considerably in the four hours they'd been talking and eating and talking. Across the room, an older gentleman leaned toward his dinner date, one hand cupped over his ear like an old-fashioned hearing aid. "Do you think you could turn the music down?"

"Or off," Nina echoed while Erin gave the idea a big thumbs-up.

Their waiter glanced toward the bar, where a handful of singles nursed drinks. "I doubt anyone would mind."

He hurried off to get their coffees and desserts. In seconds, the music abruptly cut off. Silence descended like a heavy blanket on a cold winter's evening. Diagonally across the table, Michelle rested folded hands on the tabletop. "Now that it's finally quiet enough to hear ourselves think, I have some news." She squeezed her fingers tightly. "I'm not sure if I can get through this, so just let me put it out there before we start talking about it."

Reggie tensed. Concern stirred in her gut. Her mouth went dry. Michelle had to be talking about the problem Erin had hinted at earlier in the evening. Once again, she studied the woman she'd known practically her entire life. Michelle wasn't sick, was she? Terrible possibilities raced through her mind. She swallowed hard and whispered a silent prayer that everything would be all right.

"I'm putting the house on the market."

"You—why?" Reggie sputtered in sync with Nina's shocked gasp. She swung toward Erin, but her sister's blank expression gave nothing away.

Michelle held up a hand. "I didn't tell you earlier because I didn't want to put a damper on the evening. But I don't have a choice. I have to sell it. Allen and I poured everything we had into his new start-up. When he died, so did any hope of recouping that investment. The only thing left was a small insurance policy. I've been living off that, but the money's almost gone. I have enough to make it for another couple of months, and that's it."

"Where will you go? You're not—you're not moving out of the area, are you?" Despite her best efforts, tears welled in Reggie's eyes.

"Right now, anything's possible," Michelle answered. "I'd like to stay close—I grew up in Fairfax. My friends are here." She smiled, her focus shifting to Erin. "Most of them, anyway." When Erin shrugged, she continued. "But I don't know if I'll be able to afford to live here." She took a deep breath and spoke as if she were in a confessional. "There's not a whole lot of equity in the house. I'll use whatever I get from it to get a smaller place. Probably an apartment. No matter what, I'll need to find a job. Which won't be easy."

Reggie added her two cents to a chorus of protests.

Michelle shook her head. "If you know an employer who's looking for a middle-aged woman who's spent the last twenty-five years raising a family and doesn't have a single reference, let me know," she said, chuckling. She unclenched her fingers. "Whatev. The job thing— that's still a little farther down the road. Right now, my main focus is on getting the house ready to put on the market. It needs a boatload of repairs. We put some things off, thinking we'd tackle them once the new business got off the ground. And frankly, I've let things slide this past year. But it's Catch-22. Every dime I spend on repairs should increase the value of the house.

The more I take out of my savings to cover things like new paint and getting the driveway pressure-washed, the more I'll need to take the first offer that comes along or risk losing everything. My handyman is supposed to come on Monday to get started."

"Not Timmy!" Reggie protested. The man had been overcharging Michelle for shoddy work for years now. Personally, she would have fired him long ago.

"I don't know anyone else to call," Michelle said softly.

That did it. They couldn't let their friend throw her money away. "You mentioned paint and pressure-washing. What else needs to be done?"

"I have a list."

"Of course, you do." Michelle was the kind of person who put "get in the car" on her list just for the pleasure of marking the item off her list when she ran errands on a Saturday morning. "Let me see it." Reggie held out her hand.

"I don't have it with me. It's back at the house." Michelle frowned.

"Well, give us the highlights, then. What are the biggest jobs?"

"Okay." Michelle ticked items off on her fingers. "The mantel in the living room has to be refinished. The pool needs to be prepped for summer. There's a leak in the overhang over the kitchen door. We probably ought to repaint the living room some nice, neutral color. All the shrubs should be cut back, trimmed, or whatever people do to shrubs this time of year."

"I'm not hearing anything major here."

"No," Michelle admitted. "It's all pretty basic Harry-Homemaker stuff. There's just, well, there's a lot of it. I took three pages of notes. I think I could handle most of it myself if I had enough time. Trouble is, I need to get the house on the market ASAP. Before I run out of money and the bank forecloses."

Reggie let her gaze circle the table until she came to Erin. How much help they'd be to Michelle depended on how long her sister planned to be in town. When Erin gave a barely perceptible nod, she nudged the girl beside her. "You in?"

"I'm in," Nina nodded.

"What's going on?" Michelle asked.

As the self-appointed spokesperson for the group, Reggie fielded the question. "You might still need that handyman. But before you spend any money, let's see how much we can accomplish this weekend."

"You?" Michelle's face registered surprise mingled with the tiniest amount of hope. "I can't ask you to do that. What about your own jobs? And Sam? Wouldn't you rather be home with him?"

"Oh, please," Reggie said. "Sam's so busy at work, he won't even miss me." Which was especially true now. "If I get an early start tomorrow, I can handle all the outside stuff— trim the bushes, mulch, do whatever yard work you need—this weekend."

"I have to go in tomorrow, but I'll take Saturday off—I have plenty of vacation on the books. And the restaurant is dark on Sundays, so I'm all yours," Nina put in. "I'm pretty handy with paint." She moved an imaginary brush through the air.

Erin shrugged. "No one knew I was even coming here, so I don't have any plans." She tapped her finger to her chin. "Oh, and I can swing a hammer with the best of them. When you travel as much as I do, something's always breaking down. You learn to be self-sufficient."

Michelle's eyes welled. Someone handed her a tissue. "You guys. I don't know how I'll ever repay you."

"Repay nothing," Reggie assured her. "That's what friends are for."

Besides, now that Sam had moved out, she couldn't think of one thing she'd rather do than spend time with the people who meant the most to her.

Eight

Michelle

"Ummm. I can still taste that limoncello." Michelle licked her lips. Their waiter had carried the tray of tiny cordials to the table along with the bill. She'd had no idea whether the chef had sent the round of aperitifs as a thank-you for Nina's compliments or if the restaurant was trying to make amends for the two men who'd interrupted their dinner. Either way, the refreshing taste had been the perfect way to end the evening. She double-checked her seat belt. "Tha's good. Oops!" She clamped a hand over her mouth and stared at Erin through wide eyes. "Did I jess slur?"

"We drank more than I'm used to," Erin agreed. "It's a good thing we're not driving."

"Nope. We promised the twins when they were babies. Never ever drink and drive." Michelle leaned back and closed her eyes. How many rounds of drinks had there been? Four? Five? At least the world didn't spin. That was always a good sign.

She pried one eye open. "Do you need d'rections?" she asked the driver. She and Reggie had both called Ubers while Kevin was finalizing their bill. The cars had pulled up to the door of the restaurant at nearly the same moment. After a round of hugs, Nina and Reggie had climbed into one, while she and Erin had taken the second.

"No, ma'am." The driver, a heavily accented Jamaican, tapped the cell phone mounted on his dashboard. A map to her house was highlighted in green.

She turned to Erin. "We couldn't have had a better night. The food, the company, the restaurant, it was all simply perfect." She sighed happily.

"Even with our uninvited guests." Erin made air quotes.

A laugh started deep in Michelle's belly and worked its way up. "I have to admit it. It felt good to catch someone's eye. It's been a while."

"I hear ya." Erin nodded. "When I first started guiding, I'd get hit on all the time. Mostly guys. Sometimes women. Now, not so much."

"Why is that?" she asked, perplexed. "Sure, we might have a few miles on us, but we're still in pretty good shape for our age."

"Guys our age don't want women our age," Erin pointed out. "They want perky twenty-somethings."

"Gaah!" Michelle said. "Remember us in our twenties? Too many hormones. Everything was all drama, all the time."

"Speak for yourself," Erin chided.

"Oh no. You're not sliding by that easy. Remember when you and Ron broke up? You cried on my shoulder for a solid week."

"True." Erin stared out the window.

"Do you ever hear from him?"

"Ron? No. Last I heard, he'd moved out west. Texas, maybe?" She shrugged.

"You ever wonder how things would have turned out if you'd stayed together?" She'd avoided asking the question for a dozen years. Maybe it was the alcohol, or maybe Allen's loss, but something had loosened her tongue.

"Oh, puh-leeze. We were like oil and water. We never really had a chance." Erin leaned closer. "Great sex, though. The best ever."

"TMI! TMI!" Giggling, Michelle clamped a hand over her mouth. She hiccupped. "It's not the sex I miss," she confessed. She and Allen had been intimate right up to the night before he died, but their lovemaking had never set the world on fire. "It's the closeness, the companionship. The brush of his hand on my shoulder. Watching TV together in the evenings. How he'd hold me whenever one of the kids screwed up. I miss that." She sighed.

"I bet Ashley's ears are burning right about now."

When Erin's elbow jabbed her side, Michelle laughed. "Oh, that girl! She can push my buttons."

"Don't worry, Mom," Erin coached. "Give her twenty years. She's a good kid. She'll turn out all right."

"Is this the right place, ma'am?" Their driver pulled to the curb.

"Yep." Michelle pulled up the Uber app on her phone and added a tip. Sliding across the seat to the door, she frowned. "I don't remember leaving all those lights on, do you?" She was actually pretty certain she had shut everything off. Now, lights glowed from every downstairs window and two on the second floor.

"No cars," Erin observed.

"Do you think someone broke in?"

"Don't be silly," Erin scoffed. "Burglars use flashlights."

A little less steady on her feet than she'd been when they left the house five hours earlier, Michelle stepped onto the winding walkway. It only took two steps toward the front door before she decided that the odds of breaking an ankle in her current state were higher than she liked. She slipped out of her heels. After picking them up, she carried them with her the rest of the way.

At the door, she fished her keys out of her purse. She only had to stab the purple house key at the lock twice before it slid into the hole. "Here we go," she whispered.

The door swung open to the dulcet tones of her red-haired daughter. "Well, it's about time you got home! Where in the world have you been all night?"

Michelle's toes sank into the plush oriental rug in the entryway while she stood stock-still and stared at her daughter. Granted, she'd had more than her usual share of alcohol tonight, but she remembered Ashley telling her specifically she would not make it home this weekend. She peered closer. "Ashley?"

"Yes, Mother. Ashley. Your daughter. Are you drunk?" She sniffed. "Have you been out *celebrating?*" She didn't wait for an answer but stormed around the room. "Oh, that's rich. You call and lay this huge guilt trip on me and Aaron about having to spend the anniversary of Daddy's death all alone. You left us no choice. We had to drop everything and rush home to be with you."

"Ashley, stop walking around in circles. You're making me dizzy." Michelle put her free hand to her head. She waited until Ashley stilled. Angry, her daughter gripped the back of one of the Queen Anne chairs. "As for the phone call, yes, I did call to remind you of the significance of this day. But only so you and Aaron wouldn't look at the calendar and be blindsided by the date. I certainly did not beg you to come home."

"Well, it sure sounded that way to me, Mother." The cloth around Ashley's fingers dented. "But when we get here, guess who's nowhere to be found? We were sitting here worried sick. Had you been in an accident? Had you done something to yourself? But no, here you are rolling in at one in the morning after spending the night out having a good ol' time."

Michelle drew herself as tall as her five-foot-three-inch frame would allow. Oh, how she wished she wasn't standing barefoot in the entryway holding a killer pair of high heels.

Heels that would give her some very-much-needed height just when she needed it the most. Ashley's suggestion that she'd harm herself was ridiculous. Yes, she'd loved her husband. And yes, rattling around in this big house alone sucked. But life went on, and so would she. She opened her mouth to explain all that. What came out instead was, "Aaron's here? Where is he?"

"He got tired of waiting for you and went to bed."

Of course, he had. Whenever possible, her son avoided the drama his sister was so fond of. Movement behind her caught her attention, and she turned a little too quickly. The world tilted, then righted itself. "Sorry about this, Erin." She'd all but forgotten her friend. Erin had wisely opted to remain on the front porch when Ashley launched into the tirade she'd probably been stewing over for several hours.

"Say hello to your aunt Erin, Ashley." She beckoned the twin's godmother inside.

"Aunt Erin's here?" Ashley's voice rose an octave.

Erin slipped in beside Michelle, her presence solid and supportive. "Hey, Ash."

Ashley folded her arms across an ample chest. "At least you had enough sense not to—"

Michelle's hand sliced through the air,

cutting off her daughter's rant in mid-stream. She'd heard enough. It was late, and she didn't need to hear any more of Ashley's complaints. "I'm sorry you had to wait so long. If you'd let me know you were coming, I would have been here."

"It was supposed to be a surprise, Mother," came Ashley's dry response. "Some surprise."

"Yes, well." Michelle massaged her temples with her free hand. "We'll talk more in the morning. For now, I'm going to get some water and go to bed. You might want to do the same thing. Regina will be here first thing in the morning."

"Why?" Ashley demanded. "Are you having a party?"

"A work party. There's a lot to do if I'm going to put the house on the market by the end of the month."

Ashley's normally pale complexion went alabaster-white. She stood so still, she looked as if she'd been carved out of marble. Disbelief colored her green eyes, which widened. "You're selling the house?"

Michelle groaned. She hadn't meant to say that. The words had just slipped out. "I have to, Ash. Your father—" She stopped herself before she could talk ill of the dead. "I can't afford to keep it," she said simply.

"You were just going to sell our home, the only home I've ever known, and not tell me?" Ashley's face reddened.

"I had planned to drive down to Charlottesville next week and talk to you and Aaron. I'd hoped you and he would be adults about all this." She let her arms fall to her side.

"Unbelievable! First, we lose Daddy. And now you're getting rid of the one place that holds his memories. I can't—" A sob escaped Ashley's lips. "How could you?" She dashed through the room and fled up the stairs. Seconds later, the door to her bedroom slammed.

"You okay?" Erin slung a comforting arm around her shoulders.

"No." Her hands shook. The pair of shoes she hadn't realized she was still holding dropped to the floor. She drew in a thready breath. "Well, you sure called that one."

"When I said she might not take the news about the house well?"

"Yeah, that. I hate that it came out like that. I should have broken the news to her more gently."

Erin snorted. "I don't think the how or why of it matters to Ash. I love my goddaughter, but she has a very self-centered view of the world.

Not her fault. It's her age. She'll see things differently as she gets a little more experience under her belt. But right now…" Erin sighed. "She was never going to take it well."

"I suppose you're right." Michelle nibbled on her lower lip.

"You want to stay up and talk for a while? I think there's an open bottle of wine left over from this afternoon. I can pour us a glass."

"No." The fight had exhausted her. "I'm beat."

"That's fine. I'll grab us a couple of bottles of water. Tomorrow morning, I'll make myself scarce so you can talk with her and Aaron. They'll be all right once you have a chance to explain why you have to sell the house."

"I sure hope you're right." Erin meant well, but she and Ash had gone toe-to-toe so often over the years, Michelle suspected her daughter would sulk for a week or more before she finally calmed down enough for a sensible conversation. And, as much as she'd like to give the girl that much time to adjust, she couldn't afford to waste another minute in putting the house on the market.

Feeling every one of her forty-five years and then some, she climbed the stairs to her bedroom.

Nine

Reggie

*R*eggie pulled into a parking space in front of the bagel shop. Through the clear glass window, she spotted her sister sitting at a corner table. A slow breath seeped through her lips while she counted to ten. Erin's early-morning wake-up call had been unexpected. Her sister's invitation to join her for coffee had been an even bigger surprise. But she wasn't at all surprised to find her sister already sitting in the little restaurant, a cup and saucer on the table before her, a full twenty minutes ahead of the scheduled time. Reggie might have arrived early, but not early enough to beat Erin, who regularly accused people of being late when they showed up at the appointed time.

She slid from the truck. Thanking her lucky stars for the parking space right by the front doors of the restaurant, she pressed the lock button on her key fob and listened to the reassuring "click." Hedge clippers, a chain saw, rakes and an edger lay under a tarp in the bed of the pickup. She'd be able to keep an eye on her tools from inside. She'd invested in top-of-the-line equipment and spent hours each week cleaning and oiling the pieces. The last thing she wanted was to lose it all to some light-fingered passerby. Pulling up the zipper on a windbreaker that bore a Green Pastures logo, she headed for the door.

"Hey." She nodded to Erin, who looked none the worse for wear after their late night. She, on the other hand, had worn her darkest sunglasses.

"Hey, yourself." Erin stood. "I'm glad we could do this."

"Ow!" Reggie feigned a wince when Erin tugged her ponytail. "I was surprised when you called. I thought we were getting an early start this morning." She worried a cuticle between her teeth. From the little she'd seen of Michelle's yard yesterday, it'd take all weekend and then some to give the house the curb appeal a Realtor would expect.

"Slight change of plans." Erin made shooing motions. "Go. Get your coffee. I'll fill you in when you get back."

"Okay." Wondering what had thrown them off schedule before they even got started, she headed for the line that led to a low counter in the back of the deli, where two clerks were busy taking orders. Men and women in business attire dotted the restaurant, intent on fortifying themselves with caffeine and carbs before facing the weekday, rush-hour traffic. The line moved quickly, and soon Reggie studied a board that offered bagels in nearly two dozen flavors prepared in nearly as many ways. She ordered a plain, medium latte and a toasted, whole-wheat bagel dotted with ancient grains but opted to forgo the butter or cream cheese. In under ten minutes, she slid onto the chair across from her sister.

"So, what's up?" she asked, stirring a packet of raw sugar into her coffee.

"Ash and Aaron were at the house when we got in last night. They'd driven in from Charlottesville to spend the weekend with Michelle. They, well, Ash—Aaron had gone to bed—she was pretty upset that no one was home when they got there."

Reggie felt her brows knit. "Michelle never

said a word about the kids coming home. If we'd known…"

"Yeah, if we'd known, we would've canceled. But they didn't tell Michelle." Erin had ordered a healthy-looking yogurt parfait loaded with fresh fruit and nuts. She speared a strawberry. "Evidently, Ash and Aaron planned to surprise her."

"But they came home to an empty house?" Reggie picked a pumpkin seed off her bagel and chewed thoughtfully. "Poor kids. They must have been out of their minds with worry."

Across the table, Erin stared at her blankly, the strawberry halfway to her mouth. "Say that again?"

"Well, I'm just trying to imagine how I'd feel if I drove three hours to see my mom on the anniversary of my dad's death and she was nowhere to be found. They were probably worried something had happened to her, too."

"Hmmm." Erin took a long, slow swallow from her coffee cup. "Ashley did hint that Michelle might have had an accident or some-thing. The conversation was hard to follow. She was kind of shouting."

"Again. Probably the fear talking. People react differently to stress, and Ashley's always been high-strung. Remember when she got her first period? She wailed like a banshee. You'd have thought she was dying."

Across the table, Erin gave a wry smile. "That girl should have studied acting. She'd be good at it."

"What are the twins, in their twenties?" When Erin nodded, she said, "You'd think by now, Ashley would've figured out that pitching a fit doesn't actually fix the problem."

"Oh, but it does." Erin chuckled. "She gets everyone so upset that they run around in circles trying to fix the problem for her." Her cup clinked softly into the saucer. "That's one of the things I like about you, Regina. You always shed a different light on things. Here I was, just thinking Ash was being a brat."

Reggie ground her back teeth together. She'd asked Erin at least a thousand times over the years not to call her by her full name. Should she remind her sister again? Or would Erin only ignore her request like she always did? She broke off a bite of her bagel. "How'd Michelle handle it?"

"Mmmm, okay, until she let it slip that she was selling the house. Ashley didn't take that piece of news well. Not. At. All. But Michelle kept her cool a lot better than I would have. She said she was going to sit the twins down and have a heart-to-heart with them over breakfast.

When I headed out, she'd already squeezed a dozen oranges for juice and was sliding a pan of stuffed French toast into the oven."

The bagel Reggie had chosen suddenly tasted as good as dry cardboard. "You think there'll be leftovers?" With its sweet, cream-cheese filling and doused with maple syrup, Michelle's breakfast casserole was pure, melt-in-your-mouth heaven.

"I guess we'll find out soon enough. I told Michelle I'd make myself scarce for an hour or two. It's just as well." Erin tilted her head just a bit. "It'll give us some time to catch up. We hardly had a chance to talk yesterday."

Reggie nodded. Last night had been all about Michelle, as it should have been.

Erin scooped up another spoonful of yogurt. "So, what's new with you? You still working for Green Pastures? How's Sam? When are you two going to make me an aunt?"

Reggie swallowed. Glad she'd left her sunglasses in place, she blinked rapidly past Erin's final question. Though teams of specialists had all agreed that neither of them was to blame for their failure to conceive, Sam had made her swear she wouldn't tell a soul about their infertility problems. Other than an online support group where she used a fake name, she'd kept her word. Mentally crossing her fingers, she tackled the first of Erin's questions and hoped they'd either run out of time or her sister would lose interest before they circled around to the question that made her sweat.

"I'm still with Green Pastures." She brushed her fingers over the logo on her jacket. "It's not the most challenging work in the world, but it keeps me busy. I have a good boss. He's pretty flexible about my hours as long as we bring the job in on schedule and at budget. There's a ton of new construction going on west of town, so it looks like I have steady employment for the foreseeable future."

Erin blotted her lips with her napkin. "You still thinking of going into business for yourself? With your degree and experience, I'm surprised you haven't already taken that next step."

"That was the plan, wasn't it? Work for a few years with one of the bigger landscaping firms. Use that as a jumping-off platform for my own business." She pushed the tasteless bagel aside. Once upon a time, she'd had her whole life mapped out. She'd hire on at Green Pastures, the largest landscaping firm in the area, get promoted to crew manager and, as soon as she had a few years of experience under her belt, she'd go into business for herself.

But Sam had thrown a monkey wrench into her plans. She hadn't minded paying the bills and such while he was in law school, not really. Once he passed the bar, she was sure he'd return the favor while she got her own company off the ground. But, instead of the quick trip to the Justice of the Peace she'd hoped for, he'd insisted on a big wedding with all the trimmings. Her half of the costs had nearly wiped out her savings account and her hopes of starting a business of her own. She'd spent every dime she made since then trying to have a baby. Now, her marriage was on the rocks, bills were all she had to show for five rounds of in vitro, and she was still working for Green Pastures. "Things didn't work out," she said simply.

"Are you okay?" Erin lifted one eyebrow.

"Yeah." She forced herself to sit a little straighter. "Just tired from last night. We were out pretty late."

She watched Erin mull the answer over for a long minute before her sister asked the inevitable, "How about Sam? You and he doing good?"

Reggie fought down a groan. How was she supposed to answer? Should she confess that her husband of five years had walked out on her? One day soon, Sam had to come to his senses and come back to her, didn't he? As long as there was a chance they'd work things out, she couldn't share her troubles with Erin. She and her sister might not spend a lot of time together, but Erin was fiercely loyal, and she held a grudge better than anyone else Reggie had ever known. One negative word about Sam, and her sister would never forgive the man. So, no. She couldn't admit that her marriage was on the rocks.

"He's doing incredibly well at work," she said, dodging the question by focusing on the man she'd married. "He's been given his first big solo case, which means he's putting in longer hours than ever. But it looks like all his hard work will pay off. The senior partners have been very happy with his progress. There's a good chance he'll make junior partner if everything continues to go well." She took a breath and turned the tables. "How about yourself? Where are you headed when you leave here?"

"I'm not sure." Erin dragged her finger through a water ring and traced a circle on the table. "For the first time in I-can't-remember-when, I'm not entirely pleased with the idea of hitting the road with nothing more than what I can stuff in my duffle."

"You've probably seen all there is to see on earth." Her sister had traveled the world ten times over. She, meanwhile, hadn't ever left the States. "Maybe you should try to get a seat on the next space launch."

"Not hardly." Erin snorted. "But you're right. I've visited every continent at least once and had some amazing experiences. I've been pelted by tomatoes in Spain during La Tomatina, watched camel-wrestling in Turkey." She grinned. "And learned to keep my distance. They spit, and it's nasty. One time in the Philippines I helped villagers pick up an entire house by hand—no cars or forklifts—and move it out of the way during the rainy season."

Reggie shook her head. "You've been so many places, done so many things. I bet you've had some amazing meals, too."

"Don't get me started on the food." Mirth danced in Erin's eyes. "I've eaten everything from haggis in Scotland to fried locusts in Israel." She shook her head. "You might consider eating slices of cold pork fat disgusting, but in the Ukraine, it's a delicacy called salo."

Reggie fought an urge to clamp a hand over her mouth. "You must have a cast-iron stomach and the constitution of a..." She stopped herself. She'd intended to say "the constitution of a horse," but horses actually had delicate digestive systems. She finished, "Well, I don't know what."

She peered at her sister. "And now you're thinking of settling down? For real?"

"I'm thinking about it," Erin said. "But that's all it is right now—a thought."

"Wow! Even that is a huge change. Mom and Dad would flip out if you lived closer. Me, too." She grinned. It was probably too much to hope for that Erin might actually move back home. Of all the places she visited in her travels, her sister rarely spent more than a week at a time in their little corner of Virginia. But it would be nice if she put down roots someplace close enough that they could actually see each other from time to time.

"Speaking of the folks." Erin swirled the last of her coffee in her cup. "I'm planning to head out there and spend next week with them. How are they enjoying the new place?" Their parents had sold their home in Fairfax shortly after her dad retired. Now they lived in a gated, fifty-five-plus community near Harper's Ferry, where the cost of living was considerably less than in the DC suburbs.

"I—I haven't seen them much lately. Between Sam's work schedule and mine, we haven't had the time." Reggie bit her lower lip. That last part wasn't exactly true. Her husband grudgingly spent obligatory family meals with her parents on the holidays, but from the get-go, he'd given two thumbs down to the idea of weekly dinners with her parents. Worse, he turned so mulish if she went by herself that she'd long since decided that wasn't a battle she wanted to fight. But with Sam out of the picture, at least temporarily, she was free to go and do whatever she wanted. "Maybe I could come out while you're there? At least for the weekend? We could have a little impromptu family reunion."

Erin grinned. "I bet Mom and Dad would like that. But we should probably tell them we're coming. Otherwise, we might get there and find out they have other plans. Like Ashley and Aaron did to Michelle." For the first time since they'd been sitting in the restaurant, Erin glanced at her phone. "Speaking of which, we ought to get going."

"Right." Reggie glanced outside. Sunlight bathed the parking lot that had been shadowed by darkness when she pulled in. She took her keys from the pocket of her windbreaker. "You want a lift?"

Erin stretched as she stood. "Sure. This was a little farther from Michelle's than I remembered."

Reggie shook her head. A five-mile hike in the pre-dawn darkness sounded exactly like her footloose sister. "Well, let's get a move on.

Daylight's wasting," she said, imitating a character in one of the old Westerns their parents had forced them to watch when they were kids. She shook her head.

Her tumbleweed of a sister was thinking of putting down roots. Who would have thought?

Ten

Michelle

*M*ichelle's gaze landed on the pitcher of freshly squeezed orange juice. Water droplets condensed on the rounded surface and slowly dribbled down the glass. Beside it, the twins' favorite breakfast casserole sat on a trivet, the cream cheese filling hidden beneath the crispy brown edges of the French toast. Wanting to make the occasion special for her children—and yes, to soften the blow—she'd pulled out her nicest set of breakfast dishes and set the table with cloth napkins.

All for nothing.

Ashley had still been so upset when she dragged her overnight bag down the stairs this morning that she'd deliberately let the wheels smack onto each tread. She'd stopped in the kitchen just long enough to fill a travel cup with coffee before she headed into the garage without saying a single word. Aaron had appeared in the kitchen right behind his sister, a backpack slung over his shoulder and a sheepish look on his face. He'd looked longingly at the breakfast Michelle had laid out on the table for them. He'd even taken a step toward the breakfast nook. But he'd changed directions when his phone buzzed with a text.

Michelle assumed it had been the bossier of the twins telling him to hurry.

At least Aaron had had the courtesy to offer a lame excuse. A problem with a group project he had to deal with before Monday, he'd murmured. Not that Michelle had believed him for five seconds. No. Ashley had decided they were heading back to campus, and as the dominant twin, she was getting her way. As she usually did.

Michelle couldn't very well order them not to go. They were adults, after all. Headstrong and selfish, with a lot of growing up left to do, but adults all the same. She'd refused to beg them to stay and talk to her. It nearly broke her heart to watch them pull out of the driveway while things were so unsettled between them. But Aaron had promised to call soon. Though she'd rather have the conversation face-to-face, she'd fill him in on the reasons for the move. He was a good kid. He'd understand. In time, he might even help Ashley come to grips with the change. But if not, at least she'd know her babies had made it to Charlottesville in one piece.

A throaty roar sounded from the front of the house. Her pulse leaped. Had Aaron's car developed an engine problem? Had he convinced his sister they needed to turn around? She hurried to the living room, where she pulled back the drapes. Her heart sank. The ancient pickup pulling to the curb out front belonged to Reggie. Almost before it stopped, she and Erin both climbed out of the vehicle and began unloading flattened cardboard boxes, tools and equipment from the back. Together, they hauled everything up the steep driveway and piled it in the garage. Seconds later, the door to the laundry room swung open.

"I heard you were making your famous stuffed French Toast. Did you save some for…?" Reggie's voice died as she strode from the laundry room that served double duty as a passageway between the garage and the house. She paused at the threshold to the kitchen. "Are we too early?" she asked.

"No," Michelle called. With a heavy sigh, she

relinquished her hope that the kids had come to their senses sooner rather than later. "You're right on time if you're hungry." She retraced her steps to the back of the house.

Erin joined them in the kitchen. "The twins aren't still sleeping, are they? 'Cause we can come back later."

"No." Michelle blinked away the tears that threatened. "They left. They headed back to the university first thing this morning."

"Oh," Erin said, her voice freighted with regret.

"Oh, no," Reggie echoed.

"Did you have a chance to talk with them first?" Erin eyed the beautifully set table.

"I wish. But Ashley couldn't wait to get out of here. I learned long ago there's no sense in arguing with her when she gets like that. Aaron said he'd call later. I'll bring him up to speed over the phone. It won't be ideal. I wanted to have this conversation with them in person. But it is what it is, I guess." Despite her efforts to remain upbeat, her shoulders rounded.

"I'm so, so sorry," Erin said. "Is there anything I"—she glanced at Reggie—"that we can do?"

"Not unless you want to adopt a couple of twenty-one-year old, selfish, willful children."

When Reggie threw up her hands and Erin backpedaled, she tsked. "I didn't think so. Guess I'll have to deal with them on my own. Lucky me."

Erin scuffed one sneakered foot against the wood floor. "Are you, um, still going to put the house on the market?"

"Well, yeah." Michelle grinned and rolled her eyes. "I can't let Ashley have her way this time. No matter how much I want to."

"Smart move," Reggie said while Erin's lean but muscular arms wrapped Michelle in a hug.

"I'm proud of you," Erin whispered. "I know this is hard, but you're sticking to your guns. I thought for sure you'd give in to Ashley."

"No." She shook her head when her friend dropped her arms. "I can't afford to do that. Whether the twins ever accept the situation or not, I have to be the adult here and do what's best for all of us. I've already wasted too much time ignoring this mess and hoping it would go away. And I refuse to grovel or beg them to stay. I didn't create this situation. I'm simply picking up the pieces. The kids'll realize that sooner or later." Though she hated that they weren't mature enough to look past their own disappointment. She thought she'd raised them better than that. She'd never allowed her children to sass her the way other parents did. From the time they'd been old enough to reach the counters, she'd insisted the entire family spend one Saturday a month serving meals at their church's soup kitchen. From their actions this morning, though, she had to admit her kids had failed Kindness and Generosity 101.

"I'm glad you're looking at things so clearly. You're right, you know."

Michelle shrugged. "It's either sell now or let the bank take it. At least, if I sell it, I'll get a little something out of it."

"Well, then." Erin rubbed her hands together. "Where do we start?"

"How about by eating some of this breakfast so it doesn't go to waste?"

"You don't have to ask me twice. But if you don't mind, I'll grab mine to go." Reggie ducked into the roomy walk-in pantry behind the laundry room. She emerged moments later with a stack of sturdy paper plates. "I want to get a start on the front yard while it's still cool outside."

"Sure. That's fine. Let me get you some juice." Michelle took a pair of plastic cups from a cupboard. "How about you, Erin?"

"I'll pass for right now, thanks. It looks good though. Maybe lunch?"

"It'll keep." Michelle waited, expecting

Reggie to scoop up a serving and leave, but the younger woman just stood in the middle of the kitchen like she was putting down roots. "What is it?"

"Michelle, you know how much I love your home, right?'

"Uh-oh. That doesn't sound one bit ominous." She tried not to squirm beneath Reggie's penetrating gaze. "Yes. You've told me often enough. So what's wrong?"

"Nothing, it's just…"

"Out with it," Michelle ordered. Might as well get it over with. Today didn't seem to be her day anyhow. She was already on the outs with the twins, and now Reggie clearly had something on her mind.

"It's just that you have a lot of stuff." Still holding the paper plates, she made air quotes. "You should ask your real estate agent, but I've worked with a couple of different staging companies. They're usually working on the model homes while we're laying sod. They all have this rule…and, um…"

Michelle followed along as Reggie's gaze swept over the kitchen counters. She prided herself on keeping a tidy kitchen and had cleaned up behind herself as she prepared breakfast this morning. The granite sparkled.

She'd treated the empty farmer's sink to a good scrubbing. The appliances gleamed. She didn't see a thing out of place, but something had put that frown on Reggie's face.

"It's the rule of three. No more than three objects on any given surface," Reggie said in a rush. "On your kitchen counters, you have two sets of canisters and enough appliances to open a home goods store." She paused. "Are all those rabbits really necessary?"

"I'll have you know those rabbits are Lladro." The porcelain figurines were as much a part of her kitchen as her pots and pans.

"I get that they're expensive. But you must have twenty or thirty of them in here."

Erin tapped her finger to her chin. "I never understood your fascination with them."

"The funny thing is, I don't even like rabbits." Michelle pressed her hand to her mouth. "When we moved into the house, Allen's mom gave us that big one over there as a housewarming present." She pointed to the largest bunny, which sat atop the refrigerator. "I was spending a lot more time in the kitchen back then, and I plopped it down on the counter where I could see it. Next thing I knew, guests were bringing me more of them. The kids even chipped in their allowances to buy me one for my birthday. They kind of multiplied like… rabbits."

Erin hooted, and soon all three of them were laughing. When the last chuckle died away, Reggie grew serious. "I still think you should store them and about half this other stuff. Put it all away somewhere. I brought boxes. And tape. They're in the garage."

"You're probably right," Michelle agreed. She'd put Nina to work on that project tomorrow. For today, she had another task in mind. One she'd need Erin's help with.

"Now, about that French Toast." Reggie scooped a small serving onto a plate. "Any special instructions for the yard? Any plants you don't want me to touch?"

"No. But I'd really appreciate it if you could help out with the rose bushes. I tried yesterday, but I think I was doing more damage than good." Michelle brandished the long scratch one of the thorns had made on her forearm.

"Roses, right. They're first on my list." Reggie hefted her plate and headed for the laundry room and the garage. "I'll be outside."

Once the door swung closed behind her sister, Erin rubbed her hands together. "Now, where do you want me to start?"

Michelle pulled a box of plastic wrap from

the drawer, yanked out a longish piece and covered the barely touched casserole dish. Could she do this? She squeezed her eyes shut for a long second. It had to be done. She took a breath. "I need to clean out Allen's closet, and I can't do it myself. I could use your help."

Eleven

Nina

A heavy weight sat on her chest. Nina slung one arm over her head. "It's too early, Mr. Pibbs," she moaned.

The cat made biscuits in Nina's pajama top. "Meow." His plaintive cry filled the tiny apartment. "Meow," he cried again.

"Are you hungry?" She ran one hand over the animal's soft fur while she cracked one eye open wide enough to see the clock on the empty vegetable crate she'd painted blue and used as an end table. Eleven o'clock. She groaned. She'd slept late. She'd intended to go into the restaurant early today, get a head start on her work so she could take Saturday off. As it was, she'd barely make it to the restaurant before her shift started in an hour. She struggled into a sitting position, a move that would have been infinitely easier if Mr. Pibbs had jumped off her. Instead, he dug his claws into her pajamas, insisting on coming along for the ride.

She swung her feet to the floor. Her mouth was drier than a desert. Her head felt as big as a watermelon. She had clearly had too much to drink last night. She smiled. But they'd had a good time, hadn't they? Lifted Michelle's spirits? That was worth a little hangover, wasn't it?

"Come on, Mr. Pibbs." She tucked the fur baby into her arms and carried him into the tiny kitchen area. "I'll get you some nice, tasty breakfast as soon as I have some water." Juggling the cat, she opened a bottle of water and shook two Tylenol from the supply she kept on an open shelf over the sink. She downed both in short order, then set about getting Mr. Pibbs's breakfast.

The instant she set his bowl of his favorite cat food on the floor, the big kitty leaped from her arms, his attention riveted on his tuna. Nina emptied and refilled his water bowl and did the same with the dry kibble Mr. Pibbs usually ignored until he was absolutely starving.

A half hour later, showered and wearing the Café Chef Jacques jacket over chef's pants and a black T-shirt, she blew air kisses to Mr. Pibbs.

"Stay out of trouble," she warned, though at twelve, the big kitty yawned at the thought of exercise. His idea of a workout consisted of following the pools of light as sun moved from one window to another in the tiny apartment.

Her phone buzzed with a text message before she reached the sidewalk in front of the five-story walk-up. She glanced at the screen, expecting a message from Michelle or Erin. Instead, Chef Jacques's name appeared in the screen, followed by a cryptic, "my office."

Nina gulped. Getting called into the head chef's office was never a good thing. Especially not hours before the demanding head cook usually reported to work. She quickened her pace, covering the ten-minute walk to the restaurant in half her usual time. After clocking in on the ancient time clock next to the employees' entrance, she stepped into the lounge, where shrugged off the windbreaker and hung it in her locker. Then she pulled a freshly laundered chef's coat from the rack. After slipping her arms into the snug-fitting jacket, she smoothed her hands down the front. She checked her image in the mirror mounted on the wall. Every hair in place, every wrinkle banished. She was as ready as she'd ever be.

Thirty seconds later, she wrapped on

Jacques's open door. "You wanted to see me, Chef?"

"Come in. Shut the door."

"Yes, Chef."

Jacques didn't have to look up from the ledger he was writing in for Nina to read the tension that radiated from the burly figure behind the desk. For the second time in the space of thirty minutes, she gulped. Clearly, something had put a bee in Chef's toque, but she'd done nothing to upset him. Why, she hadn't even been at work yesterday. She stilled, her hands folded in front of her as a sign of respect for the most powerful man in the kitchen. An eternity passed before a pair of dark eyes bore into her from beneath bushy eyebrows.

"Six plates came back last night," Jacques said. Fury resonated in his voice. "Six."

Years of working in some of the best kitchens in the DC area had taught her the importance of remaining poised and in control. Yet, despite herself, Nina sucked in a breath. Café Chef Jacques prided itself on excellence. On the rare occasion, a patron might request an extra turn on the grill for their steak or object to the chorizo in their penne chicken breast. But to have actual dinners returned to the kitchen was practically unheard of.

"Do you care to tell me why?"

The man's deep, guttural tone warned her that she ought to know the answer. But how could she? There hadn't been a single complaint lodged against her station on Wednesday, and she hadn't stepped foot in the restaurant on Thursday. She swallowed. "I have no idea, Chef."

A smile that didn't hold a single ounce of warmth formed on her boss's lips. He yanked the door to a mini-fridge open and took out a quart-size plastic container. Nina froze when the head chef slammed the tub down on his desk. One glance was all it took for her to confirm the date and her name on the lid. Her mind raced. She'd stayed late on Wednesday to replace the batch of pepper sauce Chad had ruined. The new dish had been perfect, even better that the first batch, in fact. She'd stake her reputation on it.

"There was something wrong with the sauce?"

"See for yourself," Chef sneered. He handed her a wooden tasting spoon.

Nina studied the thick liquid. Exactly as she'd expect them to, bits of pepper and tomato floated in the topping Chef used in creating his signature swordfish. She gave the cup a tentative stir. The texture was perfect, not so heavy that it'd sit on top of a piece of fish like jellied aspic but not so thin that it'd puddle on the plate. So far, so good. She dipped and sampled.

Salt! The taste overwhelmed the fiery peppers. The rich tomatoes were buried under it. Wishing she could spit, she swallowed.

"Well, that's unfortunate," she said. The container was undoubtedly the one Chad had doctored, but she'd thrown his away. Hadn't she?

"So you agree there's a problem?" Jacques folded his arms across his chest.

"Yes, Chef." Of course, she agreed. She'd be a fool not to. Anyone with a single taste bud on their tongue would acknowledge the dish had been oversalted.

"Care to explain how this crap got in my cooler?"

That's exactly what she'd like to know. All items prepared ahead of the actual dinner service went into a dedicated refrigerator. The containers lined the shelves in date order, with the most recent additions toward the back. They sat there, ready and waiting, until Chef needed them.

She shook her head. "I don't know, Chef."

"But these are your initials? You wrote the date on the cover?"

She swore softly. Every item in his cooler bore the initials of the cook who'd prepared it.

"What was that?" Chef Jacques lifted the container. "You made this?"

"Yes, Chef, but…" She'd marked the lid before Chad had stopped by her station. Catching herself just in time, she pressed her lips closed. She'd been on the verge of pointing out that the new sous chef had wrecked her perfectly good sauce. However, throwing the owner's nephew under the bus wasn't going to help her make friends with the man. And she needed to stay on his good side. As the restaurant's second-in-command, Chad wielded tremendous power in the kitchen. He could make her life miserable. It'd be better for her to take the hit than blame him. Aware that her shoulders had sagged, she straightened. "Yes, Chef. That's my work."

Chef Jacques folded his hands on the top of his desk. "I expected better of you, Nina. Having those plates come back made the restaurant—and me—look bad. If a food critic had gotten one of them…Well, I don't have to tell you how much that could have hurt us. This type of carelessness is unacceptable. It cannot happen again."

LEIGH DUNCAN

"Yes, Chef." Miserable, she clasped her hands together so tightly, her fingers ached. She'd worked hard to gain this man's trust. It was killing her to know she'd let him down, whether the fault was all hers or not.

"The restaurant was forced to replace the ruined entrees at no charge."

Nina sipped air. She'd expected as much. Not comping the diners risked damaging the restaurant's reputation. "I'll reimburse the costs, of course." She bowed her head.

For the first time since she'd been called into the chef's office, the man blinked at the unexpected offer. He recovered quickly. "As you should. I'll take $300 out of your next paycheck. You're also on a two-day suspension."

Much as she wanted to protest, she refused to argue. She couldn't, not without shifting at least part of the blame to Chad. "Yes, Chef. Thank you, Chef," she murmured.

The big man waved a hand, dismissive. "You can go now. Use the time between now and Monday to think about what happened. This cannot happen again," he repeated. His voice dropped. "Because, believe me, one more incident like this and I *will* fire you."

"I understand, sir." She was actually surprised that he hadn't let her go on the spot.

The restaurant business could be very unforgiving at times.

On her way to the locker to change into her street clothes, she reviewed the steps she'd taken the last time she'd been in the kitchen. After Chad had ordered her to do the impossible and "fix" the sauce he'd ruined, she'd known she couldn't very well dispose of his mess while there was a chance he might spot her. While she waited for him to disappear for a bit, she'd pushed the container to the back of her station. There, it had sat while she prepared the fresh batch, along with the andouille cream. Each sauce required multiple steps and infinite patience. Between those tasks and the busy dinner rush, she hadn't finished her work until nearly two. By then, she'd been at the restaurant nearly fourteen hours, and every bone in her body ached. Still, she'd checked to make sure the supplies her assistants might need the next day were on hand. Then, she'd cleaned her station a final time before shrugging out of her chef's jacket and heading home to Mr. Pibbs.

She had to admit, she hadn't exactly looked for the container of ruined sauce. Not that she needed to. The restaurant maintained a strict rule that only the cook who'd prepared a dish could put it in the cooler. She knew she hadn't placed it in the fridge. And she was pretty sure it hadn't sprouted legs and gotten there on its own. So who had moved it?

In the tiny break room, she tossed the barely worn chef's coat into the laundry. Charlie walked in as she was retrieving her windbreaker from her locker. He took one look at her slipping into her jacket instead of out of it and shook his head.

"How'd it go with Jacques?"

Tears stung her eyes. "Does everyone know?" she whispered, even though she already knew the answer. News of returned meals must have spread up and down the line like a fast-moving fire.

When Charlie nodded, she said, "Two day suspension and a $300 fine."

"Ouch!"

"It could have been worse." She took a chance. "You didn't notice anyone hanging around my station, did you?"

Charlie rubbed a massive hand over his bald head. "You mean besides Chad? He stopped by several times. Come to think of it, I saw him rearranging the shelves in the cooler that day, too." Charlie glanced over his shoulder at the closed door behind him. "But that didn't come from me."

"Don't worry. I won't say a word." Internally, though, that was a different story. She gave herself a swift kick in the mental pants. She'd considered Chad inept, but the man wasn't stupid. He'd known full well what would happen if the oversalted sauce made it onto a customer's plate. Which, in her book, moved him from an annoyance to a threat. She closed her locker. Lifting one eyebrow, she looked Charlie straight in the eye. "Watch your back." She kept her voice low. "And Chef's."

Monday. She had until Monday to formulate a plan for dealing with Chad, she thought as soon as her feet hit the sidewalk. Until then, she'd put her free days to good use by spending them with her friends.

Twelve

Michelle

"Hey! What are we doing for dinner?" Nina asked as she traipsed from the kitchen into the family room.

Michelle lowered the volume on her iPhone. The strains of Luke Combs's "Refrigerator Door" faded. "I've ordered in pizza and salads," she answered.

"You didn't want me to make something?" Nina put one hand on her hip. Her lips pursed.

"And mess up that kitchen? Are you crazy?" Her friend had spent hours treating the kitchen and breakfast nook to the kind of deep cleaning Michelle's housekeeper never got around to doing. Thanks to Nina's attention to detail, every inch of granite and stainless gleamed. Not a single fingerprint smudged the cabinets and shelves.

A stubborn stain Michelle had battled for two years had vanished as if by magic. Cracked grout had been replaced, the windows re-caulked, the glass panes washed until they sparkled. And that wasn't all. The entire house looked like it had been given a facelift. "You've all worked so hard this weekend. Buying dinner is the least I can do to repay you."

"Did you order from Lil Italian?"

The hopeful lilt in Nina's voice told Michelle she'd made the right choice. She nodded agreeably. "Nothing but the best for you, Nin." They'd have to go to Chicago or New York to get a better pie.

"Okay, then." Nina's glance floated over the empty sofa and chairs. "Where's everybody else?"

"Reggie's in the shower. Erin's putting the last of the boxes in my car." While the youngest of their group worked in the yard, she and Erin had emptied Allen's closet with a minimum of tears. Tomorrow she'd drop the boxes off at Boots to Suits, a charitable clothing program for veterans. "She sent me in to place our order."

"I'll get cleaned up when Reggie's done." Nina cocked her head. "Why are you listening to music on your phone? You have an awesome system. Why not use it?"

Michelle felt her face heat. "It's not exactly working right now. A thunderstorm knocked out the power a few months ago. When it came back on, none of the remotes worked."

"Months ago?" Nina's voice registered shock.

"I was able to get the ones for the TVs working again," Michelle said in her defense, "but Allen always handled the stereo system. I haven't been able to figure it out." She sighed. "I was sort of planning to ask Aaron to fix it while he was home this weekend." Leaving things so unsettled with the twins stung. "That didn't happen."

"Your stereo has Bluetooth. The remote probably lost the connection. You just need to pair them up again."

"You're speaking a foreign language," Michelle said softly. It embarrassed her that she didn't understand how the electrical gizmos in her house worked. No one would ever have mistaken Allen for Harry Homemaker, but he'd made it clear that maintaining all the electronics was his responsibility, just like doing the laundry was hers. She hated to admit it, but changing a light bulb taxed her abilities. As for the music system, with its daunting array of lights and switches, she didn't even know where to begin. "I've heard the words. But I have no idea what they mean."

"No problem. I have the same equipment at home. I actually bought it on Allen's recommendation when I upgraded my system a few years ago. I'll give you a crash course."

"I'd like that," she said, standing. She didn't do it often, but every once in a while, she'd liked turning up the music until it blasted through the speakers, the heavy bass practically rattling the windows. Her iPhone wasn't up to that task.

"We'll have you up and running in no time." Nina linked their arms. Together, they headed into Allen's office, where a bank of equipment sat on sturdy, wall-mounted shelves. She pointed to a big black box. "Okay. That's the receiver. Think of it as air traffic control for the entire system." A green light glowed when she flipped a switch. "Now that it's on, you can…"

For the next fifteen minutes, Nina pointed to various devices, explained their purpose and how to use them. Some—like the subwoofer— had names that made Michelle laugh. Others, like the amplifier, were easier to understand but more complicated to work. She took careful notes on the back of an envelope as Nina walked her through the process of pairing the remotes. It wasn't as difficult as she'd feared. When they finished, Michelle wasn't entirely certain she understood all the ins and outs of the system, but she had instructions she could follow if a power outage knocked everything off-line again. Or, if all else failed, she could call on Nina instead of waiting for her son's next trip home from college.

"Thanks," she said when they finished. "It feels good to be in charge again."

"Great!" Nina grinned. "Why don't you pick us out something to listen to while I go grab a shower."

"Will do. And thanks again. I really appreciate your taking the time off this weekend to help out. I honestly thought it would take months to get the house ready to list. But after all we've accomplished, I'm going to give my Realtor a call first thing tomorrow."

"You do that." Nina paused. "As for my time, well, I honestly didn't have anything better to do."

"Oh?" Michelle shoved a stray hair behind her ear. Come to think of it, hadn't Nina said she couldn't get the day off on Friday? Yet she'd shown up by mid-morning and immediately pitched in with the rest of them. "You didn't have to work?"

"That was the plan." Nina's eyes cut to one side. "I made a mistake. A costly one. Chef suspended me without pay for the entire weekend."

Michelle clamped one hand over her mouth. "Oh, no! I'm so sorry! I thought everything was going great for you there." It seemed like only yesterday she and Reggie had taken Nina out to lunch to celebrate her promotion to head saucier. "Are you going to be all right?"

"I hope so. I keep telling myself it's not a big deal. It does happen all the time." Nina's shoulders rounded. A worried look formed in her eyes. "Not ever to me before, though." Her smile wavering, she shrugged. "There's always a first time, right?"

A mounting concern tightened Michelle's tummy. Nina had worked hard to get where she was. Her friend was one of the most conscientious people she knew. Whatever had gone wrong, she'd bet her last dime, someone else had a hand in it. "Mind if I asked what happened?"

Time stretched out as Nina seemed to wrestle with the answer. Michelle was about to tell her not to worry about it, that she was entitled to her privacy, when her friend leaned forward. Her voice dropped to a whisper.

"There's a new guy at work—the sous chef. He's related to the owner—a nephew or something. Anyway, the guy is a real piece of work. He rode the pastry chef's back so hard last week, he had her in tears. Twice. Wednesday was my turn."

"And?" Michelle prompted.

"There's this red pepper sauce I make especially for Chef."

"Oh, yum. I know just the one you mean." The spicy dressing had topped a swordfish dish she'd had for lunch last year. At the time, she'd wished she could skip the fish and have a whole bowl of the sauce. It had been that good.

"Right. I was just finishing up a new batch when the sous chef—his name is Chad, by the way—when Chad stopped by my station. Long story short, he ended up ruining the entire container. Then he had the gall to tell me to 'fix it.' Yeah, the only way to do that was to start over. Which I did. Only, somehow the bad batch—the stuff Chad ruined—got served to a bunch of customers. When I got in to work on Friday, Chef was livid. I didn't blame him. I would be, too."

"Ouch," Michelle said. "Did it get put in the fridge by mistake?" Over the years, she'd heard enough stories about the busy restaurant to understand some of her friend's usual routines.

Nina shook her head. "The thing is, I only put away one container of sauce, and it was still there when I got to work on Friday. I checked.

140

I've been over and over it in my head. Chad must have put that bad batch in the fridge. That's the only way Chef could have gotten his hands on it. Whether he did it deliberately or he just wasn't familiar with the way we do things at the Café, I can't say. Yet. But if he did it on purpose, I'll be looking for a new job soon."

Concern rippled through Michelle's chest. "There must be something you can do. What if you talked to the head chef again, told him what you told me?"

"I wouldn't dare go over the sous chef's head. The chain of command in the restaurant is pretty rigid. Besides, it wouldn't do any good," Nina scoffed. "Even if Chef took my side of things, if it comes down to a choice between me and the owner's nephew, we both know which one will be walking out the door."

"Let's cross our fingers and hope Chad made an honest mistake."

"I'd hate to leave the Café, but..." Nina shrugged. "It wouldn't be the first time I've been forced to move on. I'm sure it won't be the last."

Michelle shook her head. Nina deserved so much more. "You really ought to open your own place. The Bolognese you fixed for us last night was to die for. And that charcuterie board the other night completely blew me away."

Nina pressed two fingers to her mouth and blew a kiss heavenward. "From your lips to God's ears," she said with a wide grin. She sobered quickly. "Sure, I'd like to run my own kitchen one day. But the odds are better that I'll win the lottery. Which isn't likely since I don't play." She held out her hands like twin stop signs. "Enough about me. One way or the other, I'll deal with the situation at work. But that's tomorrow's problem. Right now, I'm going to dash upstairs. I bet Reggie's out of the bathroom by now."

A half hour later, Erin lounged sideways in the big leather club chair, her feet dangling over one of the hobnailed arms. She rubbed her midsection. "Any word on that pizza yet? I'm starving."

"Yeah." Reggie, who'd staked out a spot on the couch, looked up from her iPhone. "Me, too."

Nina punched a button on the remote. The TV screen went dark, cutting off the host of the cooking show in mid-sentence. "He's doing it all wrong," she muttered. She returned the remote to its basket on the coffee table.

"I called them again," Michelle said. "The girl said they were running behind. It should be here in ten minutes. I'll get out the plates."

She'd started to rise when Nina motioned her

back into the chair. "It's all taken care of. I turned the oven on, too, in case we want to keep the pizza hot while we eat our salads."

"Well, since it's going to be a while…" Leather cushions creaked as Erin squared herself in the roomy chair. The moment her feet hit the floor, she said, "I was planning to bring this up while we ate, but I can't wait another minute. I have news."

Reggie gave her phone a disgusted look and placed it, face down, on the end table. "Oh? Have you decided where between Tanzania and Mozambique for your next trip?"

Erin shook her head. "Nope. This isn't about me." A Cheshire-cat grin stretched across her face.

"This sounds interesting. Don't keep us in suspense." Nina kicked off her shoes. She folded herself until she sat cross-legged on the couch.

"What's up?" Michelle asked.

Her arms in front of her, Erin interlaced her fingers and stretched. "Well, I was loading those boxes in your car…"

Michelle nodded. Packing up Allen's things hadn't been easy, but having Erin's help made a world of difference.

"And one of your neighbors stopped by to ask if you were moving."

Michelle bit her lower lip. She hadn't intended on spreading the word just yet, but she supposed it didn't matter. Her neighbors were bound to find out eventually. "Did you get her name?"

"No, but she has a border collie who could use some obedience training. She was straining at the leash the whole time we were talking. I'm pretty sure the woman called the dog Maisey."

"That's Mary Thomkins. And yes, her dog is a handful. Smart and willful. It's a tough combination." Michelle nodded. Why the younger woman had chosen such an active breed when she had three preschoolers at home, she'd never know. An older rescue—a lab or a greyhound—would have been a better fit. "She lives four houses down."

"Mary. Good to know. Anyway, Mary's brother and his family are relocating to Virginia from the Triangle." Home to three prestigious universities, Durham, Chapel Hill and Raleigh formed what was known as the Research Triangle in North Carolina. "Bo, that's the brother, and his wife have two boys about the same age as Mary's oldest children. I guess Bo and Mary are pretty tight. Bo wants to buy a house close to Mary's so the cousins can grow up together."

Michelle fought to keep her mouth from dropping open. "How in the world did you find all this out?" Mary had been one of the brigade of casserole-bearing neighbors who'd dropped by in the weeks immediately after Allen's passing. It was especially sweet of her considering, other than warning the woman to pick up her dog's poop, she doubted she and Mary had spoken more than a dozen times.

"She's a really nice lady. A bit talkative, but wait till you hear the rest. Unless you're not interested." That catlike grin put in another appearance as Erin went completely still.

"C'mon, Erin. You can't leave us hanging." Nina grabbed one of the throw pillows from the couch and tossed it at Erin.

"Hey!" Erin batted the pillow to the floor. "Okay, okay." She leaned forward the slightest bit. "Michelle probably knows this already, but it turns out houses in this particular neighborhood don't go up for sale very often."

"True," Michelle said slowly. Other than the occasional job transfer, divorce or death—as in her case—people who bought in the well-established neighborhood tended to stay put. The nearby schools regularly earned an A+ rating. Houses boasted large backyards, perfect for young families. The solidly built, brick homes had an air of stateliness about them that appealed to older couples, as well. People also appreciated the sidewalks along the winding, shaded streets and the many pocket parks and bike paths.

"The bottom line is, when I told her you might be putting this house on the market soon, she got super excited. She and her brother want to come and see it tomorrow."

"You're kidding." Michelle took a beat while Erin assured them all she was quite serious. Her mouth went desert-dry, and she sank against the cushions. Was she really doing this? It was one thing to talk about selling the house she'd called "home" for nearly a quarter of a century. Something else entirely to have a potential buyer walk through the doors.

"Why not? The house is perfect," Nina assured.

"It is that," she agreed. "Thanks to all your hard work." In three days, the four of them had crossed one item after another off her to-do list. They'd even imposed Reggie's rule of three on every horizontal surface in the house. Well, except for the twins' bedrooms. Other than washing their windows, they hadn't touched Aaron or Ashley's personal spaces. "I guess I could call the real estate agent tonight. There's one who handles most of the resales around here, and…"

"Whoa! Stop right there." Reggie held up a hand.

"What?" Michelle turned to Erin's sister.

"If you involve a real estate agent, you'll have to fork over five or six percent of the selling price. On a house like this"—Reggie waved a hand—"that's a considerable amount of money. Money that could go straight into your pocket."

"Our parents didn't use an agent when they sold their place," Erin put in. "Dad downloaded a boilerplate contract from one of those for-sale-by-owner sites. There's a ton of them out there. The title company handled all the paperwork. It was pretty simple, really."

Nina nodded. "There's no reason you can't do it yourself."

"You're assuming Mary and this Bo are going to fall in love with the house," Michelle protested. Her friends were wonderful, but they'd made a couple of pretty big leaps.

"Why wouldn't they?" Erin asked.

"It's in tip-top shape," Reggie pointed out.

"The swimming pool alone is a huge plus," Nina added.

Michelle rubbed her fingers over the raised pattern covering the Queen Anne chair. "I guess it wouldn't do any harm to show the house to them. I can always contact a Realtor later if, for some reason, they don't make an offer."

"That's the spirit," Erin said, her smile widening.

"Hold on. An occasion like this deserves a toast." Nina stood from her chair with the gracefulness of a gazelle. Her footsteps light on the hardwood floors, she dashed into the kitchen. She returned less than a minute later brandishing a bottle of wine and four glasses. Seconds later, she poured them each a generous serving of the rich red liquid. Picking one up, she held it aloft. "Here's to a quick sale!"

"To starting the next chapter in your life." Erin clinked her glass to Michelle's.

"To a fresh start," Reggie echoed.

Hints of blackberries and raspberries rolled across her tongue as Michelle drank deeply of the rich, red liquid. An oaky finish lingered long after she'd swallowed. Her breath shuddered. She still had some time. It wasn't like she'd have to move out tomorrow. Why, Bo and his wife hadn't even looked at the house yet. Worst case, they'd hate it and she'd be back to square one. But her heart told her that wasn't the case. Mary's brother and his wife were sure to fall in love with the house, just as she and Allen had known it was the place they wanted to raise their family the moment they'd stepped out of the car, some twenty-odd years ago.

She wiped a sudden dampness from her eyes. Her friends were right. The time had come to embrace the next chapter in her life. She'd given herself a year to grieve for Allen, and though she'd never truly get over losing him, it was time to move on. Time to take that next step. She didn't know what that might be, exactly, but she refused to let worry overwhelm her. For now, she'd focus on the possibility that a new door was opening for her. And thanks to her friends, she had the courage to walk through it.

Brightening, she plunged into the ongoing conversation of all the things that needed to happen before the move. They all agreed that getting the twins on board was crucial, but when the rest encouraged her to call Aaron right away, Michelle reminded them of the big project her son needed to complete by tomorrow morning. She promised to contact him in the afternoon instead. From there, the discussion shifted to moving boxes, of all things. Erin suggested they place bets on the number she'd need, and they were in the middle of doing that when the doorbell rang.

"The pizza. Finally," Michelle said. She patted

her pocket where she'd slipped her credit card and headed for the front door.

"Hey, glad you finally made it," she said, opening the door wide. She canted her head. The young woman on her porch held neither pizza boxes nor tote bags full of salads. The small SUV parked in front of the house didn't even sport one of Lil Italy's lighted signs.

"Can I help you?" she asked.

"I hope so." Curly brown hair framed the face of the girl, who looked to be about the twins' age. She smiled warmly. "Are you Michelle Robinson? Michelle Boudreau Robinson?"

The instant her full name rolled off the girl's lips, Michelle stiffened. Her grip on the door-knob tightened. Was the young woman with the police? Had something happened to one of her children? Instant panic sent her pulse racing. Her gaze shifted to the vehicle at the curb. There was no police insignia on the door, but that wasn't proof, was it? She eyed her visitor. The girl wore a navy blazer over a white blouse and jeans. Definitely not a uniform. Nor the expected suit coat detectives always wore on TV. So not the police, then. Her breathing eased just a bit, but she kept her guard up. "I'm Michelle Robinson," she said warily.

"Michelle Boudreau Robinson. Born on August fourteenth, 1976? The adopted daughter of Harold and Sarah Boudreau?" The girl recited the information as if she'd memorized a script.

"How did you..." Michelle froze. The stranger on her front porch knew far too much about her. Though she'd never hidden the fact that she'd been adopted, it wasn't exactly front-page news, either. Allen had known, of course. It was the kind of thing people shared about themselves before things got too serious. She'd told him as they walked across the quad shortly before the holiday break that first year they were together. He hadn't been the least bit concerned by the news. The twins knew, too. She'd never wanted to keep her past a secret, not that she could in this day in age, when even the most trivial act left a permanent digital footprint. Though she'd confided in her closest friends, the topic was hardly one she'd bring up with the cashier at the grocery store, the beautician who styled her hair, the mechanic who worked on her car. It was none of their business, just like it wasn't any business of the young woman on her porch.

"I think we're done here." Her hand firmly on the door, Michelle let her voice rise. "I'd like you to leave now."

"Is everything all right out there?" Erin called from the family room.

"Just a salesperson." Michelle called over one shoulder, inching the door closed. "She's going now."

"Wait, wait!" Concern pinched the girl's features. "I'm sorry. So sorry." She took a step back. "I went about this all wrong. It's just—well, this is the first time I'm doing this. I'll go if you want me to, but—" Her face fell. "But I'll probably get fired. I really, really need this job. Give me two minutes, please."

Michelle hesitated. She pictured Aaron or Ashley making a mistake and how scared they'd be to lose their job. Sympathy stirred in her chest. She took a breath. "Who are you, and what do you want?" she asked slowly.

"My name's Casey Lyon. I'm a junior private investigator for Harper Investigations." She straightened an ID card clipped to the lapel of her jacket. Slipping one hand into a pocket, she withdrew a business card and held it out. "Here's my card. You're welcome to call the home office to verify that I work for them."

Michelle took the slip of paper and tucked it into her pocket. She'd call to check Casey's credentials, all right. But she wouldn't use the number the girl had provided. She'd look the company up online first. She'd heard enough horror stories about scam artists to know that anyone with a computer and a printer could make professional-looking business cards. "Let's say your company verifies that you're here on legitimate business. What do you want?"

Casey's expression turned earnest. "My firm has been hired by the estate of Nancy Simmons of Sugar Sand Beach in Florida. In her will, Ms. Simmons left everything she owned to her only child, a daughter, whom she put up for adoption shortly after the baby's birth in 1976. Our investigation of the birth, adoption and marriage records of that child lead us to believe that you are Nancy Simmons's daughter. And sole heir."

"Say what?" Michelle relinquished her hold on the door. Her head swam. She pressed her fingertips to her temple. Awareness that the room behind her had grown entirely too quiet pressed in on her. She shot one look over her shoulder. Sure enough, Reggie, Nina and Erin perched on the edge of their seats, as still as mice. She motioned them to join her, a move she didn't have to repeat twice. "Hold on a second," she told Casey while her friends gathered around her. "Now would you repeat what you just told me?"

Casey's eyes widened as the three women

formed a protective semicircle around Michelle, but to the girl's credit, she repeated her message without faltering. "Before we go any further, I have to ask: Are you the Michelle Boudreau Robinson we've been looking for?"

Michelle's mouth worked, but no words came out. In the silence that followed, someone nudged her in the ribs.

"Did you know about any of this?" Nina asked.

"Not a clue," Michelle whispered. "I'm not sure what to do."

"Would her driver's license be proof enough?" Erin asked.

"That'd be fine, for now," Casey said.

"Reggie, get my purse from the kitchen, will you?" The star in the upper right corner of the ID card meant she'd been REAL-ID certified by the DMV when she'd renewed her license last year. Though it had been a royal pain, she'd gone through the time-consuming process of combing through all their records to locate her birth certificate and marriage certificate, her passport and the deed to the house. Once she'd found everything she'd needed to prove her identity—it still amazed her that she hadn't had a better handle on such important paperwork—she'd stored the originals in her safe deposit box at the bank.

But she'd tucked copies in a folder in Allen's office.

Michelle turned to Casey. "You say this Nancy Simmons was my birth mother?"

"We believe she was, yes," Casey answered. "You didn't know?"

"Only that I was born in Florida. I tried to find out more about my biological parents after my adoptive parents passed. I thought, since Mom had saved copies of the paperwork they'd filed to adopt me, it'd be a piece of cake. But I didn't get very far. I'm told it was a closed adoption. Evidently, Florida has very strict rules about opening those files." Her parents had moved to Maryland shortly after her first birthday.

"They're some of the toughest in the nation." Casey shook her head. "The only way we were able to track you down was through some information Ms. Simmons had in her possession. Even with that, it took a while. But I'm glad we found you. If we hadn't, since Ms. Simmons had no other living relatives, everything would have passed to the state of Florida."

Footsteps behind her signaled Reggie's return. The youngest of her friends rooted around in her purse. "You want your wallet?"

"Yes, please." Michelle flipped open the

Brighton trifold Allen had given her for Christmas last year. She slid her license from the protective plastic shield and handed it to Casey. "Will that do?"

Casey studied the plastic ID for a long minute. When she looked up, her face bore a broad smile. "Eventually, you'll need to produce your original birth certificate, passport, and whatever papers you have relating to your adoption. But this is good enough for right now."

On the sidewalk below the house, a neighbor stared up with unabashed curiosity while her dog piddled in the grass. Michelle gave her a dismissive wave. She had no doubt whatsoever that word her house was going on the market would spread. But the news Casey had brought to her doorstep was not something she wanted to share with the world. Not yet, anyway.

"Won't you come inside?" Stepping away from the door, she motioned Casey to join her. "Let's sit in the dining room and talk about all this."

Erin and Reggie chose seats on either side of her while Nina fetched drinks for everyone. Once they were seated around the solid teak table, Michelle took a long sip of water from the bottle Nina thoughtfully placed in front of her. Clearing her throat, she addressed Casey.

"So, what can you tell me about this Nancy Simmons?"

Her heart hammered. For as long as she could remember, she'd wanted to learn more about the woman who'd given birth to her. But, like a mosquito bite between her shoulder blades, the information had been just out of reach. Now, she finally had a name, the name of a woman who hadn't loved her enough to keep her but had still left all her worldly possessions to her.

"I wish I knew more, but really, I don't have a lot of information to share with you. I do know Nancy Simmons spent her entire life in Sugar Sand, a tiny beachfront community between Destin and Panama City. She died five years ago. Since then, her attorney has been trying to locate her heir. He hired our firm to search for you last fall. I've only been on the case about three weeks."

Michelle let her eyebrows knit. Five years. Her birth mother had been dead for five years. "I wonder why it took so long to find me. It's not like I'm living under an assumed name." She'd lived in Fairfax most of her adult life. Her identity wasn't a big secret.

"Like I said, Florida adoption laws," Casey said with a shrug.

Through the large picture window overlooking the front yard, Michelle spotted a car pulling into the driveway. A light mounted on its roof proclaimed it to be the much-awaited delivery from Lil Italy.

"It's about time," Erin whispered.

"Here." Michelle reached into her pocket and took out her credit card. "Can you deal with the pizza while I talk with Casey?"

"Sure." Erin pushed back her chair and eased away from the table. She headed down the hallway to intercept the driver. Moments later, footsteps sounded on the hardwood floor and paper bags rustled as she carried their delivery to the kitchen. The oven door opened and closed. Another minute passed before she appeared in the doorway.

"All set," she announced. "Pizza's in the oven. Salads in the fridge." Erin slid onto the chair next to Michelle's. She rubbed her hands together and gave Casey a pointed look. "You said you needed to track her down because of an estate. What exactly are we talking about?"

Casey's gaze scoured the other women at the table. She turned to Michelle. "Do you want them to hear all of this?"

Michelle glanced at the four faces of women she trusted to give her advice and stand by her side. She didn't have any secrets from them.

"You might as well. I'm just going to tell them all the minute you leave anyway." She cast an affectionate grin at her friends.

"Must be nice." Casey gave a somewhat wistful smile. Reaching into a shoulder bag, she retrieved a small notebook and flipped pages until she found what she wanted. "There's not much money left in the estate. Over the past five years, attorney fees, taxes and maintenance have eaten up most of the cash, I'm afraid."

"Oh, pooh!" said Reggie. "So much for my hopes that you'd whisk us all off on a round-the-world tour."

Michelle reached for Reggie's hand and gave it a squeeze. Much as she hated to admit it, the younger woman wasn't the only one who was disappointed by Casey's news. For a brief moment there, she'd felt the faintest hope that there'd be enough money in the estate to let her hang on to her home. Apparently not. "I appreciate your being frank with us, Casey." Ignoring her usual no-elbows-on-the-table rule, she cupped her chin in the palm of her hand. "It just seems like a lot of trouble and expense to go through to track me down when there's nothing left."

"Well…" Casey's head tilted. "There is the property."

Her last word caught everyone's attention. Reggie coughed. Nina's back straightened. Erin's face jerked toward Michelle's. An expectant hush fell over the room as Michelle leaned forward. "What property?" she asked.

"Um, didn't I mention that?" Casey's eyes grew wide.

"Um, no." Reggie smirked.

"Oops. My mistake." Casey's cheeks flamed. "Yes." She cleared her throat. "Property," she said, as if giving herself a reminder. "Ms. Simmons owned five acres of beachfront property in Sugar Sand. And there's a house."

"Wow!" Erin practically fell onto the back of her chair. "Way to bury the lead."

"You're saying I own a beach house?" Michelle asked, perplexed.

"You will," Casey said with a voice full of assurance. "Once we get all the paperwork and the back taxes straightened out, it'll all be yours."

And there it was—the catch.

Michelle told herself she'd known there had to be one. Casey's spiel was just a little too good to be true. Next, she supposed, the girl would name some exorbitant amount of money she'd have to pay in order to inherit the property. Like those emails that crowded her inbox. The ones supposedly from a concerned employee of a national bank in some third-world country. The sender usually claimed to have gotten their hands on millions of dollars which they wanted to give her…for only a *small* finder's fee. A fee which, of course, she'd have to pay up front.

Yeah, no.

She arched one eyebrow and gave Casey the same look that used to stop the twins in their tracks. "And how much are these taxes?"

Casey swallowed visibly. "Eight thousand dollars will keep the state from selling the property to the highest bidder at the tax lien auction next month."

Michelle nudged her left eyebrow another quarter inch higher. "But that's just the tip of the iceberg, right?"

"Well…" Casey squirmed, actually squirmed, in her seat.

Michelle glowered at the girl. "Be honest now."

Casey held up her hands in a sign of surrender. "Two years ago, Ms. Simmons' attorney took what little cash remained in the estate and put it into one last effort to find her heir. That means the taxes—eight grand a year— haven't been paid since then. With fines, the grand total is closer to twenty thousand."

"You want a check right now?" Michelle

snorted a laugh. Even if she had that kind of money lying in her checking account, she wasn't dumb enough to give it away. There wasn't a doubt in her mind that once she ponied up the money, other mysterious bills would surface. Or there'd be other obstacles. Or her mythical inheritance would simply disappear. But she had to give Casey credit—the girl had her patter down pat. She'd almost believed her. Almost, but not quite.

"Wait, no!" Casey protested, her demeanor all innocence. "Definitely not. I couldn't take your money if I wanted to. And I don't want to."

Surprised that the girl had passed up an opportunity to close the deal, Michelle squinted at Casey. Had she misjudged her visitor? Her voice level, she asked, "What exactly do you want, then?"

Casey ticked off items on her fingers. "First, we need to verify that you are who we think you are. To do that, I'd like to see your birth certificate, passport and your marriage certificate. You said you had copies of the original paperwork related to your adoption?" At Michelle's nod, she continued, "Those certainly help bolster your claim. If you don't mind, I'll take pictures of all of that for our records."

"I don't keep the originals here at the house. Will copies do?"

"Yes." Casey's curls shook when she gave her head a firm nod. "As long as you can produce the originals when the attorney asks for them."

"That won't be a problem." If things ever got that far, that was. Casey seemed like a sweet kid, but didn't all con artists have an air of innocence about them? Michelle doubted a skeezy-looking person would be very successful in running a scam. "What else?"

"That's just about everything. You'll need to sign a form saying I've relayed the information to you. There's no obligation, nothing to pay," Casey repeated. "I'll give you the phone number of Ms. Simmons's lawyer—he's also the executor of her estate. That's it. I'll be on my way. You're free to get in touch with the attorney. Or not. That's totally up to you."

Michelle racked her brain for any red flags. But with no money exchanging hands, she couldn't see where Casey had anything to gain. She glanced around the table. At some point, Erin had stepped away. She eyed Reggie and inclined her head to Erin's empty chair.

"Upstairs," Reggie mouthed. She pointed a finger toward the ceiling.

Michelle turned to Nina. "Do you see any harm in showing her the paperwork?"

"Not really. If she had something shady up her sleeve, she'd insist on you giving her money up front."

"True," Reggie agreed. "She could probably get copies of your birth certificate from the courthouse."

"Okay, then." To Casey, Michelle said, "Sit tight. I'll be right back." She hurried into Allen's office, riffled through the file drawer in the big desk. The folder she wanted was right where she'd left it. Trying to ignore, for the moment, the astounding information that had been thrown at her over the last thirty minutes, she grabbed what she needed and returned to the dining room. "Here," she said, spreading the papers out on the table. "This is everything I have."

True to her word, Casey snapped a few pictures. Michelle took the form the girl handed her and went over it line by line. Satisfied it contained no mention of fees or obligated her in any way, Michelle scrawled her name and the date on the bottom line. Moments later, with the attorney's contact information in her hand, she showed the young woman out.

Michelle watched Casey climb into her car and drive away before she slumped against the door, suddenly feeling completely drained. After all these years, was it possible that she'd finally learned the identity of the woman who'd given birth to her? "Nancy Simmons was my mother," she whispered, trying the words on for size. They felt awkward in her mouth. If it turned out to be true, the idea that she'd left everything she owned to a child she'd never met was just as astounding.

Thirteen

Michelle

Michelle's head swam. She pushed away from the door and strode into the family room, where she picked up the glass of wine she'd been drinking before Casey knocked on the door. "Here's to you, Nancy," she said lifting the glass. She drained it in a single gulp. Heat spread down her throat until it warmed her belly.

"Hey, you," Nina said, poking her head into the room. "I was wondering where you'd gotten off to. Crazy day, huh?"

"You might say that." Michelle shook her head. "I never, not in my wildest dreams, imagined this."

"You want to talk about it?"

Michelle forced herself to take the deepest

breath she could manage. "I think we'd better eat. I bet everybody is starving." She clamped her hands over her stomach. "I know I am."

"Sounds good. I'll lay out the salads."

"And the pizzas, if they're hot," Michelle added. "I think I'm going to need more sustenance than rabbit food."

"I hear ya." Nina linked arms with hers. Together they walked into the kitchen, where Reggie was dealing silverware and napkins onto the table.

"Where's Erin?" Michelle asked, looking around the room. The fourth member of their little group was nowhere in sight.

"I don't know," Reggie answered. She placed a stack of extra napkins in the center of the table. "She disappeared a little while ago. I thought she'd just ducked into the little girls' room."

Michelle backtracked to the foot of the stairs. "Erin?" she called.

"Coming, Mom."

Erin's immediate response sent a ripple of much-needed laughter through the kitchen. Seconds later, the missing member of the foursome skidded into the room on stockinged feet. "Wait till you hear what I found out," she said, pinning Michelle with a look that was all business. She tapped the laptop she carried.

167

"Our friend Casey there might just have been telling the truth."

"About which part?" Michelle asked dryly. "That Nancy Simmons was my birth mother?" She still couldn't wrap her head around that idea. "Or that I've inherited beachfront property in Florida?" She shook her head. "Things like that don't happen in real life." At least, they didn't happen to her.

Erin frowned. "I still think you ought to look at what I've found."

"Okay, but can we eat first? Everybody's starving."

"Now that you mention it, I could eat, too." Erin's frown shifted into a smile. "Is there any better smell than a Lil Italy pizza?" She lifted the lid to one of the pizza boxes and inhaled deeply. "Mmmmm. Pepperoni and mushroom, my favorite."

"This one's vegetarian," Nina said, holding open another box. The rich scents of yeast, tomato and basil filled the air. She flipped up another lid. "Oooh, and a white pizza." She slipped one hand under a slice that came up dripping mozzarella and ricotta sauce. She took a bite before slapping the piece on a plate. "Oh, my. That's good."

"Hey! Save some for me!" Reggie slipped a

wedge-shaped spatula under a slice of the vegetarian. "I'm going to have one of everything."

"Good idea," Michelle agreed while Erin set her laptop aside on the kitchen counter.

In no time, all four women had served themselves. Michelle savored her first bite. The crisp buttery crunch of the crust mingled with the best marinara this side of the Atlantic. The sharp tang of spicy pepperoni went perfectly with the earthy taste of the mushrooms. She drank in the smell of Parmesan and mozzarella and sighed. "Oh, so good."

Erin pronounced her slice "the best ever" before giving Nina a sheepish look. "Except yours, of course."

Nina waved away the apology. "No. Not even mine can compare to Lil Italy's."

Reggie stuck a fork into the salad she'd heaped on her plate. "And their dressing. I wish I had the recipe."

"You and every other cook in town." Nina nodded. "I've tried a dozen variations. I think they put crack in it."

Reggie, who'd just taken a sip of water, clamped a hand over her mouth. When her eyes crinkled with laughter, Michelle grabbed napkins and handed them across the table. Reggie took them gratefully. She blotted her eyes and mouth.

"That's my story, and I'm sticking to it." Nina just shrugged when the remark set off another round of laughter.

Everyone was too hungry for much more joking around, and for the next few minutes, no one said a word while they demolished their pizzas and salads. When only nibbled-on crusts and a few sprigs of lettuce remained, Michelle pushed away from the table. She patted her tummy. "I needed that."

"I think we all did," Reggie agreed. She wiped a tiny bit of grease from her mouth with a napkin. She let her gaze linger on Michelle. "Want to talk about the elephant in the room now?"

"Let me take care of this mess first." Michelle swiped her own lips. She gathered up the empty pizza boxes for the recycling bin. While Nina cleared the salad containers and Reggie stacked their plates in the sink, Erin opened another bottle of wine.

"None for me," Reggie said as Erin began filling glasses with ruby red-liquid. "I'm driving." She helped herself to water from the dispenser on the fridge.

Once they were all seated at the table, Michelle nodded to Erin. She did her best to breathe normally while Erin fired up her laptop, but it was no use. She had the sense that, whether it turned out that Casey had been telling the truth or not, her life was about to take an unexpected turn.

"All set?" Erin asked from her seat at the foot of the table. At Michelle's breathy "Yes," she spun the laptop around so everyone else could see the screen with a quick, "So this is Nancy Simmons's obituary. She was sixty-three when she passed."

So young. Michelle swallowed. She couldn't read the text from where she was sitting, but unless Nancy had aged better than most, the accompanying picture had been taken when the woman had been a few years younger than Michelle was now.

"Wow, Michelle!" Nina swore softly. "You look a lot like her."

"Yeah, you could be sisters," Reggie agreed. "The shape of your mouth is the same as hers. You both have the same high cheekbones."

Michelle's eyes watered. The similarities were uncanny. Looking at Nancy Simmons's photograph was almost like looking in the mirror. Or it would be if big hair, polka-dot dresses and clunky jewelry hadn't faded from the fashion scene in the '80s.

"Here. Let me tell you what the write-up says."

Erin spun the laptop around. "Nancy was born in '57 to James and Margaret Simmons. She was injured in the same car crash that killed her parents when she was eighteen. She never walked again."

"That explains the wheelchair," Michelle pointed out. She'd spotted the chrome handles in the picture. "How awful for her. Losing both her parents and her ability to walk at the same time? It's..."

"Heartbreaking," finished Reggie.

Michelle nodded. She wiped the corners of her eyes, where tears had welled.

Reggie took a sip from her glass. "It says here she graduated from Destin High School. There's no mention of college. She never married. Nothing about a job or children. But she was very involved in charitable activities. President of the Sugar Sand Beach Women's Society. Active in the First Baptist Church. Patron of the library. Chairperson of the Destin Hospital Board of Directors—that's the next town over. Yada yada. Died of natural causes. Let me check the date—yep. Five years ago." Erin turned the laptop around again. "That all squares with what Casey said." She clicked a few keys.

Michelle stroked her chin, contemplative. "Sounds like she didn't let the wheelchair stop her from living a productive life."

"Pretty amazing," Nina agreed.

"Here's another picture."

They all leaned forward when Erin turned the laptop so they could all see the screen. This photograph was more recent, Michelle noted. Nancy's wardrobe had definitely changed for the better. The woman in the picture had paired loose, light-colored pants with a darker sweater. She'd tucked her hair into a broad-brimmed hat and donned overlarge sunglasses. The wheelchair still figured prominently, but it had been upgraded to a motorized version. "She looks like the kind of person people would want to be around."

"She has a nice smile. Friendly. Outgoing," said Reggie.

"I think she was," Erin said, chiming in. "I found another article that said more than two hundred people attended her funeral."

"That's quite a turnout," Michelle said. Maybe half that many had shown up to pay their respects after Allen passed. She paused. "So I guess we're thinking this Casey person might have been on the up-and-up?" She shook her head, trying to come to grips with the idea.

"But wait. There's more," Erin said with a sly grin. With the laptop once more facing her, her fingers flew across the keyboard. "It's amazing what you can learn from public records. According to the Walton County Property Appraiser's website, Margaret and James Simmons bought five acres of property in Sugar Sand Beach in 1922. The house they built there had eight bedrooms. In 1924, the house appraised at six grand, which I think was pretty substantial for the time. Ownership transferred to Nancy Simmons in 1975, right around the time her parents died. And yeah, before you ask, there is a lien on the property. As near as I can figure out, taxes haven't been paid in two years. That's about sixteen grand, plus penalties. So Casey was telling the truth about that, too."

Unable to process so much information at one time, Michelle folded her arms across her chest. "I still think there's something awfully fishy about this young woman showing up on my doorstep on a Sunday evening to tell me I've inherited property in Florida. Oh, and by the way, the owner was your long-lost biological mother." Despite her protest, though, she couldn't help the little shiver that passed through her at the possibility.

"It's a lot to take in," Nina commiserated. Compassion filled the look she cast toward Michelle. "How is it you're not tearing your hair out? I would be if it were me."

"How do you want to handle it? You know, we've got your back whatever you decide." Reggie leaned forward, her arms folded on the table.

"Can you find anything out about this attorney?" Michelle dug into the pocket of her jeans for the slip of paper Casey had given her. Coming up with it, she slid the name and number of the lawyer across the table to Erin.

"Hold on a sec."

Michelle sipped from her wineglass while Erin surfed the web in search of information. In less time than she expected, her friend looked up.

"Found him," she announced. "He's in Destin, about twenty miles from Sugar Sand Beach. He's a partner in Rollins and Rollins, which has been in business for forty years. I've only taken a cursory look, but he seems legit. Served as vice president of the Florida Bar Association. Currently a member in good standing."

The image of a portly, white-haired man took shape in Michelle's mind. She drummed her fingers on the tabletop. "Well, I suppose the first step is to get in touch with this Mr. Rollins and hear what he has to say."

"So you're going to call him?" Erin asked.

"I think I have to, don't I?" Michelle toyed with her glass. The wine spun around, coating the sides. "Whatever is going on, I owe it to myself to find out the truth. But I'll be careful." She waved a hand, heading off the concern she read in her friends' eyes. "I'm going to have Erin sit in on the call." She turned to her closest friend. "You'll be around, won't you?"

"You couldn't force me to leave," Erin said with a grin.

"Sounds like a plan to me." Reggie scraped her chair back and away from the table. "I hate to end the party, but I have to work tomorrow." She turned to Nina, who'd arrived by Uber earlier. "I'll drop you off, Nin, if you're ready to go."

Nina stifled a yawn. "I want to be at the restaurant early, maybe find out more about our new sous chef." She made a face. "You'll let us know when you hear anything?"

"I'll call as soon as I talk to Mr. Rollins. If you're busy, I'll leave a message." Her friends didn't normally take personal calls while they were at work.

Nina eyed the kitchen. A stack of empty pizza boxes sat on the counter beside the stove.

Takeout containers filled the trash can. Utensils and glassware had been piled in the sink. The table needed to be cleared and wiped down. "Why don't you let us stay for a minute and clean up. You have that couple coming by in the morning."

"No, I'll get it. You've all done enough this weekend. I couldn't possibly let you do one more thing," Michelle insisted. Working together, they'd accomplished more in three days than she could have possibly done by herself in three months.

After she'd walked Nina and Reggie out and Erin had disappeared upstairs to read before she turned in, Michelle eyed the messy kitchen. She really didn't mind cleaning up after dinner. It wouldn't take more than fifteen minutes to take out the trash and recycling, spritz everything with a little cleaning spray. Besides, with everything so up in the air, she had a feeling it was going to be a long night. Nothing was certain—there were still a lot of hurdles to clear before she fully accepted that Nancy Simmons was, in fact, her biological mother—but so far, everything Casey had told them had panned out. A faint hope bloomed in her chest as she filled the sink with soapy water. She had no idea what five acres of Florida beachfront

177

property went for these days, but it had to be worth something. Selling it might generate enough money to let her hang on to her home.

She bit her lower lip. Was that what she wanted, though? To stay here…alone?

A year ago, she and Allen had planned to live out their lives in this house. When she'd looked to the future, she'd pictured the two of them hosting Thanksgiving dinner in the dining room, her children and, hopefully, grandchildren gathering in the family room to open presents at Christmas, Easter egg hunts in the backyard, Memorial and Labor Day celebrations with friends and families. Even without Allen, she could still have all that, but in between those holiday celebrations stretched countless lonely days and nights. She had to admit she hadn't liked rattling around in the big, empty house much this past year. Was that really how she wanted to spend the rest of her life?

She shook her head. The opportunity for a different future had dropped in her lap tonight. She had no idea whether it'd pan out or not, but she couldn't deny that, for the first time in a long time, she felt excited about the possibility for something…more.

Fourteen

Michelle

We don't want to keep you." The tall man in designer jeans and a ribbed, cotton pullover grasped his wife's hand. "But we would like to find out more about the house."

"And let you know our plans," added the diminutive figure beside him.

"Of course," Michelle said. Bo and his wife, Anna, had shown up a half hour early for their tour of the house. The minute they'd stepped into the foyer, she'd known they'd make an offer. Two days ago, she would have been thrilled. But Casey's visit had changed things. Until she knew what exactly she stood to inherit from her mother's estate—if indeed, Nancy Simmons was her biological mother—she couldn't sell her home. Could she?

"Let's sit in the living room," she suggested to the young couple. She preferred the family room with its raised brick hearth and vaulted ceilings, but she had too many good memories of that room to sit there and keep her wits about her while selling her home. The home she and Allen had hoped to grow old together in. She squared her shoulders. This was not the time for an impromptu trip down Memory Lane. She gestured toward the arched entry into the formal parlor.

"We really like your house," Bo said, his long legs folding as he lowered himself onto the tufted cushions of the sofa. He propped one elbow on the rounded armrest. "You say the roof is new?"

"It's two years old. The furnace and central air units were replaced last year. The appliances are still under warranty."

"What about the pool? Does it require much upkeep?"

"Very little in the winter—there's a tarp that keeps the leaves out. In the summer, weekly treatments. But there are several local companies who can do the work for you at a very reasonable rate." A binder in the kitchen had the names and contact information for all the repair and service people she used. When, and if, she sold the house, she'd be sure to pass the information along to the new owners.

"Your home is lovely. It has most of the features we're looking for. But we're just getting started." Sitting primly beside her husband, Anna spoke for both of them. "Mary said we could stay with her as long as we'd like."

Michelle smiled. She bet these two were a hoot when it came time to buy a new car, what with Bo seemingly all in on the deal and Anna playing devil's advocate. The salespeople probably had a hard time figuring out who they should negotiate with. She, however, didn't have that problem. She'd seen Anna's eyes light up at the in-ground pool in the backyard. She'd heard the woman's approving murmur when the couple had discovered a whole kitchen's worth of extra cabinets in the laundry room.

"So you're all staying with Mary?" she smiled sympathetically. "Five children? To say nothing of Maisy. She's nearly as smart as a child."

"I'll say," Anna conceded with a weary voice. "She's crate-trained, but she gets out any time she wants to." Anna skimmed one hand over the chenille upholstery on the sofa. "This is the first bit of peace and quiet we've had since we got here."

Bo took his wife's hand. "You're the one who insisted on bringing the children along on our house-hunting trip. Your parents would have kept them."

"I couldn't be away from them that long." Anna sniffed. "Tyler's only three. Devon's six, but he's miserable when you don't tuck him in at night."

Bo beamed as he patted Anna's hand. "I don't like to miss that, either."

"Can I get anyone something to drink? Coffee? Water?" Erin leaned into the opening into the living room.

"No. Thanks," Bo answered. Anna simply shook her head.

Michelle motioned Erin to join them, and her friend quickly slid onto a Queen Anne's chair identical to the one Michelle had chosen. "Erin's visiting for a few days. She's my oldest and dearest friend."

"Nice to meet you, Erin. You're the one who told Mary the house was going up for sale, right?" Anna smiled brightly.

"That's right." Erin's khaki slacks whispered as she crossed her legs. "So, what'd you think?"

Michelle swallowed a laugh. She'd been right to ask Erin to join them. She could count on her friend to get right to the point.

"We're definitely interested," Bo said.

"If we can negotiate a fair price and a reasonable closing date," Anna added.

"About that." Bo's posture went just a tad stiffer. "Whatever house we choose, we need to be settled before the school year starts. Devon will be in second grade. Going to a new school and making all new friends will be hard enough without having to walk in halfway through the first semester. We'll need to close in early August."

Michelle quickly calculated. Given the precarious state of her finances, Bo's timeframe was a little beyond her comfort zone. However, once she had a contract on the house, she could probably work things out with the bank. "July or August should work," she said. "As long as there aren't any contingencies."

"None from our end," Bo said.

Relieved that the sale of Bo and Anna's current house wouldn't be a factor, Michelle breathed a little easier.

"As for price…" Anna took a deep breath and looked up at her husband, who nodded. "We need to go back to Mary's and crunch some numbers. Would it be all right if we call you tonight?"

"Take as much time as you need," Michelle said, exhaling slowly. Putting off the rest of the negotiations until after she spoke with Nancy Simmons's attorney was probably in all their best interests.

The couple quickly said their goodbyes and, promising to get back in touch within a day or two, left soon after.

"Were you disappointed that they didn't put in an offer right away?" Erin asked while Bo and Anna followed the walkway to the sidewalk.

Michelle turned to the friend who stood beside her. "Not really. I mean, it would have been nice, but I really want to speak with that attorney—Mr. Rollins?—before I commit to anything." For all she knew, she was pinning her hopes on a worthless piece of Florida swampland.

Erin flexed her fingers. "You're probably right, but I sort of wished they'd mentioned a figure. At least then, we'd know if they were even in the right ballpark." Below them, Bo and Anna disappeared from view. "So, are you going to call this Rollins guy now?"

Michelle smiled at Erin's eagerness. "In just a minute. I made a list of questions to ask him before I went to bed last night."

"Of course you did," Erin said dryly.

Michelle stuck out her tongue. "I like lists. So sue me." By now, she told herself, she should be used to getting teased for her insistence on working from a list. "I want you to look it over. See if I forgot anything. While you do, I need coffee."

"I'll fix it while you get your notebook," Erin offered. "Which pods do you use?" Michelle kept a varied selection of single-serve pods on hand for guests.

"Surprise me." On impulse, she leaned in and gave Erin a quick hug. "I'm so glad you're here. I don't know how I'd get through all this without you. Or Nina and Reggie," she added as she stepped back.

"It's nothing. You'd do the same for us," Erin insisted, but her face colored slightly. "Now, where's your notebook?"

When she admitted she'd left it on the nightstand in her room, Erin headed for the kitchen while she headed up the stairs. Two cups sat on the table by the time she returned, her notebook in hand. She handed it to Erin and doctored her cup.

"Looks good to me," Erin said after paging through the list. "I'm sure other things will come up while you talk to him, but this will definitely get you started." She gave Michelle's cell phone a light tap. "No time like the present."

A sudden nervousness rushed through her as Michelle lowered her favorite mug to the table. Coffee that really was stronger than she liked soured her stomach. But Erin was right. She had nothing to gain by putting off the call that could change everything...for the better.

Fifteen

Nina

"Hey Charlie, what are you doing out here so early?" Most days, the grill cook dropped off his kids on his way to the restaurant, which meant he rarely arrived before nine on a weekday. "Don't Dimella and Malcolm have school?"

A ray of bright sunshine beamed down between the buildings. The light glinted off Charlie's bald pate. "Yep. Their mom's takin' 'em. Figured you'd be in early today. Thought I'd better bring you up to speed on what happened while you were out." He patted the empty crate beside him. "You're gonna want to sit down for this."

"Can it wait a sec? I want to punch in first."

Things were going to be tight enough as it was this month. She was out three days' pay on top of the ruined meals she'd promised to cover. The last thing she needed was to clock in late. Not that she didn't have savings. She did, and they were considerable. After all, Mr. Pibbs didn't eat much, and she grabbed most of her meals at work. But she'd rather work a few extra shifts and tighten her belt than dip into the money she'd set aside.

"You wanna hear this before you go in. Trust me." Charlie stretched his long legs in front of him.

Nina stifled a groan. So much for her plan to get an early start on the day. Charlie had settled in like he did whenever he had a long story to tell. Taking her knife roll from under her arm, she sank onto the crate he'd indicated. "What happened now?"

"Rene's gone."

"You've got to be kidding!" Nina exclaimed, incredulous. The pastry chef had outlasted two head chefs and a change of ownership. And no wonder. Give her a half-cup of sugar, and she'd spin it into a web that made plain chocolate cake so beautiful patrons regularly forked over twenty dollars for a slice.

"Someone complained about finding a hair in their crème brûlée. Chad fired her on the spot. Claimed he'd already warned her twice."

"Chef let him get away with that?" Nina sucked in air so hard, it made her chest hurt. She'd expected better of Jacques. The chefs and cooks on his line might not agree with the rules, but they knew better than to break them. Even Charlie wore a net, and he didn't have a hair on his head.

"Yeah. I think somebody set her up. I started to say something, defend her, y'know. But Rene waved me off." Charlie rolled a shoulder as if it wasn't that big a deal. "That's not all. Two of the dishwashers and three of the busboys either quit or was fired."

"So in addition to losing the best pastry chef in Arlington, we're short-staffed?" The situation grew more incredulous by the moment.

"Wait." Charlie grasped his knees with both hands. "Cha-ad," he said in a singsong voice, "has already replaced Rene, the bus boys and the dishwashers with—wait for it—"

Nina didn't have to wait. The answer was a hard, round pit in the middle of her stomach. "Family members or friends. Am I right?"

"Ding. Ding. Give the girl a prize. I swear,

he had this new pastry chef—name's Paul—waiting by the phone, ready to call in on a moment's notice. The guy was in place within the hour."

"Is he any good?" Nina asked hopefully. Talented pastry chefs like Rene contributed substantially to a restaurant's bottom line.

"He's all right, I guess." Charlie lifted one hand and rocked it from side to side. "The guy slathers everything in whipped cream."

"Let's hope he's a whiz of a baker, then."

"There've been some changes in the front of the house, too. Sarah, that girl with the long, blond hair? She's gone. A waiter and one of the bartenders, too."

He waited while Nina placed them. Some staff turnover wasn't unusual when a new head chef came on board. Not so much with a new sous chef, though it wasn't unheard of. But—she paused to count. "That's nine altogether? Doesn't that seem like a lot?" Unease rolled silently through her midsection. So many changes could change the whole character of the restaurant. Especially if the new people had been chosen for their loyalty to Chad rather than their skill in the kitchen.

She searched the face of the man who'd sacrificed his own time on the clock in order to speak with her. Much as she appreciated hearing the news before she walked inside the restaurant, Charlie had to have more on his mind than bringing her up to speed. "What else?" She braced for more bad news.

Charlie's posture softened. "You know I think you're pretty good with them sauces, don't you?"

Nina grinned and punched the big man lightly on the arm. "You might have mentioned it a time or two."

"Well, I think Chad's gonna try and replace you next. The last three days, while you've been out, he's complained—a lot—about how you took off without notice and left him high and dry. Coupla times he said if you did it again, he'd fire you."

The unease that had shifted through her belly solidified into a hard knot. Her voice barely a whisper, she stared up at Charlie. "I don't suppose he mentioned that I'd been suspended. It wasn't exactly my choice."

"That never came up." Charlie's massive head hung.

"Well, crap." Nina swore softly.

"That 'bout sums it up," Charlie agreed. "I wanted to warn you. I don't think it would take much for him to let you go. Probably without a reference. He wouldn't give Rene one."

Nina's stomach burned. A good recommendation could spell the difference between landing a new job at the same level or having to drop back down the ladder a few steps. Not that Rene had to worry. She had a solid reputation as one of the finest dessert chefs in the area. Other restaurants had tried to lure her away from Café on numerous occasions. Her own position was far more precarious. She'd already screwed up once and been forced to start over at the bottom. It had taken her ten long years to get where she was now.

Charlie hesitated. "So, what are you going to do?"

Nina fiddled with one of the buckles on the knife roll Michelle, Erin and Reggie had given her last year when she'd been promoted to lead saucier. If everything Charlie had said was true—and he had no reason to lie to her—the handwriting was already on the wall. One way or another, she was leaving the Café. How was up to her, but she didn't have many options. She could report to work and let Chad fire her. Without a reference and with her history, she'd face the nearly impossible task of finding a similar position in any other restaurant in town. Or she could knock on Chef Jacques's door, turn in her resignation effective the end of the week, and beg him for a personal recommendation.

Hadn't he said himself that her work had always been exemplary? She shrugged. If Jacques turned her down, she'd be no worse off than she was if she let Chad fire her. And quitting offered one outstanding benefit. She'd be walking out on her own terms, her chin held high. Not slinking out the back door.

She expelled a huge breath and stood. Tucking her knife roll under one arm, she offered Charlie a tremulous smile. "I hate this. Hate letting Chad win this one. But I don't see much point in fighting him. I'll hang around till Chef comes in, turn in my resignation and hope for the best."

"Chef's in his office." Charlie tilted his head toward the door to the restaurant. At Nina's raised eyebrows, he explained, "He came in early to work on the menu."

"It's nearly summer, isn't it?" She nodded. The café's menu changed with the seasons. She wondered if the new one would include the swordfish with the brighter, lighter sauce she'd been working with Chef to create. Her composure wobbled a bit when she realized she wouldn't be around long enough to find out.

"It might take you a while to find a new position. You gonna have enough to get by? I don't have much, but I can lend you a little if you—"

She cut him off. "Thanks. I appreciate the offer more than you know. But I can't take your money. You said yourself, you'll need it to get those kids through college. I'll be fine." She'd learned the importance of saving the hard way. Since the last time she'd had to start over, she'd set aside a portion of every paycheck. In ten years, she'd built a nice little nest egg. Not enough to open her own place—not by a long shot—but enough to get by for six months or a year without putting either herself or Mr. Pibbs on a diet of cheap ground beef and pasta. She paused. "How about yourself?"

"I think I'm gonna be okay. Chad hasn't bothered me none. Not since that first day when he was all over my case. Still, I got some feelers out. Ain't gonna lie. I'd hate to leave here."

"Any kitchen would be proud to have you, Charlie." She extended her hand. Tears threatened to clog her throat when the big man grasped her palm in a warm grip. "Promise me, we'll stay in touch no matter what?"

"You know it."

"Thanks," she said. And squaring her shoulders, she walked through the staff entrance to Café Chef Jacques one last time.

Thirty minutes later, after Jacques assured her he'd provide a good recommendation to anyone who called, Nina checked her phone. A bright red circle told her she had a message waiting. She quickly read a note from Michelle telling her the meeting with the potential buyers had gone well enough that she expected them to make a formal offer. Despite the rocky start to her own day, she smiled, glad that at least one of her friends was finally having some good luck.

She stared at the phone in the palm of her hand. Now that she'd joined the ranks of the unemployed, she ought to call the agent who'd helped her land the job at Café Chef Jacques. She hadn't fooled herself. Positions as lead saucier didn't open up every day. Not even in busy Fairfax County. In all likelihood, she'd end up doing temporary work—filling in while another cook took vacation or was out sick—until she found the right spot. Trouble was, temp work didn't pay as well, which meant the longer she stayed out of work, the more she'd have to dip into her savings. So she really ought to make that call right away.

Instead, she thumbed through the apps on her phone until she found one for a ride service. With her career on hold, her day was already shot. She'd spend what was left of it surrounded by the people who meant the most to her. She followed her ride on the app, and when the driver pulled to the curb, she gave him Michelle's address.

Sixteen

Michelle

"What time are you supposed to hear from that lawyer?"

Michelle studied Erin leaning against the door to Allen's office. "He said he'd call at one."

Erin pulled her cell phone from the pocket of her slacks. "It's five past," she said after a glance at the screen. "Are you ready?"

Michelle surveyed the desktop. Steam rose from a fresh cup of coffee. A pen and a spare—just in case—sat beside a blank note pad. She tapped the list of questions she'd prepared. She and Erin had been over them twice. She nodded. She was as ready as she'd ever be.

Her cell phone vibrated with an incoming call. "RRA" and a number with an 850 area code flashed on the screen. She gulped. "Here goes nothing," she muttered. Her hand shook as she picked up the phone. She crossed the fingers of her free hand, thought better of it and reached for her pen.

Meanwhile, Erin sank onto the folding chair beside her.

"Hello. This is Michelle Robinson."

"Michelle. So nice to hear from you. I'm Dave Rollins, senior partner in Rollins and Rollins. I'm sorry I wasn't able to take your call earlier. I was with another client."

"That's quite all right," she assured the attorney. She hadn't expected his receptionist to put her through to the lawyer immediately. No matter how anxious she was, she understood he had other clients, other obligations. "If you don't mind, I'm going to put you on speaker. I have a friend with me—Erin Bradshaw. I'd like her to listen in on our conversation."

"You're absolutely welcome to do that."

"Thank you." Michelle punched the button. "Okay, that should do it."

"Hello, Ms. Bradshaw."

"Call me Erin." Erin turned toward Michelle. "He sounds nice," she mouthed.

Michelle gave her head a quick shake. She'd had the same thought. Dave's deep timbre and warm Southern accent had gone a long way toward easing her jitters.

"Erin, then." Dave Rollins cleared his throat. "Just to be clear, I have you on speakerphone, as well. CoraBeth Burke, a paralegal in our firm, will be taking notes while we talk. Is that all right with you?"

"Yes," Michelle answered. Her interactions with attorneys had been few and far between, but as near as she could tell, having an assistant in on the call was perfectly normal.

"Good. This next part is going to sound a little formal, and I apologize for that, but it's necessary in order to make sure everything is perfectly aboveboard. Now, for the record, my firm handles the estate of Nancy Simmons, a lifelong resident of Sugar Sand Beach. According to her will, Ms. Simmons left her entire state to her only child, a girl, whom she put up for adoption shortly after the child's birth in 1975. It's my understanding that you, Michelle Boudreau Robinson, have recently come to believe you are Nancy Simmons's daughter and sole heir. Is that correct?"

"Yes," Michelle said, sounding as uncertain as she felt. "I mean, according to the woman from Harper Investigations, I am. I'm, um, still a little bit in shock, I guess. I had no idea Nancy

Simmons was my birth mother or that she'd passed away. I'm having a hard time believing that she left anything to me in her will, let alone such a huge gift." She took a breath. Might as well lay all her cards on the table. "To tell you the truth, I'm having a very hard time believing all of this isn't some sort of scam."

"I understand your concerns. I'd probably have the same doubts if someone claiming to represent my dead mother's estate approached me out of the blue. Can I assume you've visited the Rollins and Rollins website?"

"Yes. It's quite nice." One day over the summer, Aaron, a computer science major, had pointed out some of the differences between the cheaply designed website of a local game arcade and the more substantial one run by a national department store. She'd been pleased to find that the attorney's office had more in common with the latter. "I've also made inquiries with the Bar Association and searched for you on the internet." Michelle grinned when, beside her, Erin silently claimed the credit by aiming her thumbs at her own chest.

"So you know Rollins and Rollins is a reputable firm."

"By all accounts." Her cheeks heated. Dave Rollins sounded so sincere, she hated to admit she still wasn't a hundred percent convinced.

A creak of leather sounded through the receiver, and Michelle imagined the portly, white-haired gentleman she'd seen on the firm's website resettling himself in his office chair. "I understand this is a lot to take in, Michelle. I want you to know that Ms. Simmons was a highly respected member of our community and a good friend to many. That's why, after the available cash in her estate ran out, our firm began handling her affairs pro bono. You should also know that absolutely no money will change hands in my dealings with you. If at any point you'd feel better hiring your own attorney to act on your behalf, you're perfectly welcome to do so."

The reassurance put her last niggling qualms to rest, and Michelle told him so.

"Now that that's settled, let's return to my original question—have you, Michelle Boudreau Robinson, recently come to believe you are Nancy Simmons's daughter and sole heir?"

"I have." Michelle paused. Still unable to accept that, after all this time, she might know the identity of her birth mother, she asked, "And she left everything to me?"

"Well, we still need to prove that you are, in fact, the daughter Ms. Simmons put up for adoption. But yes, she did leave everything she owned to her only known blood relative. That would include the Simmons family residence in Sugar Sand Beach, as well as the five acres surrounding it. Several outbuildings. A couple of motor vehicles, including a pickup truck, a golf cart and a boat."

Erin straightened, her eyes taking on a sudden glint. "A boat?" she mock whispered.

Michelle put one finger to her lips. A boat was the least of her concerns. Dave Rollins sounded very reserved and professional. She had the impression he'd have plenty of hoops for her to jump through before handing her the keys to the estate.

The man on the other end of the line cleared his throat. "Harper Investigations faxed over their report this morning. I've seen the photos of your paperwork."

Michelle held her breath, waiting for the attorney to continue.

"Everything looks in order. This is all preliminary, of course. We'll need to see the originals. And we'd like you to take a DNA test to confirm your relationship to Ms. Simmons."

Michelle stopped scribbling notes. "DNA?"

"It's a simple blood test. We have a sample of Ms. Simmons's DNA. We'll ask the lab to compare it to yours. We'll arrange for that test while you're here."

"While I'm there?" she echoed, feeling a little like she'd just fallen overboard and couldn't swim.

"The agent didn't explain that to you?"

"Um, no. Maybe she didn't know about it? She said she was fairly new with the company."

"Not your problem," Dave Rollins soothed. "But, yes. It's one of the stipulations of the will. You'll need to come to our office in person to prove you are who you claim to be. We'll have our in-house team review all the pertinent paperwork—originals of the same paperwork you gave the investigator. Our office will cover the cost of the DNA test. Once your identity has been verified, I'll be able to proceed with transferring Ms. Simmons's assets into your name."

"Sounds like there's a trip in my future, then." She shoved one hand through her hair and let the sleek strands sift through her fingers. So much for the slightest hope that cashing in on her birth mother's estate would resolve her problems at home. With all she had going on here, any trip to Florida would have to wait at least until she'd sold the house and found a smaller, less expensive place to live.

"Yes," Dave said with a laugh that was little more than a rumble. "If you'd like, I can recommend a hotel near the office. In the meantime, I'll go ahead and set up the appointment for the DNA test for one day next…"

"That's too soon, I'm afraid," Michelle interrupted. "I'll have to get back with you on the dates. I'm not sure when I'll be able to break free. I was thinking maybe in October. Or over the winter?" As a matter of fact, a short winter vacation in sunny Florida sounded just perfect.

"Well…"

Michelle stared at the phone when Dave Rollins fell silent. "Well, what?"

"You're aware there's a tax lien against the property?" he said slowly.

"Yes, Casey mentioned that." Catching Erin's eyes, Michelle tapped her pen against the top of the desk. Here it comes, she thought. "She said something about eight thousand dollars."

"That's the minimum," Dave Rollins corrected. "It'll take closer to twenty thousand to pay off the entire lien. That bill must be taken care of as soon as possible."

"And you can't pay the taxes out of the estate?" Michelle queried.

"There's only enough cash reserves left for incidentals. As I mentioned, we're handling this case for free out of respect to Ms. Simmons." As if he hated to be the bearer of bad news,

Dave Rollins slowed. "The property tax has been in arrears for some time. The house and the acreage around it are scheduled for a tax sale. There won't be anything left to inherit unless the account is brought up to date before that happens."

"And when is this tax sale?"

"The end of the month."

So soon?

Her hand fisted until her nails dug into her palm. "Let me be sure I've got this right," she said, her voice tight. "You expect me to rush to Florida and pay this tax bill with no promise that I'll inherit anything?" She had to give Casey and Dave, if those were their real names, credit. They'd hooked her and nearly reeled her into their elaborate scam. But she hadn't been born yesterday, and she didn't have s-u-c-k-e-r printed on her forehead.

"No. Gosh, no." Dave Rollins spoke in a rush. "I'm so sorry. I didn't make that clear." His words slowed. "Once we have your DNA, it will take less than twenty-four hours to get the results. That will tell us whether or not you're actually Nancy Simmons's biological daughter. Assuming your other paperwork checks out and the results from the lab come back positive, I'd immediately transfer the assets to your name.

Then and only then would you go to the Property Tax office and bring the account up to date."

Okay, so maybe this wasn't a scam after all. Still…

"Twenty thousand dollars, though. That's a lot of money." She didn't have much more than that in savings. "I'm not sure…"

"Maybe this will help, Ms. Robinson. I'll text you a recent photo of the Simmons property. As you can imagine, five acres on the beach is a valuable commodity. It may not be worth as much here in Sugar Sand Beach or Destin as it would be if it were located, say, in Miami or Tampa, but any number of developers would like to get their hands on it."

Dave had no sooner finished speaking than Michelle's phone dinged with an incoming text. Braced for a picture of cypress knees and murky wetlands, she paged over to the message app. Instead, when she tapped the icon with her thumb, an entirely different image filled the screen. This one showed a long stretch of pristine white sand bordered on one side by waves that gently lapped the shore. On the other, palms and palmettos competed for room in a tangle of undergrowth that covered a gently sloping hill. At the top, sun glinted off the metal roof of a rambling, wooden turn-of-the-century house.

Michelle's mouth worked but nothing came out. She shot a desperate look at Erin.

Her friend leaned forward. "Mr. Rollins? Erin here. We're going to need to call you back. Would you be available in, say, two hours from now?"

If the request confused him, the lawyer recovered quickly. "Yes, of course. You have my number?"

"Yes," Michelle managed, though she couldn't help but wonder who, exactly, had whose number.

Seventeen

Michelle

Propped up on pillows, Michelle lay on her back in the king-size bed she'd shared with Allen. She braced her thumbs on her cheeks while she massaged her temples with her fingers.

So many problems.

She still hadn't heard from either of the twins. She could only assume from their silence that they were both still angry about the other night. For the umpteenth time, she wished the two of them hadn't stormed out the way they had. Despite their youth and immaturity, Ashley and Aaron were the only family she had left, and she hated it when they had even a minor spat. This one was anything but minor.

In a perfect world, the three of them would at least sit down and discuss the decisions she faced. She might not follow their advice, but she would definitely appreciate their perspective. But this wasn't a perfect world, and she didn't have time to sit around and wait for her children to get over their collective snit.

For one thing, she needed to reach a decision on the Florida trip in a matter of hours. What was she going to do about that mess? She took her hands from her forehead and held them out in front of her, palms up. On one hand, she could wipe out her savings in the hopes that lightning would actually strike twice and she'd find buyers for both her home in Fairfax and the land in Florida. She figured the odds of that happening were somewhere between nil and next-to-none. On the other hand, her stomach turned at the thought of letting the state take possession of the Simmons family home.

If she had the means to prevent that from happening, didn't she owe it to herself to try?

Her eyelids fluttered, and she squeezed them shut. She was getting ahead of herself. She didn't know whether Nancy Simmons was her bio-logical mother. Casey certainly seemed to think so. Dave Rollins, not so much, but skepticism was probably in an attorney's job description.

In all likelihood he was just as leery of being taken in by someone pretending to be Nancy Simmons's long-lost daughter as she was afraid of being duped by some con artist. He, at least, had a way to find out the truth. The DNA test would tell him all he needed to know about her relationship to the Simmons family.

She needed to take that test. And, according to Mr. Rollins, someone from his office had to witness her taking it. Which meant she had to make a quick trip to Florida. *Well, so be it.*

She opened her eyes, sat up, and swung her legs over the side of the bed. Excitement shimmied through her midsection. In just a matter of days, she might have a partial answer to a question she'd been asking ever since her sixth birthday, when her parents—her real parents—told her they'd adopted her as a baby. She wouldn't kid herself. It didn't hurt that the knowledge came with a valuable piece of property attached. But what if the opposite were true? She shrugged. If the results came back negative, she wouldn't be much worse off than she was now. The cost of a plane ticket and a couple of nights in a hotel seemed like a small price to pay for the chance to find out the identity of her birth mother.

She slipped her feet into a pair of colorful

Gucci loafers she'd bought on sale at Neiman Marcus several years earlier. In the hallway, the low murmur of conversation caught her attention. Curious as to who'd stopped by, she followed the voices downstairs to the kitchen, where, much to her surprise, Nina sat talking quietly with Erin. Coffee cups and what was left of a plate of cookies littered the table.

"Nina?" Michelle asked. "I thought you'd be at the restaurant today."

The tall, thin cook lifted one shoulder. "There was a…complication. I'll fill you in on all of that later." She motioned with her hands, shoving her own problems aside. "Erin's been bringing me up to speed on what's happening around here. Sounds like you've had a *very* busy day. A buyer for the house? Congratulations!" She lifted her coffee cup.

Despite Nina's reluctance to provide details, Michelle would have pressed her for more information if Erin hadn't leaned into her line of sight. She pointed to the digital clock on the built-in microwave.

"It's almost time to call Mr. Rollins. Do you know what you're going to say to him yet?"

Michelle took a deep breath. "I don't have a choice. I need to go to Florida and take that DNA test. It's the only way I'll ever know for sure whether or not Nancy Simmons was my birth mother. What happens next will depend on the results."

A broad smile broke across Erin's face. "Road trip!" she declared.

"Count me in," Nina added. "I could use a little vacation right about now."

"Wait. You want to drive to Florida with me?" Michelle reeled back in surprise. When she'd decided to make the trip, she'd figured on flying down one day, spending a night or two, and flying back.

"Why not?" Erin asked. "It's only a little over fifteen hours by car. With the three of us taking turns behind the wheel, we can drive straight through. If you flew, you'd have to change planes in Atlanta or Charlotte and fly into Fort Walton Beach. It's about an hour away, so you'd have to rent a car. That's a big hassle, and it'd cost twice as much as driving."

Michelle grinned. "Sounds like you've really thought this out." Not that she was surprised. Erin was a world-class traveler.

"What do you think?" Erin prodded.

Michelle let her grin widen. "I think I can't think of any better way to spend the time than hitting the road with my besties."

"What about Bo and his wife?" Nina asked.

"Aren't you afraid they might change their minds about the house?"

"It's only a few days. Not like we're taking off for months. I'll ask them to hang on to their offer till we get back. I'm pretty sure they'll agree as long as I promise not to sign with a Realtor in the meantime." She scanned her friends' faces. Erin's brows had drawn together like they did whenever she was concerned. Nina's lips had tightened into a straight line. "Okay," she sighed. "If they insist on putting the house under contract, we'll handle everything by email. Will that work for you?"

"Sounds like a plan," Erin agreed.

"When do you want to head out?" Nina wanted to know.

"I need to run a few errands tomorrow—go to the bank, touch base with the kids. How about first thing Wednesday? We can meet with Dave Rollins on Thursday, get the results Friday and head back Saturday."

"That'll give me plenty of time to talk to my neighbor." Nina pushed her hair behind her ear. "I'm sure she'd be happy to check in on Mr. Pibbs while I'm gone."

"I'll let Reggie know," Erin said. "She and I were going to visit Mom and Dad later this week. We'll need to push that back a few days."

With their plans set, Michelle said, "I'll call Mr. Rollins, let him know we'll be in Destin the day after tomorrow." And not long after that, she'd learn the answer to the question of whether or not Nancy Simmons was her birth mother.

Eighteen

Reggie

Reggie unlaced her boots and toed them off by the front door. Sam complained whenever she left any kind of footwear in the entryway and had insisted she keep her shoes in the closet. Which didn't turn out well when the shoes in question were mud-encrusted boots. So even though she hated leaving them on the balcony overnight—where who knew what could crawl inside them—for the past five years, she'd dutifully carried her work boots through the apartment at the end of every day and left them on the other side of the sliding glass door. And every morning, she'd clapped them together over the balcony and prayed that whatever creepy crawlies had found shelter in them would fall out. But she hadn't heard a peep from her husband in nearly a week, so as far as she was concerned, there wasn't much point in following his rules any more. Before she left for the job site this morning, she'd spread newspapers at an out-of-the-way spot near the door. Leaving her boots to dry on the papers overnight, she removed her thick socks.

She didn't bother checking her phone. When she'd tried to get in touch with Sam, her calls had gone straight to voice mail. He'd ignored her texts. How long was this going to go on? If they were going to save their marriage, they needed to work things out between them. And soon.

Carrying her socks, she trudged into the bathroom. After a full day of laying sod, nothing felt better on her sore and aching muscles than a long, hot shower.

Later, her hair wrapped in a towel and wearing her favorite pair of pajamas, she scrounged around in the refrigerator for leftovers. Regret zinged through her when she thought of the roast she'd fixed for Sam last week. She'd cried herself to sleep that night, their delicious dinner still sitting untouched in the kitchen. The next morning, unwilling to risk giving herself a severe case of food poisoning, she'd thrown every scrap of that meal in the trash. Which was a pity. She could go for some pot roast and pie right about now.

LEIGH DUNCAN

Rooting around in the bottom drawer, she unearthed two not-quite-mushy potatoes. A couple of eggs and a half-quart of milk one day past its expiration date made up the rest of the contents of the fridge. Clearly, she needed to make a grocery run. But not tonight. Not when she was already in her jammies.

Hungry for something more substantial than scrambled eggs, she reached for the slim notebook where menus of local restaurants had been neatly hole-punched and arranged in alphabetical order per Sam's directions. Choosing her favorite, she started to place her usual order. Before anyone picked up on the other end, she canceled the call. She and Sam got delivery from the Chinese place around the corner at least once a month. He was a creature of habit, her husband. Claiming that spicy takeout food gave him indigestion—though apparently the jalapeno poppers he scarfed down while watching football did not—he insisted they share the same two dishes every time. But Sam wasn't here, and she didn't really love the moo shoo pork or sweet-and-sour chicken. What she did like was spice. And lots of it. She ran one finger down the menu, found the dishes she preferred and hit redial.

"I'd like an order of Szechuan Beef and

another of General Tso's Chicken, please. With fried rice, not white. And a pint of hot and sour soup," she added at the last minute. It was enough food for an army, but unlike Sam, she didn't mind eating leftovers two or three nights in a row.

Waiting for the delivery, she wandered through the apartment, plucking dead leaves from the philodendron on the windowsill in the spare bedroom they'd turn into a nursery one day, watering the orchid in the front window, pinching back the fiddle-leaf fig on her nightstand so it wouldn't get too leggy. In the kitchen, she picked a cherry tomato from the tiny window garden and promised herself that one day, she'd have a real garden. With the usual rows of tomatoes and zucchini and cucumbers, of course. But she'd also try her hand at heirloom tomatoes, pole beans and, maybe, even some okra. She'd spread crushed eggshells to encourage anything with more legs than she had to go elsewhere, plant marigolds and citronella to discourage other pests and, if worse came to worse, bathe her fruits and veggies in a mix of vegetable oil and soap. She imagined working in the garden with a baby on her hip, teaching a curious toddler to care for the plants, picking vegetables with a pre-teen, the two of them laughing and telling stories while they preserved the bounty for the winter.

The doorbell rang, interrupting her pleasant daydream. Her stomach rumbled a reminder that she hadn't fed it in far too long. She slipped a few dollars from her wallet for the tip and, her mouth watering in anticipation, headed for the door.

She froze, her muscles tensing when she spotted an altogether different type of delivery person through the peephole. Wearing a black baseball cap emblazoned with the logo of the Quick Messenger Service, the man outside her door held a slim package in one hand. It certainly wasn't big enough to be the dinner she'd ordered.

She shook her head. When Sam had the flu last fall, his boss had used the same courier service to send casework for him to look over while he recuperated. She'd been livid when her husband, who barely had the strength to stand, had dragged himself out of bed to work on the files.

"Yes?" she said, opening the door a crack while leaving the chain in place.

"Is this the Frank residence?"

"It is, but…" She cut herself off. Telling a perfect stranger she was home alone wasn't exactly the smartest move she could make. "It is," she repeated firmly.

"I have a delivery for Regina Frank." He hefted a manila envelope.

She didn't know anyone who'd send her paperwork, much less pay for an expensive courier to deliver it to her front door. Unless… Her stomach sank. "Sam, what have you done?" she whispered.

"I'll take it." She slipped the chain free and opened the door wide enough to scrawl her name across the courier's electronic pad.

Dry manila crackled as she took the package. It had some heft to it, and she tightened her grip. She closed and locked the door behind her. For a long moment, she stood in the entryway, staring down at the envelope. Her name on the front in Sam's distinctive script sent chill bumps racing up and down her arms. Her stomach turned over. She clenched her teeth and ripped open the envelope the same way she'd rip off a Band-Aid—fast. Crossing to the living room, she dumped the contents on the coffee table. A thick, unyielding sheaf of papers slid out. She flinched as Sam's apartment key bounced off the papers and rattled against the tabletop for half a second before it lay still. Bile rose in her throat. She swallowed, hard. Gingerly, she turned over the stack of papers. A note in Sam's neat script had been paper-clipped to the front.

Reggie,

Virginia law requires us to be legally separated for six months before the divorce can be finalized. To start the clock, I'll have to file a Separation Agreement with the court. I've filled it out. Sign it. Send it back ASAP. I've generously agreed…

There was more, but she couldn't see the words through her tears. She sank onto the same sofa where she and Sam had once curled up together.

Separation.

Divorce.

"No," she whispered. Those things happened to other couples. Miserable couples. Couples who fought all the time. That wasn't them. They loved each other. They were trying to have a baby together.

How could Sam want a divorce? He'd said as much, but she hadn't believed him. Not really. She thought they'd at least talk it over, see a marriage counselor, try to fix whatever had broken.

She wiped the tears from her eyes and flicked aside his note. Briefly, she scanned the separation agreement that lay beneath. She sucked in a breath while the truth washed over her. Her husband didn't want to be married to her anymore.

More tears rolled down her cheeks.

She didn't know how long she sat there before the doorbell rang again. Hope rose in her chest. Had the courier had realized his mistake and come to retrieve the papers that were meant for someone else? But no. There'd been no mistake. There was no other Sam Frank living in Fairfax County. No other Regina Frank in this apartment complex.

Wiping her eyes with the backs of her hands, she rose on legs she wasn't sure would support her. At the door, she took the bag the delivery man handed her and somehow remembered to tip him. The spicy scent of onions and hot Chinese peppers filled the apartment. Her stomach wobbled precariously.

No longer hungry, she tried not to breathe as she shoved the food, bag and all, onto the top shelf in the fridge. She'd already thrown out one entire meal this week, thank you very much. Though she didn't think she could force down a single bite of tonight's dinner—or that it would stay down if she did—she wouldn't let more food go to waste.

Whenever she or Erin had been sick as kids,

their mom had fixed them hot tea and toast. Though a broken heart didn't exactly qualify as the stomach bug, hot tea sounded like just the prescription for what ailed her. Taking a stainless-steel saucepan from the cabinet, she ran filtered water from the dispenser in the fridge until the water came halfway up the sides. She set the pan on the front burner and turned the knob to high. The rings of the electric cook top turned a bright cherry red in a matter of seconds. While waiting for the water to simmer, she gathered her favorite mug, a packet of Earl Grey and a bear-shaped squeeze bottle full of honey. She dropped the bag of spicy Earl Grey into the cup. Once the water simmered, she poured it over the bag, making sure she held onto the tag at the end of the string so she wouldn't have to fish it out later. She hated when that happened. When the bag floated to the top as she'd known it would, she drizzled the honey over it just like her mother had taught her to do decades earlier. She spent the next few minutes mindlessly dunking the teabag up and down in the cup until the water turned a rich cinnamon color. She waited until the orange scent filled the kitchen before she took a sip of heat and comfort.

Carrying her cup, she forced her feet to take her into the living room. She sighed heavily as she sank onto the cushions of the couch. Sam insisted they use coasters whenever they drank beverages. It was one of the many rules he enforced with near-religious zeal. Even though she rarely put her cup down until she'd emptied it, she automatically reached for one of the stone disks scattered across the top of the coffee table. She caught her bottom lip between her teeth, slowly returned the coaster to the table and picked up the stack of papers her husband had sent over. For the next half hour, she sipped tea while she waded through the legalese. She finished both the tea and the last sheet of paper at the same time and leaned back into the cushions.

The separation agreement required them to divide their marital assets and debts, and the itemized list Sam had included covered practically everything they both owned and owed. Considering her husband's profession, she supposed she should have expected nothing less. There were a few surprises, though. That he wanted her to shoulder the bulk of the fertility clinic bills was one of them. When she saw that, her heart, which felt like it had been filled with lead, grew heavier still. She'd always thought they shared the same desire to start a family, that he wanted a baby as much as she did. But asking her to cover the costs of doctor visits and treatments made it abundantly clear she'd been alone in efforts to get pregnant.

The things he wanted out of their marriage were almost as revealing. She'd expected him to ask for the few items he'd owned before they wed—a basketball the Harlem Globetrotters had signed the night he'd watched them play in Atlanta, the afghan his grandmother had crocheted for him. At first glance, the rest lined up evenly, but a closer look revealed anything but a fair division. While she'd get the plastic tumblers, he'd take the crystal. He wanted the oversize TV in the living room, leaving her with the tiny one from their bedroom. And so on and so forth down to the last two items on his list— the kitchen table they'd rescued from Goodwill for her, and the desk he'd insisted they splurge on when he passed the bar for him. She glanced into the spare room, where the desk sat beneath the window, and her stomach clenched. She'd resented the darn thing ever since Sam put it in the room that was supposed to be their nursery.

She steepled her hands and pressed her index fingers against her nose, her thumbs under her chin. What was she supposed to do now? Sign the papers and throw in the towel? Or fight for him, for them?

She supposed at least part of the answer lay in how long ago Sam had given up on them. Had he been planning to call it quits for a day? A month? Six months? She lifted the corner of the thick document and fanned the pages through her fingers. By the looks of the paperwork, Sam had had his mind made up for quite a while. No one, not even her meticulous husband, was this thorough on a whim. For all she knew, he'd already moved on, had found someone new. In which case, did she even want him back?

The questions came at her so fast and furious, they made her head spin. She rubbed her temples. She needed to make a decision, but she didn't know where to start. Didn't know what she even wanted. She wished she had someone to talk to.

The thought had barely crossed her mind when her cell phone buzzed. Hoping against hope that an apologetic Sam would be on the other end of the line, that he'd tell her leaving had been a big mistake, that he'd beg for her forgiveness, she slipped the device from the pocket of her robe and checked the screen.

Erin.

She pressed the green button to accept the call. "Hey."

"Hey, yourself. You got a minute? I want to tell you what the lawyer said."

Her lawyer? But that was impossible. Erin wasn't psychic. She didn't know her husband had walked out on her. Had Sam called her sister? Reggie's gaze landed on the separation agreement. A sob threatened to bubble up from her middle. She fought it down and gave her sister a cautious, "What lawyer?"

"Dave Rollins. He's Michelle's attorney. Or, more to the point, he's handling Nancy Simmons's estate. The woman we think was Michelle's mother."

"Oh, yeah." Her breathing smoothed out. She hadn't mentioned a word about her troubles. Not to Erin or Nina. And definitely not to Michelle. Not on the anniversary of her husband's death, when she'd needed the full support of all her friends. As for Sam, he wouldn't reach out to her sister, either. She doubted he had her phone number, much less kept tabs on her whereabouts.

"Listen, Regina. Are you okay? You sound a little…off." Concern rode heavily on Erin's voice.

That's one way to put it.

"Sorry. I'm a little distracted. I was just, um—" As much as she ached to confide in her big sister, she couldn't dump all her problems on Erin. There was too much to explain. Starting with the fact that they'd never even discussed her infertility issues. She closed her eyes, imagining how she'd break the news. *Uh, Sam walked out on me after the fifth round of in vitro failed. Not that I ever told you about the other four.* No, that wasn't exactly the conversation she wanted to have over the phone. Not right now, at least. She ran a hand down the sleeve of her robe. "I was getting ready to turn in."

"It's awfully early," Erin pointed out. Doubt filled her words.

"It was a long day, and I'm beat," she said into a silence that stretched out a full five seconds. She grimaced. She didn't know how her sister did it, but Erin had always been able to tell when something was bothering her. Tears stung her eyes, and she whispered a prayer that this one time, her sister would just let it go. She was barely hanging on by a thread as it was. Admitting that she'd failed at marriage just like she'd failed to have a baby, well, that would break her completely.

At last, Erin cleared her throat. "Well, since you're *sleepy*, I'll give you the Readers' Digest Condensed version."

She didn't have to hear the sarcasm in her sister's voice to know that Erin hadn't bought her story for one second. Whatever. She faked a yawn. "Okay, let me have it."

"The bottom line is that there's a very good possibility this Nancy Simmons is Michelle's biological mother. She has to take a DNA test to be sure, but if it proves that Nancy and Michelle are related, Michelle stands to inherit a nice piece of property in North Florida. There's a house on it and everything."

"That's..." At a loss for words, she stopped. "That's amazing. How soon will she find out for sure?"

"That's part of the reason I'm calling. The lawyer says the test has to be done in his office. So Michelle and Nina and I are heading down there day after tomorrow."

"To Florida?"

"Yeah."

"How long will you be gone?"

"Just a few days. It's about a fifteen-hour drive. We'll have to stick around until the blood work comes back, but the attorney says it won't take more than twenty-four hours. We want to have time to check out the property anyway since Michelle might owe taxes on it. Say, two days in Destin at the outside. After that, we'll turn around and drive back. Altogether, that's four, five days?"

Reggie was pretty sure Sam meant for her to sign the separation agreement right away.

Hadn't he said as much in his note? But deciding how to divvy up everything they owned—and their debts—wasn't something she could do in five minutes. Especially when she hadn't even come to grips with the fact that her marriage might be over. A five-day road trip with the people she trusted the most in the world sounded like just what she needed. "Sounds like fun," she said, forcing an upbeat note she didn't feel into her voice. "Do you have room for one more?"

"You want to come, too?"

"If it's okay." She hated to beg, but the opportunity to get out of town for a while was too good to pass up.

"Don't you have to work?"

"It'll still be here when I get back." Or, if worse came to worse, she'd find another job if she had to.

"You're sure?"

"I'm sure," she answered despite her sinking heart. Her sister's tone said she knew Reggie was hiding something. Somehow, she was going to have to find the courage to tell her sister and her friends that her marriage had fallen apart.

"It's fine. We'd love to have you, but…"

"Yes?" she asked slowly.

"You will tell me what's going on, right?"

"Yeah," she sighed. "I will." People always said two heads were better than one. She hoped they were right about that, 'cause she had a feeling she was going to need all the help she could get to figure out her next move.

Nineteen

Erin

Thursday morning, Erin sat on the front porch sipping coffee. She wanted to take advantage of a last chance to be outdoors before being cooped up in the car during the long trip to Florida. The spicy perfume of blooming azaleas floated in the air. She inhaled deeply, enjoying the clove-like scent. Though the first hint of sunrise barely glowed on the eastern horizon, lights seeped through closed bedroom curtains as some of Michelle's neighbors rose and began to get ready for the workday. A day that probably included a long commute into DC. A throaty rumble broke the quiet of the still neighborhood. Instead of fading like it would if the driver had gotten an early jump on the rush-hour traffic, the sound grew louder. Erin checked her watch when her sister's pickup truck rounded the corner at the end of the block. Regina was right on time.

She tossed what was left of her cold coffee onto the mulch in the flower bed when her sister pulled the ancient vehicle onto the driveway. The creak of rusty car doors echoed as Regina and Nina stepped from the truck. Both women waved hellos before they took overnight bags from the open truck bed and lugged them to the Cadillac Escalade that sat, idling, at the curb. The phone calls and texts that had flown between the four women over the last twenty-four hours had covered a variety of subjects, but no one had questioned the decision to use Michelle's big SUV for the trip. Still under the factory warranty, the car made the obvious choice. Plus, its heated leather seats and extra leg room made it a far more comfortable ride than the tiny electric car Nina rarely drove or Regina's pickup. As for her own Jeep, Erin had left it parked beside her little bungalow in the Keys.

"Good morning," she said, addressing Nina while Regina headed back to her truck.

"Morning," Nina said. She stretched, her long, dark hair flowing loose over her back. "I can't believe I'm up this early. Whose idea was it to leave at the crack of dawn?"

"Blame me," Erin said as she stood. The most experienced traveler in their group, she'd taken responsibility for planning their route. "We need to leave by five if we're going to check in to the hotel before midnight." In addition to the fifteen hours' driving time, she'd allowed three hours for rest stops and dinner at a restaurant Nina had suggested.

"Aye-aye, captain," Nina grumbled good-naturedly. She lifted a well-worn travel mug. "Coffee ready?"

"Help yourself."

When Nina headed inside, Erin waited for her sister, who'd taken a few gift bags from the back seat of the pickup.

"Whatcha got there?" she asked as the shorter woman neared.

"A little something to make the trip just a bit more pleasant." Regina shifted the handles of the bags. "Let's go inside and I'll give you yours."

"How sweet," Erin said, holding the door open. She gave her sister a one-armed hug and tried unsuccessfully to brush aside her concerns when Regina stiffened momentarily. Something was definitely bothering her sister. Though she obviously didn't want to talk about it, Erin determined to get to the bottom of whatever was troubling her before the trip ended. For now, though, she'd give her sister some space. Not that there'd be much of that, what with four of them in the car. She didn't care how roomy and luxurious Michelle's car was, she'd traveled enough to know that twenty hours on the road strained even the closest friendships.

Inside, they topped off travel mugs while Michelle rushed around, checking doors, turning off lights and double-checking the oven to make sure she'd shut it off. When they were finished, Erin insisted each of them make one last trip to the powder room. She followed her own advice, returning just as Regina checked the names on her gift bags and handed one each to Michelle and Nina.

Michelle squealed happily when she pulled out a treasure trove of her favorite treats. She clutched the package of Swedish fish, the latest romance novel by Hope Holloway, and a bag of salt-and-vinegar chips to her chest while offering profuse thanks. Nina's gifts had likewise been selected with care and included her favorite brand of chocolate bars, a pack of barbecued potato chips, and the most recent issue of *Bon Appétit*. Erin was almost afraid to look in her gift bag. She'd been away so long, she doubted her little sister knew which sweet treats she preferred or that she'd never met a chip she liked, but her eyes watered when she spotted a bag of orange-colored marshmallow candies tucked inside beside a book of word puzzles.

"How did you know?" she asked Regina. Despite the early hour, she ripped the plastic open and popped one of the spongy peanuts in her mouth.

"Remember that time Mom and Dad took us to the candy store in Baltimore? That was all you wanted—a big bag of circus peanuts." Regina grinned, her happiness at choosing correctly evident. "The word puzzles—we used to do them together when we were kids."

"I remember," Erin said, swallowing. "This was really nice."

"What did you get for yourself?" Michelle asked.

"Hard caramels." Regina held up a familiar yellow bag. "And another word-puzzle book. There's a six-pack of water in the car, too."

"Speaking of which…" Erin tapped her phone. While Michelle unplugged the coffee pot, the rest of them gathered up purses and sweaters and trouped to the car. Erin had plugged their route into the car's navigation system the day before, so Nina, who'd claimed shotgun, only had to press Go and, with Michelle behind the wheel, they headed south.

"I'm bored," Regina whined. Her voice struck the same plaintive note she'd had when their parents had loaded them into the family sedan for a long, Sunday drive.

Erin grinned. "Are we there yet?" she asked, snapping her seat belt in place.

Michelle caught her reflection in the rearview mirror. "Don't make me stop this car," she scolded, sounding very much like the harried mother of rambunctious twins. "You two hush and settle down, you hear me?"

They were well below Atlanta before the traffic, which had remained relatively heavy throughout the trip, thinned considerably. The sun was sinking by the time Erin prodded the seat back with one foot. "Can we stop for dinner soon? I'm hungry for something that isn't orange and sweet." She shot a quick look at the figure beside her. "No offense, Regina."

Without looking up from her word-puzzle book, her sister said crossly, "Call me Reggie. You're the only person on earth who calls me Regina."

Just as Erin thought it would, the endless

miles had put everyone on edge. She tried to lighten the mood. "I think someone else is hungry, too," she said with a grin.

"Another ten miles," Nina said from her spot behind the wheel.

Erin shrugged. She could handle ten more miles. In the captain's chair beside her, Regina buried her head deeper into her book.

Still, Nina kept driving until nearly sunset, when she pulled off the interstate near a mom-and-pop that had a reputation for the best fried chicken in the state. The cook swore her mouth had been watering for a taste ever since they left Fairfax.

Heat and humidity wrapped them in a warm Georgia embrace when they stepped out of the car into a parking lot crowded with cars bearing local license tags. At first glance, Erin wasn't impressed with the diner. A neon sign advertising the World's Best Chicken buzzed and hummed from the roof of the squat, cement block building. The plate-glass windows staring out over the highway like two wide eyes provided the only other break in the monotony of the restaurant's stark white exterior. But Nina had never steered them wrong before, and besides, she'd meant it when she said she was hungry. Her body had long since burned through the breakfast they'd grabbed at a Tex-Mex drive-through just outside of Richmond. She couldn't eat sweets like she used to, and to avoid a sugar high, she'd allowed herself only two circus peanuts during the long drive. Trailing her friends into the tiny restaurant, she reminded herself that during her many travels, she'd eaten in far worse dives.

She was pleasantly surprised, then, when they stepped inside. The first thing she noticed was the cool, dry air that carried the tantalizing aroma of fried chicken. Beyond a small waiting area, cedar tabletops gleamed beneath drop lights. Booths along both walls had been padded with a tufted leatherette that looked comfortable enough. They'd only lingered in the entryway a few seconds before a young brunette with big hair, bright blue eye shadow and a gingham checked apron straight out of *Steel Magnolias* led them to an empty booth.

"Fried chicken is our specialty," she said, her Southern accent so thick, Erin needed a knife to cut through it. "We also got fried pork chops, catfish—that's also fried—and Brunswick stew. Everything comes with two sides." She pointed to a chalkboard mounted on the back wall. "Can I get y'all tea or coffee?"

"I can hear my arteries crying out for mercy,"

Erin whispered when their hostess had scurried off to grab four sweet teas.

"Mine, too," Nina nodded. "But they'll just have to deal. I'm having the chicken."

After the waitress delivered four tall glasses of tea to their table, Erin sipped hers and smacked her lips. "So sweet it makes my ears wiggle," she declared.

In the end, they all opted for the restaurant's claim to fame. Twenty minutes later, their waitress settled a platter piled high with crispy, golden-brown chicken on the table. Around it, she dealt substantial servings of potato salad, cole slaw, green beans, fried green tomatoes and okra until their food covered every bare inch of wooden surface.

"Need anything else?" their waitress, a carbon copy of the hostess, asked before sauntering off once Nina assured her they'd be fine.

"There has to be two whole chickens here." Regina took a meaty drumstick from the pile.

"We're never going to eat all this food," Michelle gasped. She speared a breast nearly twice the size of Erin's hand.

Nina took another breast, while Erin helped herself to a thigh. She reached for her knife and fork, but a glance around the restaurant stopped her.

At the table in the center of the room, a group of men in bib overalls, work boots and baseball caps bit into pieces of chicken they held in their hands. Across from them sat three women in soft knit pullovers they'd worn over pants with elasticized waistbands. While she watched, one of the women used her fingers to deftly strip the crispy skin from a breast. Her dining companions didn't so much as blink an eye when she plopped the morsel into her mouth. A family of four sat one booth over. There, a pair of towheaded boys dueled each other with chicken legs.

"When in Rome." Erin shrugged. Lifting the thigh in both hands, she took a bite. She made a pleasurable sound as her teeth sank into the salty, crunchy crust. The chicken was so tender, it practically melted in her mouth. "Oh, so good." She nudged her sister, whose gaze shifted between the utensils on her napkin and the piece of chicken on her plate. "Try it, Regina." She lifted the thigh to her mouth and took another bite.

"I mean it, Erin," came a hissing sound. "Call me Reggie."

"Oh. You were serious?" Erin slowly lowered what was left of her chicken to her plate. So much for her theory that her sister had been hangry.

"Everyone else calls me Reggie." She placed her hands flat on the table.

Erin tilted her head. Searching the faces of their friends, she asked, "For real?"

When Michelle and Nina stopped devouring their chicken long enough to nod, she wiped her mouth with a napkin. Something had been bothering…Reggie…lately, and if calling her sister by her full name was even a small part of it, she'd work hard to correct it.

"I'm sorry," she said, turning to her sister. "I didn't realize it was that important to you. I'll do my best…Reggie." She'd probably slip up from time to time. She had, after all, been using her sister's full name for thirty-five years.

She reached for the bowl of potato salad. In her travels, she'd probably come across more variations on the simple dish than there were methods for frying chicken. This one looked particularly interesting. Potatoes cooked so long they'd practically turned to mush swam in a creamy dressing with what looked like enough pickle bits and chopped onion to kick it up a notch. She held the peace offering out to her sister. "Have some?"

Reggie hesitated only a second or two before accepting the dish with a wan smile. "Thanks." She scooped a generous helping onto her plate, picked up her fork and tried a taste. "Yummy," she declared.

Everyone relaxed and dug into their dinners as the sudden tension faded around the table. In minutes, the four of them were laughing and telling jokes again. Michelle had been right—they'd barely put a dent in the mountain of fried chicken by the time each of them declared they couldn't eat another bite and pushed back from the table. Erin eyed what was left with sorrow as she politely declined their waitress's offer to box up the remains to take home.

"Please give our compliments to the chef," Nina said. "The chicken truly was the best I've ever tasted."

"But we're traveling and we don't have a cooler to keep it in," Michelle explained.

"The Quick Stop next door has them Styrofoam ice chests," the waitress pointed out.

The suggestion met with instant approval. Soon, their leftovers carefully wrapped and placed in a plastic bag, Erin, Reggie and Michelle headed for the car while Nina dashed next door, where she paid ten dollars for the necessary supplies to keep the World's Best Chicken on ice until they reached their destination. As she slid onto the front seat for her turn behind the wheel, Erin just hoped their hotel room had an ice machine or a mini-fridge.

The sun had sunk well below the horizon by the time they got back on the road again. Traffic quickly thinned as vacationers and salesmen ended their travels for the day and checked into hotels. In the last of the fading daylight, headlights came on, their beams punching holes in the dark. By nine, when she followed the GPS's directions off the interstate and onto a four-lane highway that led toward Destin, Michelle and Nina slept soundly in the back seat, and few other vehicles shared the roadway. From time to time, lights outlined one of the big rigs that appeared out of the darkness behind her. Even though Erin drove a steady five miles above the speed limit, the Escalade shook as, by ones and twos, the semis thundered past.

In the passenger seat, Reggie closed her book of word puzzles. She slipped it and her pencil into the purse at her feet. Erin took a breath. With two hours left until they reached their destination, this might be the best—and last—chance she'd have of finding out what had been bothering her sister.

"Hey."

A good wingman, Reggie instantly straightened. "You want something? Water or a snack?"

"I'm all right. Thanks. I just wanted to tell you again, I'm sorry about the name thing. I had no idea it was so important to you."

"It's not. Not really. I think you were right. I was a little bit hangry." Reggie laughed softly.

"It had been a long time since breakfast." Knowing they were planning a longer break for dinner, they'd all decided to forgo lunch. "But if it's important to you that people call you Reggie, I want to do that, too."

"Well, it's true that everyone else does."

"Good to know." She waited a beat, then forced herself to plunge ahead. "So, I get the name thing, but I also get the sense that something else has been troubling you. I see it in your eyes. You haven't been yourself. You hardly ever laugh anymore. And I was wondering…did I do something to upset you?"

"No. It's not you. Not at all."

Though the instant response sent a wave of relief through her, it also confirmed that there was a problem in her sister's life. "Do you want to talk about it?"

"I need to talk to somebody." Reggie shifted on the leather seat until she pressed her back against the door.

Out of the corner of her eye, Erin saw her sister glance into the back seat. She knew without being told that Reggie was checking to see if Michelle or Nina were awake. But after driving most of the day and then eating a huge dinner, she had no doubt, the two of them were dead to the world and would remain so until they reached Destin.

Apparently Reggie drew the same conclusion. Her voice low and so soft Erin had to strain to hear it, she said, "I think my marriage is over."

Erin's breath escaped in a long, slow hiss. She'd expected Reggie to tell her she'd run into some kind of problem at work—a missed promotion, too much pressure or a coworker who didn't give her the respect she deserved. She'd been prepared to deal with a secret gambling addiction. She'd even braced herself for problems with the folks—after all, they weren't getting any younger. But trouble in her marriage? The answer had come at her out of the blue. As far as she knew, Reggie had never so much as hinted things were rocky at home.

"What..." She thought better of what she'd been about to say and clamped her lips closed before she could ask what went wrong. Though it had happened so long ago she hardly ever thought of it anymore, she'd been through her own divorce. Back then, she hadn't wanted to share the gory details. What she'd really needed was for someone to tell her she was going to live through it. "Oh, honey. I'm so sorry," she said instead. "Are you all right?"

"I—I think I am. I mean, those first few days were rough. But I'm better now."

"Is there anything I can do? Do you need anything?" Whatever her sister needed, she'd get it for her.

"I don't think so. Not right now, anyway. I feel so stupid. I didn't see it coming. He just came in from work one day, packed his bags and walked out. Said he was done with us." Her breath caught. "With me."

"He didn't give any reason?" She hesitated, but the question had to be asked. "Is there someone else?"

"I honestly don't know. I've been going over it and over it in my mind, but nothing he said makes any sense. I mean, I knew things had been tense between us lately. We've had, um, we've had money troubles. I've been working overtime to help out. Between that and this big case he's working on, we're hardly ever home at the same time anymore. I thought it was a rough patch. That we'd work through it. But then he—he just walked out. Who does that?"

Someone who has something else—someone

else—on the side, Erin thought. Her sister didn't deserve this. Reggie was the sweetest person she knew. Why, look at the gift bags she'd brought for everyone. Such kind and thoughtful gifts. She, Michelle and Nina weren't exactly slouches in the good friend department, but none of them had thought to pick out special treats for the others.

"When did all this happen?" she asked.

"Last week. The night before we all went out to dinner," Reggie answered, sounding miserable.

Poor kid.

No wonder Reggie hadn't seemed like herself. She'd been keeping up a cheerful front while her world had been falling apart. Erin tightened her grip on the steering wheel. Wait till the next time she saw Sam. She'd give him a piece of her mind for what he'd done to her sister.

She nearly said as much but then caught herself. Now was not the time to trash her sister's husband. Not if there was even the slightest chance Reggie and Sam would work things out between them. Before she said something that might come back to haunt her later, she'd better find out if there was any hope of that happening.

"Do you think…Is there any chance he'll change his mind? Or do you want him to?"

She caught the slightest movement when Reggie shook her head. "No. At least, I don't think he's willing to give it—give us—another chance. At first, I thought he would, you know? I kept waiting for him to call. He'd say it was all a big mistake. That he'd been a fool and he was coming home." She choked back a sob.

Erin's heart sank as Reggie leaned down and plucked a tissue from her purse. The many times her sister had checked her phone last weekend made sense now. She'd been waiting, hoping, praying for a phone call that would let her know her life hadn't fallen apart.

And what had she done? She'd practically laid into Reggie about it. *Geez.*

"It hasn't been that long. A week?" Erin risked a quick sideways glance into the passenger seat. Her gut clenched when the beams of an oncoming car glinted off the tears on her sister's cheeks. "Maybe he'll still change his mind?"

"No," Reggie said softly. She blew her nose and sniffled. "He, um, he had separation papers drawn up. A courier dropped them off just before you called the other night."

"He didn't waste much time, did he?" She muttered a curse she used so rarely it left a rusty taste in her mouth. That settled it. At least it did as far as she was concerned. With roughly half of all marriages ending in divorce, she'd seen a lot of breakups. Usually, the couple limped along in a sort of limbo—separating and reconciling, then separating again—until one of them got serious about someone new. In all those times, she'd never—not once—known either party to jump right into a legal separation unless they had someone waiting in the wings. Sam, bless his rotten heart, had found someone new.

Did Reggie know?

Deliberately, she loosened her grip on the steering wheel and shook her hands, one by one, to restore the circulation in fingers that had grown stiff. Whether Reggie had figured it out or not, she couldn't be the bearer of *that* bad news. In the fragile state she was in right now, her sister was more likely to shoot the messenger than thank them. Best to leave Reggie to figure it out on her own so that, when the time came, she'd be around to lend her sister a much-needed shoulder to cry on. For the time being, she'd do as much as she could to help.

"You mentioned money problems." Erin gave her ponytail a tug. That was another mystery. How did a rising attorney in a top-notch practice and one of the best landscapers in booming Fairfax County have financial trouble? Had Sam been wining and dining his new love?

She supposed that was another question for another day, too. "I can lend you whatever you need." She had plenty. With only herself to worry about, she'd built up a considerable nest egg. If need be, she could even sell the house in Key West.

"I'm okay for right now. Sam has offered to cover the rent on our apartment for the next six months." Her voice dropped to a soft whisper Erin had to strain to hear. "I could use some help looking over the separation agreement, though. If you wouldn't mind. Since we don't have"— her voice hitched—"don't have children, when it comes time for the actual divorce, I'll be stuck with whatever I agree to now."

A hard knot formed in the pit of Erin's stomach. She was pretty sure there was more to Reggie's story, but she wouldn't push. Her sister would tell her the rest in her own good time. In the meantime, though, Reggie needed someone in her own corner. "I'll be glad to read through them for you," she said. "But before you sign anything, you need a good divorce attorney to look it over."

"I don't know, Erin. Having you look over the paperwork is one thing. But an attorney?" Regina stuck the balled-up tissue in her purse. "Isn't that just an unnecessary expense? Sam knows how these things are handled. Besides, he'll be furious if I get another lawyer involved."

"Did he include his 401K or retirement funds in the paperwork he sent over?" More than twenty years had passed since her own divorce, but she still knew a thing or two about the pitfalls. She didn't want Reggie to make the same mistakes she had.

"Um, no? Was he supposed to?" Reggie asked softly.

"Yes." Erin nodded.

"I thought he was being fair. Yeah, he wanted most of the more expensive stuff for himself, but that makes sense since he makes more money than me. And he did offer to pay the rent so my salary, or most of it, could go toward paying off our credit cards…and stuff."

"Like I said, I'll be glad to look over the papers with you. But you need your own attorney. Someone who's one hundred percent on your side. Let me help you with that, okay?" From the little Reggie had said, it sounded like her soon-to-be-ex was playing with a loaded deck and expected his naïve wife to accept whatever cards he dealt her. A protective growl formed in the back of Erin's throat. Nobody was going to take advantage of her little sister, not if she could help it.

The light at the next cross street turned yellow. Erin slowed the big SUV and brought it to a stop just shy of the intersection. With her focus split between Reggie and the road, she'd lost track of where they were. She glanced at the GPS and was amazed that, while they talked, the big car had eaten up the miles. They'd nearly reached the Destin city limits. At the next light, they'd turn left. From there, it was a short five-minute drive to their hotel.

"No matter what, I want you to know I'm here for you," she told her sister when the light turned green.

"I know you are. And I appreciate it. I hate that I've been such a Debbie Downer lately."

"Hey. Don't worry about it. You probably don't remember, but I was pretty much a basket case for months after Rob and I called it quits." Although her situation had been entirely different.

She thought of something else. "Listen. I guess you haven't told them"—she hooked a finger over her shoulder to the two sleeping in the back seat—"but think about it. At times like these, it can really help to have good friends who'll share the burden with you. Those two, they're two of the best."

"You're not so bad yourself, Erin. Thanks.

And if the offer still stands, I'll take you up on that divorce attorney."

"It does. I'll make a few calls." The light turned green, and she proceeded through the intersection, her mind churning. She'd see that her sister walked away from the marriage with her fair and equitable share. "I'm glad we talked," she said as she signaled for the next turn.

"Me, too. I'm not kidding myself. I know the divorce is going to hurt, but I'm really glad you're here to help me get through it."

Will I?

Erin swallowed. Though she'd come home to help her best friend get past an especially tough day, she hadn't planned to stick around long. But then there'd been all the work to do around Michelle's house and the news about her birth mother. Now, here she was, making a road trip to Florida. Sure, she and Reggie would make a quick visit to see the folks when they got back. After that, though, she had a date with a dart and a map of the world, didn't she?

A growing weariness settled over her. Along with it came questions Erin couldn't answer.

She'd traveled the world, seen incredible sights, but at what cost? She hadn't been around to watch Ashley and Aaron grow up. The day they'd graduated from high school, she'd literally been in Timbuktu, studying a fifteenth-century mosque. She'd caught the first flight home the day Allen died, but that still meant she'd been on the other side of the world when her friend had needed her most. She'd been thrilled for Nina when, just four years after graduation, she'd been named sous chef in one of DC's better-known restaurants. By the time she learned everything had fallen apart for her friend, though, the news had been as stale as a week-old donut. Yes, she'd made it home in time for Reggie's wedding—barely—but now her sister's marriage had crashed and burned without her knowledge. She'd missed out on so much already. How much more would she miss if she left again?

Twenty

Michelle

Flanked on one side by Erin and on the other by Nina and Reggie, Michelle eyed the stately law offices of Rollins and Rollins. Pavers laid in a herringbone pattern led to the main entrance, where brick walls and tall, white columns assured visitors of the building's permanence and stability. She'd expected as much, having studied the practice's website, but seeing it in person somehow brought home the idea that, in a matter of hours, she might actually know the name of her birth mother. The thought loosed a cloud of butterflies in her stomach. Her footsteps slowed.

"Nervous?" Reggie asked.

"A little," she confessed. It wasn't every day she inherited the estate of a woman who'd disappeared from her life after nine months. Had her mother held her? Kissed her goodbye? She'd been far too young to remember. "What if this Dave Rollins thinks I'm some kind of charlatan?"

"He won't," Reggie said with so much assurance, Michelle had to believe her. "Remember, they came looking for you. Not the other way around."

"You look great, by the way," Nina said. "I like the new haircut."

Nina's reassuring touch at her elbow settled a few more butterflies. "Thanks," she said. "I splurged on a trip to the day spa before we left. Sean insisted I buy this new serum. It was hideously expensive, but he said it'd work wonders on my hair." The jury was still out on that, but she loved the cut the stylist had given her. The slightest movement sent the ends of the precision trim swinging.

"Is that a new outfit?" Reggie asked.

Michelle ran a hand over the sheath dress. "Another splurge. This one hides all the bulges." After the day spa, she'd breezed through Macy's department store. All too aware of her limited resources, she hadn't intended to buy anything. But the Ann Taylor hanging on the half-off rack had caught her eye. Its square neck and a forgiving waistline made the dress a wardrobe must-have. Plus, she'd never been able to resist a good sale.

"What bulges?" Nina asked, giving her the once-over.

"Exactly," Michelle said, feeling better about herself than she had in months. "It's amazing what a good haircut and a new dress can do to bolster your confidence."

"And friends," Reggie piped in.

"And friends," Michelle agreed. "I can't imagine going through all this by myself."

"We've got your back," Erin said, drawing close.

"That goes double for you," Michelle said, squeezing Reggie's hand. The younger woman had shared the news of her impending divorce over coffee this morning.

Bolstered by her friends' support, Michelle grasped the doorknob. The door swung open on a spacious lobby, where the sidewalk's herringbone pattern had been repeated in dark wood flooring. Beautiful seascapes dotted exposed brick walls beneath twelve-foot ceilings. Foot-high gold letters mounted on a false wall in the middle of the room announced the Law Offices of Rollins & Rollins. Slate topped a rosewood reception desk, where a neatly dressed young man welcomed them.

"I'm Michelle Robinson," she said and credited her friends when her voice didn't waver. "I have an appointment with Dave Rollins."

"Yes, ma'am. He's expecting you. If you'll have a seat, I'll let him know you're here." He indicated a cozy waiting area tucked into one corner of the lobby. "Can I get you some coffee? Or water?"

"None for me, thanks." Caffeine would only kick-start her nerves again. She glanced at Nina, Reggie and Erin, who each politely declined the offer, before the four of them trouped into the area where upholstered couches and wing chairs provided comfortable seating. A darkened television sat on a corner table. Discreetly situated on end tables, pamphlets advertised different services offered by the law firm.

"Is that him?" Reggie pointed to one of the trifolds. On the cover, a smiling Dave Rollins stared out through rimless glasses. A sober dark suit and white hair contributed to his grandfatherly look, while piercing blue eyes hinted at an intelligence anyone in need of a good attorney might appreciate.

Michelle nodded. She guessed the man in the photograph was in his late sixties and wondered if he'd been friends with her birth mother.

Assuming Nancy Simmons was her birth mother, that was.

"Ms. Robinson?"

Michelle started. Lost in her own thoughts, she'd failed to notice the tap-tap-tap of heels across the hardwood floors. She stood. "I'm Michelle." She extended a hand to a slender woman who'd swept her platinum-blond hair into a sleek updo that accentuated the angles of high cheekbones. Skillfully applied makeup gave her skin a dewy freshness. A gray pencil skirt and short, bolero-style jacket accentuated the long, lean body of a runner, though the crow's-feet at her eyes hinted she was older than she looked.

"I'm CoraBeth Burke, Mr. Rollins's paralegal." Thin lips painted a dark coral shade widened into a smile. "If you'll come with me, we'll get all the preliminaries taken care of before you meet with Mr. Rollins. You brought the necessary papers?"

"Right here." Michelle patted the side of the barely pink Kate Spade satchel she'd plucked from her closet as much for its roominess as for its color. "These are my friends—Erin, Nina and Reggie."

"Nice to meet you all." CoraBeth greeted each warmly. "Josh, we'll be in the small conference room," she said to the young man at the reception desk before leading the way to a room at the end of a long hall.

Once they were all seated at the large rectangular table in the room, where the air carried the faintest scent of lemon oil, CoraBeth settled a pair of tortoiseshell glasses on her nose. A tense silence descended on the room when Michelle pulled out the important papers she'd retrieved from her safe deposit box at the bank. The next fifteen minutes crept by with turtle-like slowness as the paralegal gave Michelle's paperwork a thorough going over. At last, CoraBeth piled the papers on top of one another and straightened the edges. "These all seem to be in perfect order," she said. She dealt the pages out in a straight line on the table.

Michelle let out the breath she'd been holding. Around the room, cloth rustled as Nina, Reggie and Erin relaxed slightly.

"Next, if you don't mind, we'll have the nurse come in and take a sample of your blood for the DNA comparison. To be legally binding, this test would normally take place in a medical setting. However, we have an agreement with the lab to take samples on the premises in cases like these."

"You handle a lot of cases that require DNA testing, do you?" Reggie asked.

CoraBeth shook her head. "Mostly, we're trying to prove paternity. My professor told us of one case where the mother swore her ex-husband had fathered her child. He was so afraid of getting stuck for child support that he convinced his best friend to take the DNA test in his place. But the joke was on both of them. Turned out, the best friend was really the father." She sighed and shook her head as soft laughter filled the room.

"I think every law school student hears some version of that story," CoraBeth confided in a conspiratorial whisper. "But it does explain why we insist on witnessing the blood draw. To weed out the imposters." To Michelle, she added a reassuring, "Not that I think that's the case here. Our nurse will take the sample straight to the lab. We should have the results back by this time tomorrow. Would you like your friends to wait in the reception area?"

"They can stay, if it's not a problem," Michelle answered. Her friendship with Erin, Nina and Reggie had spanned decades' worth of broken bones, cuts, scrapes and one emergency appendectomy. One more needle, more or less, wasn't going to make any difference.

"It's perfectly all right," CoraBeth said. She reached for a video phone centered on the long table. Pressing a button on the console with one neatly manicured finger, she asked Jonas if someone named Deborah could join them in the conference room.

Almost before Michelle had time to think about it, a woman in blue scrubs appeared in the doorway. Another round of introductions followed. The collection of the specimens—first a quick swab of her mouth, followed by the cool dab of an alcohol wipe on her arm and a slight pinch—was almost anticlimactic after the long drive and the apprehension she'd felt leading up to the moment. The nurse pressed a cotton ball against the spot on the inside of Michelle's elbow and wrapped it in stretchy blue gauze. Then, carefully setting her samples in a specially-marked envelope, the nurse left.

CoraBeth glanced at the phone. A single light blinked on the console. "Mr. Rollins is finishing up a phone call. Can I get you anything while we wait—coffee, water?"

"I'll take some water, if you don't mind," Michelle answered. Anticipation had left her mouth as dry as cotton.

"Not at all." CoraBeth pressed another button on the console, and within seconds, Josh appeared at the door carrying six bottles of water.

Michelle had barely taken a sip when the door opened again. A man who either wasn't the stout father figure pictured on the law offices' brochures or who had undergone a serious transformation entered the room. This man had grayed at the temples in a manner that gave him a uniquely distinguished look. If he carried an extra ounce of weight on his six-foot-two-inch frame, he hid it well. Beneath the jacket of his well-tailored suit—Hugo Boss or Armani, she thought—a tie in a soothing blue topped a white shirt. Suddenly wanting to make a good impression, Michelle pulled herself the tiniest bit straighter.

"Hi y'all. I'm Dave Rollins."

Definitely not the man in the picture, she thought. This Dave Rollins was at least thirty years younger, although he possessed the same penetrating gaze. He used it to zero in on the gauze wrapped around her elbow.

"You must be Ms. Robinson," he said, extending a hand while the softest of Southern accents enhanced the rich timbre of his voice.

"Michelle, please," she said, slipping her palm into his much larger one. "I have to admit," she said as they shook hands, "you're not at all who I expected."

"Oh?" Mirth deepened faint laugh lines around his mouth.

"The pictures on your website…"

"That's my father. Dave Rollins Senior." Dave smiled warmly. "He retired two years ago, but people around here equate Rollins and Rollins with him, so he remains the face of the firm. On our website. Our brochures and such." His gaze traveled the table. "I see you brought reinforcements," he said, nodding at the other three women in the room.

"My friends, yes." Michelle introduced each in turn. "Erin Bradshaw. Nina Gray. Regina Frank. We made the drive down together."

"I hope you had a pleasant trip and enjoy your visit to Destin. Will you be staying long?"

"We plan to head back on Saturday," Erin answered.

"Where are you staying?" Once more, Dave zeroed in on Michelle.

"We're at the Marriott."

"Bryce Harper is the manager there—he's good people. You need anything, you ask for him. He'll take good care of you." Dave nodded his approval. "Destin has lots to offer. Great beaches with all sorts of water activities. Bike paths. Nice shopping. Some of the best seafood in the state."

Nina perked up at that. "Anyplace in particular you'd recommend?"

Dave rubbed his chin. "Depends. If you're looking for casual, waterfront dining, I'd recommend Boshamps down at the harbor. Freshest oysters in town. For something a little more refined, try Louisiana Lagniappe. Impeccable service. Top-notch seafood."

"Thanks. We might check out both of them." Nina busily plugged the names of the restaurants into her cell phone.

Dave's focus shifted to Michelle again. "I take it you don't mind if we talk in front of your friends?"

"I'd like them to be here." Michelle gave him her warmest smile. "It'll save me from having to repeat everything you say."

"Well, that's fine. Ladies." Dave lowered himself onto a chair directly across from Michelle. He pulled a pair of readers from his suit pocket and slipped them on as, one by one, CoraBeth handed him the documents Michelle had brought with her from Virginia. The attorney treated each paper to the same thorough scrutiny his paralegal had given them. As he finished with each one, he placed it upside down on the table beside him until, at last, they were all in a neat stack.

Removing his glasses, he slipped them into his coat pocket.

Dave's piercing gaze lost a little of its intensity as he looked at Michelle. "Well, this all seems to be in order. We won't know for sure until we get the lab results, but based on what I've seen here"—he tapped the stack of papers—"I'd say you appear to have a credible claim as the daughter Nancy Simmons put up for adoption."

From the seat next to hers, Erin grasped Michelle's hand and gave it a squeeze.

Michelle told herself she couldn't get her hopes up, that the blood test could yield results that were totally different from what Dave expected. After all, it was possible that another woman had abandoned her child on the same day that Nancy Simmons gave up her daughter. In a town the size Destin had been in 1976, that wasn't likely, but she couldn't rule it out entirely. Still, it wouldn't hurt to find out as much as she could about the woman who could very well have been her birth mother. She took a breath. "Did you—or your father—know Ms. Simmons well?"

Dave's face softened. "We weren't close. I'm not sure anyone was. Nancy had agoraphobia and rarely left her house. Especially in her later years."

That was interesting, and Michelle was certain Dave noted her confusion. "But didn't she sit on the board of several charitable organizations?" When Dave hiked an eyebrow at the question, she explained, "Erin found her obituary online."

"I did," Erin nodded. "It said she sat on the hospital board, was active in the women's society, contributed to the library. It sounded like she was very active in the community."

"She was but not in the usual manner. She conducted almost all her business by phone." Dave leaned back in his chair. "My dad served on the hospital foundation with Nancy. He says the secretary would call her, and they'd leave the line open during the entire meeting." He smiled. "You might say she mastered the art of tele-commuting before it was even a thing."

"She must have had some contact with the outside world, though. Doctor visits. Groceries," Michelle pointed out. She couldn't imagine cutting herself off completely. Even in the darkest hours following Allen's death, she'd craved familiar faces, hearing the sounds of laughter, of people talking.

Dave's posture, like his voice, softened. "Destin may look like a touristy big city, but it's still a small town at heart. Sugar Sand Beach is more like a village, actually, but a strong sense of community runs through both places. Whenever someone's in need, there's always someone else willing to lend a hand. For years, the ladies at First Baptist church did all Nancy's shopping. Most of her doctors made house calls. Whenever she needed legal advice or services, someone from the office drove to her house. On the rare occasions that she had to go out, a trusted friend or two always went with her."

"Wow, that's…" Stunned, Michelle groped for the right word. She would have sworn such tight-knit communities only existed in Hallmark movies.

"Amazing," Erin finished.

"Yes," Michelle nodded.

"It's the way we do things around here." Dave drew himself a little taller in his chair. Folding his hands, he turned serious. "That brings us to the reason you're here. There are a few things I'd like to go over with you, things you should know and be thinking about, in case the lab results are positive."

Michelle felt her face warm. She'd been shocked by the hourly rate Allen's attorneys had charged for setting up her husband's new business venture. Considering that in a successful practice like Rollins and Rollins, time was money, her conversation with Dave had probably drifted too far afield. She straightened. "Of course."

As they'd discussed earlier, Erin flipped to the first page in the small notebook she pulled from her purse. She clicked her pen, ready to jot down anything important.

"When we spoke on the phone, I told you Ms. Simmons left everything—all her possessions, bank accounts, her house and property—to her sole heir, a daughter she put up for adoption in 1976." Giving Michelle his undivided attention, Dave added, "I'd like to discuss those items in some detail, if you don't mind."

"Yes, please." She leaned forward.

"Rollins and Rollins has been handling the Simmons estate on a pro bono basis ever since Nancy's account balances dropped below a thousand dollars. Her heir will have access to what's left—$436—but I'm afraid that's all the liquid cash left in the estate."

Michelle pressed her fingers together. So far, Dave was simply rehashing what he'd told her over the phone.

"That leaves the property itself, the furnishings in the house and Ms. Simmons's vehicles." At a slight nod, CoraBeth slid a map across the table to him. "This is an aerial view of the grounds. You can see, the house sits on a bluff a short walk from the beach. This"—he tapped a square box—"is the gardener's shed. It's quite roomy, roughly twenty by twenty. One half of it was converted into a small apartment some time ago."

When Michelle gave him a questioning look, he nodded to himself. "The Simmons family was quite well off. They made their money in salt—extracting it from seawater. What with the Gulf right outside their front door, they had plenty of raw material to work with. In their heyday, several of their staff lived either on the grounds or in the house itself."

"Whew! Must'a been nice." Reggie whistled.

Dave's blue eyes twinkled. "In this day and age, that's practically unheard of, but in the early 1900s, the wealthy were expected to maintain a certain image. Live-in nannies and gardeners were part of it. Unfortunately for the Simmons family, though, new production methods and foreign markets put an end to their salt extraction business in the '40's. Bad investments eroded what was left of the family fortune. Nancy still inherited a tidy sum when her parents died. Not enough for an extravagant lifestyle, but what with her disability and the agoraphobia, she didn't want that anyway."

Michelle gave a discreet cough. "The obituary mentioned injuries sustained in the same accident that killed her parents?"

Like a curtain, sadness dropped over Dave's features. "It happened before my time, but people around here still refer to the accident as a terrible tragedy. They were on their way to Fort Walton for a Christmas pageant. A tire blew while they were crossing the Brooks Bridge. Mr. Simmons lost control, and the car went over the side. Both the parents drowned. Nancy survived, but a spinal cord injury left her permanently disabled."

No one so much as twitched for a long moment while Michelle took a beat to absorb this news. Assuming Nancy was her birth mother, the young woman must have been five or six months pregnant at the time. Her own birthday fell in March, a scant three months after the accident. She tried to imagine what it must have been like for Nancy to realize she was unable to walk and alone in the world, and with a baby on the way. Small wonder she'd opted to put her child up for adoption. "She wasn't married?"

Dave lifted one shoulder and let it fall. "There was no marriage certificate among her papers. She never mentioned the father of her child. At least, not to my father or to me."

Michelle cleared her throat. "Thank you for telling me, telling us about the accident. It makes things clearer."

"I'm sure you have plenty of questions. I wish I had more answers for you." Sympathy filled his features. He waited another long moment before he tapped the map on the table before him. He pointed to another building. "This is the garage. There are several vehicles parked inside. Which brings us to the house itself. As you can see, it's quite large—eight bedrooms, six baths, a maid and a butler's rooms, a library. I could go on."

"No, that's all right," Reggie assured him. "It's a big house."

"It's been sitting vacant for over five years now, ever since Ms. Simmons's death. Immediately after her passing, we had a local handyman hang the hurricane shutters."

Caught off guard by the remark, Michelle frowned. "I'm sorry. The what?"

"Hurricane shutters," Dave said as if everyone in the room knew what he was talking about. When he saw they didn't, he hurried to explain. "Hurricane season starts in June and lasts through November. Pretty much every homeowner along the coast keeps shutters or plywood on hand in case a big storm threatens.

In this case, though, the shutters are there to discourage unwanted visitors—squatters and the like. Nancy's handyman, Chris Johnson, put them up. He's been keeping an eye on the place and taking care of absolutely essential repairs."

Michelle grabbed her bottle of water and took a drink. Hurricanes rarely struck Virginia, and when they did, they almost always fizzled out soon after they made landfall. But the big storms sometimes came ashore in Florida's Panhandle. She and Allen had made a sizable donation to the relief efforts after a bad one hit Mexico Beach in 2018. "Um, how often do hurricanes strike each year?"

Dave's smile turned contemplative. "There's no way to tell. We can go years without a big blow, then the next year get three in a row. The good thing is, the weather reports give us plenty of notice. As soon as a hurricane warning is issued for our area, business owners board up their windows, homeowners hang their shutters, everyone loads their most precious possessions in the car, and we all head inland. Destin turns into a ghost town." He frowned. "The real hassle comes later, when the danger is over. With everyone anxious to get back home, traffic creeps along bumper to bumper for hours."

She could handle a little traffic if it meant not having to live through a life-threatening storm.

She had no burning desire to sit in a house while gale-force winds tried to knock it into the next county. The pictures she'd seen were bad enough. Trees uprooted. Buildings torn down. Roads washed out. Property could always be repaired. Houses, rebuilt. But risking lives, that was something else again.

Dave peered at her. "Are you thinking of, um, moving here? Living in the house?"

Hating to dampen the hopeful note in the attorney's voice, she gave her head a slight shake. "No," she said. "I was actually thinking more of putting it on the market. Do you think there'd be any interest?"

"Yes, definitely. But…" Dave mopped his face with one hand. "That touches on a rather sensitive subject."

"How so?" Had Nancy placed some restriction on selling the property?

"As the new owner, you'd be within your rights to sell it if you wanted, but—with your permission—I'd like to interject a word of caution."

Michelle steepled her hands on the tabletop. Dave seemed like a nice guy. The kind of man who inspired people to trust him. It wouldn't hurt to listen to whatever he had to say. "What's up?" she asked.

"Sugar Sand Beach is a sleepy little beachside community. It's the kind of town where property stays in families for generations. Where your grandfather might have inherited his bungalow from his parents and plans to leave it to his son when the time comes. But..." Dave let out a long breath and shook his head. "But lately, that little slice of heaven has caught the eye of more than one major developer. Right now, a New York investment group is doing its best to buy up property in the area for a planned community that will cater to folks who come down from up north to spend the winter where it's warmer. We call them snowbirds," he said with a smile.

Michelle nodded. A couple of her neighbors fit into that category—retirees who wintered in Florida and summered in Virginia.

"Don't get me wrong. The group's plans are solid, if a little tight—houses so close together neighbors, can hold hands through their kitchen windows. Or they could if they knew each other. But with sixty percent of the properties devoted to short-term rentals, chances are slim you'd ever meet the person next door, much less get to know them well enough to be on a first-name basis. I guess that works for some people, but it's not how I want to live."

Michelle couldn't agree more. A big backyard

was one of the things that had first attracted her to the house in Fairfax.

"On the other hand," Dave continued, "I've seen the master plan. If they get all the land they want, they'll add a ton of amenities. A nice clubhouse. Churches. Since they're using local construction companies, the project means more jobs. All those new homes will spark a flurry of new businesses, too. Hair salons, veterinarians, pizza parlors and the like. Some people think it would be good for the local economy."

Sensing he wasn't one of them and was trying to make a point, Michelle prodded. "But…"

"But…" Dave gave her a sheepish smile. "It would fundamentally change the face of Sugar Sand Beach. Property values would skyrocket. Which sounds like a good thing, but not to the current owners because along with rising property values come higher taxes. The people who live there, who've held on to their land for a generation or two, they won't be able to afford to live there anymore. Most of them would be forced to sell. Soon, what used to be Sugar Sand Beach would be just another planned community along the coast, one that sits empty from April, when the snowbirds head back home, until late fall, when they head south again."

Michelle pushed her hair off her face. "I'm not sure what that has to do with me."

"The Simmons property is the lynchpin in the development plans. It's a strategic location. Butts right up to the Topsail Hill State Park. Ten years ago, the state would have snapped up the property and expanded the preserve. The economy being what it is today, that's not an option. There's talk the state might even reduce their holdings. Which presents these investors with a unique opportunity. If they can get their hands on these five acres—your five acres—they'll raze the house and launch Phase One of the development. Then, when land prices go up and the neighbors either want to get a piece of the action or can't afford to pay their property taxes, they'll gobble them up. If the state does decide to sell off some of the park land, well, let's just say they'd be foolish to pass that up. Orson Danner—he's the local point person—he never struck me as a fool."

"Well, you've definitely given me something to think about." Irritation stirred in Michelle's belly. She traced the seam of her dress with one finger. Dave made it sound like preserving the community's way of life was somehow her responsibility. That was an awful lot to ask of someone before they even knew whether or not they'd inherit the property. She firmed her lips and her resolve. "You mentioned property taxes. I know there's a tax lien against the Simmons property. How does Orson's project figure into all that?"

Dave pushed away from the table. "Unless the lien is satisfied before the end of the month, the county plans to sell the land to the highest bidder in the tax auction. Right now, that looks like Orson."

Her irritation deepened. Assuming she was Nancy Simmons's daughter, was Dave actually asking her to shell out twenty grand for taxes on a property he didn't want her to sell? She didn't have that kind of money lying around.

The attorney must have sensed her unease. His forearms propped on the table, he held up his hands. "Now, I'm not saying you shouldn't sell to Orson. Obviously, if you're proven to be Nancy Simmons's sole heir, what you do with the land is no one's business but your own. I'm just asking you to take a good, long look around before you do something you might regret later."

The attorney's conciliatory tone soothed the burn in Michelle's stomach. She mustered a tentative smile. "That sounds like a plan I can get behind."

"Why don't you ride out there this afternoon and take a look around? We can talk more tomorrow after the lab results come back." Dave reached into his pocket and pulled out a set of keys. He tapped the largest one. "There's a gate across the driveway. This key opens the padlock. The others are to the house and outbuildings."

"You trust me with the keys?" Michelle had to fight to keep her mouth from dropping open. She'd lived in Fairfax, Virginia, most of her life, and she could count on the fingers of one hand the number of people she'd hand the keys to her house. Three of them were sitting in this very room. Yet, here Dave was, handing the keys over to a near-perfect stranger.

Life sure was different in the South, and so far, she liked what she'd seen of it.

Twenty-One

Michelle

"Hmph. That was a bust," Reggie announced as they climbed into the car after leaving the attorney's office. She mimicked the lawyer's voice. "Here are the keys to five acres of prime beachfront property. It may or may not be yours. If it is yours, I'd rather you didn't sell it. And oh, by the way, that'll be twenty grand, please."

"Yeah, but what'd you think of Ol' Dave?" Erin nudged her sister in the ribs. "He wasn't too shabby to look at."

"Not the cigar-puffing good ol' boy in a seersucker suit I expected," Nina put in. "Did anyone else notice he wasn't wearing a wedding ring?"

"I saw that, but I figured, why bother?

He only had eyes for Michelle." Erin buckled her seat belt.

"Oh, get on, you." Michelle waved a hand, dismissive. "I bet he treats all his clients that way." Although she might as well admit it: She'd sort of liked being at the center of Dave's attention. "It was a lot to take in, though. My head is kind of spinning right now."

"You need coffee. We barely had time for a cup at the hotel," Nina pointed out. In their rush to make it to the attorney's office on time, they'd only grabbed fruit from the complimentary breakfast buffet. "I know I could use some."

Erin consulted the GPS on her phone. "There's a Starbucks on the next corner. Let's go through the drive-through and grab some before we go out to the Simmons place."

"Are we really doing that, though?" Michelle asked. "I won't know till tomorrow if Nancy Simmons really was my birth mother." Like the soap bubbles the twins used to play with, questions popped into her head one after another. Had Nancy given up her baby because of the accident? Or had that been her plan all along? What about the father? Combined with all the issues Dave had raised about the property itself, no wonder her head throbbed. She signaled for a turn into the coffee shop.

After placing their order for four Grande lattes in an assortment of flavors, she slowly inched through the line to the pickup window. Over the years, the four of them had made enough road trips together that they'd worked out a system of asking for individual checks at sit-down restaurants but taking turns paying for incidentals and gas. This time she accepted the credit card Reggie handed her from the back seat and swiped it through the card reader. Taking a loaded cardboard carrier from the server, she handed it off to Erin, who checked the labels on the four tall cups before doling them out.

Meanwhile, Michelle pulled into a parking space under a shade tree. The motor still running, she lifted her one-pump mocha latte from the cupholder where Erin had thoughtfully placed it. Inhaling the aroma of strong coffee mixed with chocolate a long second before she took a sip, she waited for the perfect blend of sweet and bitter flavors to hit her tongue. She swallowed. There was nothing like that first taste of hot coffee, and she took a moment to enjoy the heat that spread down her throat and into her stomach. "Oh, I needed that," she said. "Whoever suggested we stop, you're a genius."

"Here, here," echoed Erin, raising her cup in a mock toast.

Michelle took another drink. Letting the caffeine and sugar work their magic, she angled her body so she could see into the back seat. "What do you want to do today? Really. This is your trip as much as mine. You've already spent the morning at the lawyer's office, for which I'm forever grateful. But what's next? Hang out at the beach? Hit some shops downtown? Grab a bite at one of those places Mr. Rollins suggested?"

When no one answered, she scanned the faces of her friends. "What?" she asked.

"Well, speaking for myself, I'd like to at least drive out to the property and see what's what," Erin began. "Mr. Rollins's assurances aside, we could still be talking about a piece of swampland here."

"I'm curious about it, too," Nina added. "I'd love to see the furnishings. It'd be like our own private museum tour."

"I wouldn't mind taking a look at the plants," Reggie said. "You never know when a client is going to want something exotic for their greenhouse."

"You're not kidding." Michelle blinked back tears. She really did have the best friends. Here they were, giving up a full day of their vacay to spend it tramping around a piece of land that might not even be hers. "Well, I guess that settles it, then. Let's stop at the hotel and change clothes first." She ran a hand down her dress. "I might have grabbed this off the sales rack, but I'd like to get more than one wear out of it."

Fortified by coffee and wearing comfortable jeans and T-shirts, they assembled at the car twenty minutes later.

"You concentrate on getting us there. I'll drive." Erin held her hand out for the keys.

Glad not to be behind the wheel when she got her first glimpse of what might be her family home, Michelle handed them over. She slid onto the passenger's seat, and as soon as everyone buckled up, Erin headed east. At first, Destin's touristy strip malls and tall condominiums crowded both sides of the road. Those thinned as they neared the city limits. Colorfully painted beach houses replaced them. Michelle caught glimpses of blue water and white sand in the narrow spaces between the cottages. A sign at the side of the road soon announced, "Top Sail Preserve, one mile ahead."

"We're close now," Michelle said. "See where the road curves to the left up ahead? We're supposed to go straight. According to the directions, we should follow a dirt road to the entrance to the Simmons property."

A thrill of anticipation sent goose bumps rippling down her arms. She leaned forward, a blend of apprehension and hope causing her breath to hitch as Erin steered onto a deeply rutted dirt path and braked to a stop in front of a swinging gate. Beyond it, the track cut through tall saw grass and palmetto. Slash pines and scrub oaks dotted a rise that hid the house and the rest of the property from passersby.

Reggie jumped out to open the gate. Erin pulled past it, then waited while her sister closed it and locked up behind them. They moved forward, creeping along at a snail-like pace, while they followed the track a little farther.

"Whoever's driven down this road lately, they must have had a truck," Erin said when palmetto and tall saw grass sent up an ungodly racket as it brushed the undercarriage. The car rolled to a stop, and she put it in park. "Unless we want to call AAA, I think we should walk from here."

Two by two, they followed the twin ruts. Reggie slipped in beside Michelle while they headed deeper into the property. "What do you think so far?"

She eyed wispy pines and weeds for as far as she could see. "Well, to be honest, I'm thinking more and more about that swampland Erin's always talking about."

Reggie laughed. "I thought you might be having second thoughts, but look over there." She pointed to a line of low, green plants nearly hidden by the taller saw grass. "Those are hostas. And there, see those red, fuzzy blossoms? Those are chenille plants. They're too evenly spaced for it to be happenstance. And over there..." Another wave of her hand, this time to weeds with red blossoms. "That's firecracker plant. It doesn't grow wild. See those flowers with the pointy beaks? Those are bird of paradise. Someone spent a lot of money on landscaping here. I bet it was gorgeous once upon a time. With a little bit of work, it could be again."

"You don't say." With Reggie's help, Michelle could almost envision a welcoming road lined with flowers by the time they topped the small rise. In the distance, sunlight glinted off a metal roof. A turret towered over the two-story house. She sucked in a breath. "Whoa! When Mr. Rollins said the house had eight bedrooms, I knew it had to be a big place, but I never in my wildest dreams imagined this. This is..." She groped for the right word and came up empty.

"Amazing," whispered Nina.

Built in a Queen Anne style, the house, much like the grounds, needed a good dose of TLC. It didn't help that sheets of metal covered the windows and doors like Band-Aids. Or that paint peeled from gingerbread trim. On either side of brick steps, thin columns supported the roofs of twin porches that jutted out from the main house. Each sported lacy knee rails. Octagonal rooms embraced a narrow balcony centered on the second floor. She could only guess at the dimensions, but the house looked to be twice as wide as her home in Fairfax and was at least as deep. Yet, despite its size, the place had a delicate air about it, not unlike that of a gracefully aging matriarch.

"No holes in the roof, as near as I can tell," announced Erin. "She could use a good coat of paint and some repair work"—she pointed to a place in the porch railing where the wood had rotted—"but at first glance, it's relatively sound."

"I'd hate to see bulldozers raze the place," Michelle said as they drew close enough to see spider webs dripping from the eaves. "It looks like something out of *Architectural Digest.*"

They circled the place, looking for a way in, and finally found one in the back. There, someone had propped several heavy metal panels against the siding. No doubt, the panels would come in handy if a storm threatened, but for now, the door remained uncovered.

Michelle selected the oldest key on the ring.

It slipped easily into the lock. The door itself, however, must have swelled in the humidity. When it didn't budge, she put her weight behind it and gave a good shove. Wood creaked as the door swung open onto a sun porch. Or at least, she thought it was a sun porch. With the windows all boarded up, it was hard to tell.

Hot, musty-smelling air spilled out of the opening. Michelle turned aside to catch her breath. "I didn't think about the electricity. Of course, it's turned off." Going into the boarded-up house would feel like stepping into an oven. A dark one at that.

Erin edged past her. "Here," she said, whipping out her cell phone. "Use the flashlight app on your phones. We'll just take a quick look around."

The tiny lights barely illuminated a few feet in front of them. The farther away from the door they got, the darker and hotter it grew. Still, Michelle got the impression of large rooms, wide hallways, and a solidity that was oddly comforting.

Nina called from another part of the house. "Wait till you see this kitchen! It's incredible."

Michelle slowly felt her way forward until her hand landed atop the banister at the base of a wide staircase. Intrigued, she started up the steps but backed up quickly when something sticky brushed against her face. "Oh, crap! Spiders! I'm out of here." She beat a hasty retreat to the back door. Outside in the relatively cooler air, she hopped up and down while she repeatedly ran her hands through her hair. She didn't relax until she'd thoroughly finger-combed each strand without encountering anything with eight legs. "Ugh," she said, brushing a long white line from her jeans. "I hate spiders."

"Too bad we couldn't see more of the inside, but it's just too dark and hot in there!" Nina said as she pounded down the steps with Erin and Reggie right behind her. Despite only being in the house a few minutes, sweat dampened their T-shirts.

"It's just not safe to go exploring without more light," Erin pointed out. "The house looks to be in pretty good shape, but you never know. One rotten floorboard is all it'd take for someone to get hurt."

Erin's concern went a long way toward soothing Michelle's embarrassment over bolting for the outside. Her friend was an adventurous traveler. If she said it wasn't safe, it wasn't. Making sure they locked up behind them, she checked the door.

"What about the rest of the buildings? We could check those out," Reggie suggested.

"Sure. Lead the way." Michelle fell in behind Erin's younger sister. Though she doubted the garage or gardener's shed would hold much of interest, they'd come this far. They might as well have a look.

Thick vines covered the exterior of the first outbuilding they reached. Extracting the key ring, Michelle tried several different ones before she found the key that worked. The door screeched open on rusty hinges. Inside, enough sunlight streamed through gaps between the vines to let them take a good look.

"Oh, wow!" Reggie exclaimed. "Look at all this equipment. That's an expensive John Deere," she said, pointing to a tractor with an open cab. "And that mower? We use the same one at work. It's a sweet ride." She spun in a circle, taking in the back wall, where everything a gardener would need, from pruning shears to hoes, hung in orderly rows. "That stuff could use some work—the blades are a little rusty from sitting out here so long—but if someone wanted to clean this place up, they'd have everything they'd need to do the job right at their fingertips."

"This is really something, isn't it?" Michelle asked. When the lawyer said there was a shed on the property, she'd expected something like the rickety storage unit in her neighbor's backyard.

Not a miniature hardware store.

"There are living quarters, too, aren't there?" Nina crossed to a wall that divided the building in half. A door in the middle opened onto a tidy apartment roughly the same size as the one she had in Fairfax.

"Nice," Reggie pronounced, edging past Nina. She disappeared down a narrow hall. "There's a bedroom and a bath back here. Small, but perfect for one or two people."

"We should probably check out the garage," Erin said, rubbing her palms together. "Who knows what we'll find in there?"

What they found was a three-bay garage loaded with enough vehicles to open a used car lot. In addition to the serviceable pickup and roomy sedan on the attorney's inventory, a van outfitted with a loading platform for handi-capped passengers stood in one of the bays. Two ATVs filled the gaps between the other vehicles and the door. Spotting a key rack near the back of the garage, Erin grabbed a set of keys. She climbed into the pickup truck and tried to start it. Michelle felt an intense twinge of disappointment when a solid click was the only response.

"It was too much to hope for that the engine would turn over," Erin said, stepping off the running board. "I imagine, after sitting for five years, all the batteries need replacing."

"Still," Nina pointed out, "this is quite the treasure trove. What do you think all that is?" She pointed to the ceiling, where cobwebs dripped like icicles from boat-like shapes tucked into overhead racks.

"Good grief!" Erin maneuvered between vehicles until she stood directly beneath an oblong shape. "That's a touring kayak—you'd use it in the ocean. See how the other one is shorter and less pointy? It's for freshwater. These are so old, they're practically vintage. No one uses fiberglass anymore. Oh! There's a canoe, too." She aimed an index finger toward the back of the unit and grinned. "Boy, would I like to pull them down and get them in the water. See if they'll float after all this time."

"Oh, hush. You can't do that," Michelle objected. "Mr. Rollins gave us the keys so we could look around a bit. I don't think he'd appreciate it if we took any of the boats or cars out for a joyride."

"I know. I know. But you know—" Erin gave the kayaks a final wistful glance. "Maybe someday."

Michelle's stomach tightened. It had been fun, poking around the old estate, imagining it could all be hers. But who was she kidding?

She had no more business thinking along those lines than the man in the moon. Even if the lab results proved that Nancy Simmons was her biological mother, she couldn't afford a place like this. Okay, she might be able to swing the tax lien, but what about next year's taxes? Or the ones that came after that? She didn't have that kind of money, much less enough to cover the operating expenses on such a large house. Why, the air-conditioning bill alone would be astronomical in the summer.

She gave the vehicles a parting glance. Nina and Reggie had escaped the stuffy garage, but Erin still studied the boats with a dreamy expression on her face. "I think I've seen enough for now. What do you think? Lunch?"

"Mmmm. I could eat. It's nearly four." Erin dusted her hands on her jeans.

No wonder her stomach felt empty, Michelle thought. She hadn't eaten since they left for the lawyer's office, and then, she'd only had time to grab a banana from the buffet on her way out the door. Talking with Mr. Rollins had taken longer than she'd expected. More time had slipped away while they explored the property. She trailed Erin outside.

"What say we head back into town and grab an early supper?" she asked, directing her question at all three women while she locked the garage door.

"How about that Boshamps place Dave Rollins mentioned," Nina suggested.

"Oysters and beer sounds good to me," Erin agreed.

"Perfect," Reggie said. "But I think we should get a picture or two before we go."

"Maybe we should wait till we get the lab results. We don't even know if Nancy Simmons is my birth mother yet," Michelle objected.

"All the more reason to take a picture now. Once you get the results, you may have to give the keys back right away. This could be our only chance."

"Yeah, let's go for it. If nothing else, we'll have something to remind us of the trip when we get too old to remember it," Erin coaxed.

"Speak for yourself. I'm never getting that old." Nina tossed her hair behind her back.

"Okay, okay." Michelle gave in. "Where do you want us?"

"How about in front of the house?" Reggie suggested.

Following directions from the youngest of the group, Michelle and the others arrayed themselves at the top of the brick steps. Reggie propped her cell phone up on the stump of an old oak tree and set the timer. They all counted down, "Ten...nine...eight..." while she dashed up the stairs. She slid into place seconds before the shutter clicked.

"Don't move. Let me take a look first." Reggie reversed course, checked the image and rejoined them. "What do you think?"

Giving the picture a nod of approval, Michelle handed the phone off to Erin. While she waited for the others, she looked out over the wide swath of overgrown grass and palmetto that led down a gentle rise straight to a wide, white beach. Beyond it, the calm waters of the Gulf of Mexico sparkled.

"This view is priceless," Michelle sighed. The scene was picture-postcard-worthy.

"I could see myself coming out here to enjoy my coffee in the mornings," Erin said.

Reggie shaped a box with her fingers. She held it up in front of her eyes. "A little strategic trimming and chopping would make it sheer perfection."

Nina plopped down on the top step, her long legs angled down in front of her. "No wonder that developer wants this place. It's really spectacular."

"Yeah, but he's going to tear down the house," Reggie said softly.

Michelle willed herself to be strong. "There's nothing we can do to prevent that. Even if the lab results prove Nancy Simmons was my birth mother, I simply don't have the resources for a place like this."

"Besides, the house and grounds are too big for one person," Erin said, agreeing. "It's the kind of place that ought to be filled with people. Can't you just imagine it back when Nancy's parents were alive? The lights all ablaze. A dance band in one of those big parlors. Cars pulling up to the front door. People in their finest spilling out."

Michelle laughed. "What an imagination! We didn't look around enough to know if there's a living room, much less a parlor."

"In a house like this? I bet there are several," Erin said, grinning.

Michelle's tummy rumbled. Patting her midsection with one hand, she hushed it with a red-faced grin. "I think we'd better eat soon. Or they'll hear my stomach complaining all the way to Destin."

"Mine will join the chorus, I'm afraid," Nina said, pushing herself up off the steps.

"Hey, we don't have anything planned for tomorrow, do we?" Erin asked on the way back to the car.

"Nope. Did you think of something?" With its sunny skies and white-sand beaches, Destin offered plenty of options for outdoor activities.

"Well, if no one else minds, I'd like to come back out here. Get a better feel for the place," Erin said.

"Really?" Michelle raised an eyebrow. "With all there is to see and do in the area, you want to go poking around in an old, boarded-up house?"

"I, for one, would love to take a better look at that kitchen," Nina said agreeably. "I'm pretty sure the stove is an Aga, but it was too dark to make out the details."

"I'm kind of itching to explore the rest of the grounds. Five acres—that's a lot of ground to cover. I'd like to see what else is out there," Reggie put in her request.

"And I want to scope out the rest of the house," Erin added. "Get a feel for the size of the rooms. Check out the furnishings and see if anything's salvageable." When Michelle tried to point out that they'd already discovered it was too dark, too hot inside, Erin grinned. "We'll get an early start, and we'll pick up some heavy-duty flashlights so we can see where we're going."

"But what about the beach? Doesn't it seem like a waste to drive all the way to Florida and not go to the beach?" Michelle asked. She kicked at a small clod of dried mud in the dirt track.

"We still have all that leftover chicken," Nina pointed out as they reached the car. "We can grab salads and drinks at a convenience store and have an early picnic on the beach when we're done."

By the time everyone had had their say, Michelle knew it wouldn't do any good to try and talk her friends out of their plans. Besides, truth be told, she wanted to look the place over once more while she could. Considering the land could be headed to the tax auction whether she inherited or not, this was probably her last chance to see the house her birth mother might have grown up in. To seal the bargain, she made her own request. "I'm in…as long as I can get my feet wet while we're here."

"All right!" Reggie and Erin fist-bumped before taking their places in the back seats.

They were quiet on the ride back to Destin. Michelle wondered if everyone else's head was filled with thoughts of a restored Simmons house, the grounds immaculate, lacy curtains hanging in the windows, a swing on the front porch. In her own pleasant daydream, Ashley and Aaron came for long visits. She envisioned her daughter walking down a curving staircase to say "I do" to the man she loved in the front room, pictured Aaron and his bride holding their wedding on the beach. Later, there'd be grandchildren, of course, and visits to Grandma's, where she and the youngsters would spend endless summer days collecting shells and swimming in the cool, clear water.

Foolish thoughts, she told herself. A woman her age with no savings to fall back on needed to be practical. What she'd been thinking had been nothing more than a pipe dream. One that couldn't possibly come true. No matter how much she'd like it to. Though she struggled to remain upbeat, she fell into a funk thinking about her much more likely future as a sales clerk in a department store or a receptionist in an office, living in a cheap apartment too small for overnight guests, much less for entertaining the grandchildren she hoped to have one day.

But it was hard to stay blue in the company of good friends. As if they sensed she needed a boost, Erin, Nina and Reggie kept the conversation flowing once they arrived at Boshamps. After a short wait for a table and drinks at the railing overlooking the sailboats and cabin cruisers moored in the quaint harbor, Michelle's mood improved considerably. As one, the group opted to enjoy the warm breezes coming off the water and asked for a table on the covered deck. There, she and her friends plowed through servings so substantial they'd make longshoremen groan. At last, having eaten their fill of succulent oysters, fish and shrimp, they pushed back from the table.

"Oh my word, that was delish." Nina sighed. "I can't remember when I've had seafood so fresh. I swear that grouper was swimming in the ocean this morning."

"I'm stuffed," Reggie declared, patting her tummy. "I can't eat another bite. What'd you call that sauce on the snapper again?"

"A béarnaise with honey-roasted pecans," Nina explained. "I'd never had it prepared like that, but it was yummy."

"We need to thank Mr. Rollins for recommending this place," Michelle said.

"Speaking of our favorite lawyer, what time are you seeing him tomorrow?" Erin toyed with her fork.

"He said they'd have the lab results in twenty-four hours. I'm supposed to call the office around noon." Their attentive waiter appeared at her elbow, and Michelle waited until he refilled their water glasses before she resumed speaking. "If the test results are negative, and Nancy Simmons isn't my biological parent, we won't need to meet. I'll just drop off the keys with Josh."

"And if she was?" Nina leaned forward.

"I'm sure he'll have papers for me to sign." She paused. Her friends obviously had something up their collective sleeves. "Why?"

"Nothing." Erin managed a look that was just shy of innocent.

"It's obviously something," Michelle challenged.

"Did I ever tell you, you know me too well?" Erin asked.

"Quit stalling. Out with it."

"Well." Erin let out a long breath. Around the table, Nina and Reggie leaned forward. "We were talking about the Simmons house while you were in the bathroom," Erin began.

"Oh? Ganging up on me?" Michelle softened the words with a teasing smile.

"No. It's just we can't get over that place. It's a huge piece of property. The house is in remarkably good shape considering how long it's been vacant." Erin stirred her coffee.

"At least, the little bit we were able to see," Michelle conceded. Her eyes narrowed. Where were they going with this?

"Right." Erin had apparently been appointed spokesperson for the group because she continued. "It really would be a shame to let go of it.

It's the perfect vacation spot. Right there on the Gulf. Plenty of things to do—swim, snorkel, fish, go for bike rides. And that view. That alone is worth hanging on to the place for."

As Nina and Reggie's heads bobbed, Nina added, "I bet it'd look stunning once it was all spruced up."

"I'm sure it would," Michelle agreed. She steepled her hands, the familiar gesture helping to soothe her nerves. "But what would I do with a place that big? Sure, you guys could come down to visit once, maybe twice a year. But the rest of the time? It's too large—and too expensive to maintain—for just one person."

"Have you thought about turning it into a bed and breakfast?" Erin asked.

"Or an inn?" Reggie suggested.

"No," Michelle answered slowly. "A B&B. An inn. Aren't they the same thing?"

"There is a difference," Nina said. "We talk about this kind of stuff in some of my cooking classes. A B&B offers breakfast and maybe a light snack in the evening. Guests, who tend to stay a couple of nights, max, are pretty much left on their own. People stay longer—a week or two—at an inn. Those usually offer more options—bike rentals, fishing or kayaking, tours of the local sights, maybe even a spa. There might be a café or restaurant on the property, but breakfast is not included in the cost of the rooms."

"Sounds like an inn would offer more revenue streams," Michelle said, dredging up what she remembered from twenty-five-year-old business classes.

"More flexibility, too." Nina nodded. "You could start out small, add new options as the business grew."

At the next table, a busboy juggled an enormous tray of dirty dishes. They held their breaths until he passed by their table.

"I think the Simmons property would be perfect for something like that. Don't you?" Erin pinned Michelle with a look.

She didn't have much choice. She had to agree. "Yes, of course. If it was cleaned up, refurbished. Maybe a few things brought up to date. But Mr. Rollins said the only person who'd expressed an interest in buying the place was this Oscar Danner person. He wants to raze the house and the outbuildings for his new development."

"We could do it," said Nina so softly, Michelle barely heard her.

"We could," Erin said more firmly. "I have savings. We could all chip in, pool our resources and do it together."

Open an inn? The four of them?

The possibility sent excitement through Michelle like a rising tide. She released her fingers and soaked in the feeling. Running an inn would definitely put all her skills at decorating and organizing to work. The pleasant daydream she'd had earlier came back in a rush, and she smiled. But it didn't take long before reality raised its ugly head.

"Wait a minute." She flattened her palms on the table. Was this some kind of a joke? Erin, Reggie and Nina couldn't be serious. She studied their sober faces. "Do you have any idea how much money you're talking about?" she asked, not trying to hide her skepticism. "There's the tax lien to begin with. That's a huge chunk of change. Then there's the landscaping, new paint, new window treatments. Forty, fifty grand minimum. And that's assuming the house doesn't need major repairs, like a new roof or air-conditioning."

"It would be a big investment," Erin said, her tone reasonable. "But think of what it would mean to each of us." She tipped her head toward Nina. "She could open her own restaurant."

Nina nodded. "I'd start out small—open a café for breakfast and lunch. Everything farm-to-table fresh. Once the restaurant is in the black, we'd think about adding a dinner service."

"I could handle the outdoor activities," Erin

said thoughtfully. "Kayak and bike tours to start with. Once I learn more about the local conditions, we might plan some fishing trips. I'm pretty handy with a fly rod. Reggie's been talking about starting her own landscaping business. She'd be our resident gardener."

Michelle held up her hands, palms facing her friends. Someone had to put the brakes on this train before it ran away with them, and it looked like that someone was going to be her. "Let's not get too far ahead of ourselves here. We don't even know if I'm going to inherit the property. Everything hinges on whether or not Nancy Simmons was my biological mother. And if she was, we'd need a better idea of the shape the house is in before we even start thinking about what to do with it. If it needs major repairs, like a new roof or, heaven help us, if there's termite damage, it's game over. It'd be better to raze the place than throw what little hard-earned cash we have into a money pit. Then there's the not so little matter of zoning and permits. It might not even be legal to turn the house into an inn. I could go on. There's probably a zillion other reasons why this is a bad idea."

"But you'll think about it?" Erin asked.

Michelle clenched her fingers. Her friend really did know her too well. "I'll think about it," she said slowly. "But you all have to do the same thing." She let her gaze linger on each of her friends. Erin had been footloose and fancy-free ever since college. Was she really willing to put down roots in tiny Sugar Sand Beach? Nina had worked long and hard to get where she was at Café Saint Jacques. Sure, moving to Florida meant the opportunity to open her own restaurant, but was it worth the risk? She turned to Reggie. Was she willing to walk away from her marriage, no matter how troubled it might be? "Decide whether you really want to go all in on this or not. Besides the money, it would take a huge commitment." She spread her arms. "Huge."

Around the table, the faces of her friends sobered. Looking at them, Michelle gulped. They weren't alone in having to face facts. She had the house in Fairfax to deal with. She was on the outs with both her children. She didn't even know what to think about Nancy Simmons and the possibility that she might be her mother. So much of her own life was in turmoil right now, she had no business thinking of moving to Florida, much less opening an inn with three equally inexperienced people. Yet she couldn't prevent the thrill of anticipation that surged through her every time she considered going into business with her friends.

They'd left the restaurant and were nearly to the hotel before anyone spoke again.

"Hey! Pull into Home Depot for a minute," Erin called from the back seat.

"Okay. What do you need?" Michelle followed a side road to the big home improvement center.

"Those flashlights I mentioned earlier."

Michelle's heart skipped a beat. "You still want to go out to the house tomorrow?"

"Oh, yeah." Erin's wicked grin filled the rearview mirror. "You didn't think we were going to give up that easily, did you?"

Warmth spread through Michelle's body as she pulled into the nearly deserted parking lot and cut the engine. Amid hoots of laughter, Nina and Erin dashed for the store. They emerged fifteen minutes later, arms loaded with heavy-duty flashlights and several cans of bug spray. The lights of the Home Depot cut off as Michelle drove out of the parking lot.

"Just in time," she noted.

"It's a sign," Erin said. "We're doing the right thing."

Maybe. Or maybe it was simply an advertisement for the hardware store. Uncertain which she believed, Michelle headed for the hotel.

Twenty - Two

Michelle

A little after sunrise the next morning, they drove up the rutted driveway, which had been mowed since their visit the previous day. Sipping coffee in to-go cups from the hotel's breakfast buffet, they sat on the front porch, taking in the view before they headed in different directions. Reggie, eager to explore the property behind the house, opted to rely on her sister's report on the interior. While the others headed for the back door, she peeled off toward the gardener's cottage. There, she grabbed a hoe, which she declared was perfect for dispatching bad snakes and relocating good ones. Promising to be back in an hour, she waved goodbye. In seconds, she disappeared into the thick brush.

Michelle's heart pounded against her ribcage

as, armed with flashlights, she, Erin and Nina entered the sunroom. They played their beams across the windowpanes. Relief coursed through them when all the thick glass appeared to be intact. White sheets draped the furniture around them. Michelle pulled back the edge of one cloth. Beneath it, cushions covered in a bright yellow print sat atop rattan furniture.

"Those cushions will need to be replaced, but the furniture itself looks sturdy," she pointed out.

"Don't be so hasty." Nina trailed one finger across an armrest. Her hand came away grimy, and she wiped it on the hem of her shorts. "It needs a good scrubbing. That might be all the pillows will need, too."

Erin trained her flashlight on the ceiling as they walked down a short hall. "I don't see any signs of leaks or cracks."

Michelle played her flashlight over the footprints Erin left on the dusty hardwood floors. "The floors feel solid."

"A huge plus," Nina said.

A parlor off to the left featured soaring ceilings covered in white, hammered tin ceiling tiles. Draped in more sheets, tables on spindly legs and Tiffany-style lamps stood beside sofas and chairs. Michelle traced a finger through the dust on one table. The rich patina of the wood confirmed what she'd suspected—the furniture was of such high quality, it could have been on loan from a museum.

"Have you ever seen a mantel that high?" she asked in wonder. The one on the fireplace at the end of the room soared at least eight feet off the ground. Thin, half-columns stood like sentries on either side of the firebox.

"I'm impressed with this wainscoting," Erin said, pointing to the decorative white woodwork that graced the walls.

"The kitchen is that way." Nina pointed across the hall. "I'm going to check it out."

"Shout if you run into a problem," Erin cautioned to their friend's retreating back.

"Will do," Nina called over one shoulder.

Together, Michelle and Erin explored the rest of the downstairs, the beams from their flashlights bouncing off foot-deep crown molding in a formal dining room. They peeled back dusty sheets to get glimpses of tall china closets. Filled with dishes, they stood on either side of a table large enough to seat twelve. More deep crown molding lined the ceiling of a front parlor large enough for twin sofas and no less than six Queen Anne chairs. A family room had been furnished with comfortable-looking leather couches. Recliners, sturdy coffee tables and end tables clustered around a television that was probably state-of-the-art ten years earlier. Books lined the shelves of a library.

"This must have been Nancy's bedroom," Erin said, opening the door onto a sitting area with a spacious bedroom beyond. An en-suite featured strategically installed handrails and a shower large enough for a wheelchair. "Did you happen to notice any other bathrooms on this floor?"

"There was a powder room between the front and back parlors." A strand of Michelle's hair had stuck to her face. She brushed it off.

"Everything down here looks better than I expected," Erin said. .

"It's a little spooky, what with all the dust covers everywhere. But they sure helped preserve the furniture."

Erin aimed a finger overhead. "You ready to head upstairs?"

"Let's. It's already warming up in here." In the half hour they'd been inside, she bet the temperature had risen ten degrees.

At the base of a curving staircase, Erin swung the broom she'd grabbed from a closet in wide arcs. When she'd finished knocking down the surprisingly few spider webs, she warned, "Step lightly. I'd hate to see you go crashing through a rotted step. If there's damage, it'll likely be upstairs."

But, amazingly enough, the second floor was in excellent condition. Michelle paused outside the first room at the top of the stairs. Here and there, large bright rectangles marked the spots where posters had once been taped to the floral wallpaper. A few bugs lay feet-up on the gauzy canopy over a double bed. Matching dressers and a makeup table stood against the walls. "I think this might have been Nancy's room before the accident," she said while Erin explored the rest of the suite.

"You might be right. It looks like someone lifted it straight out of HGTV or Pinterest." Floorboards creaked when Erin crossed to the boarded-up window. "I bet she had a nice view of the Gulf. She had her own sitting room and bath, too."

A heavy weight pressed down on Michelle's chest. "Imagine losing both your parents and your ability to walk in a single night."

Erin fell silent for a moment before she shrugged. "She didn't let it destroy her, though. According to her obituary, she went on to do some pretty great things for the community."

"That she did." Michelle fell silent for a

moment in honor of the brave young woman who may or may not have given birth to her.

They moved farther down the hall. In addition to Nancy's room, six other bedrooms branched off from the main corridor. Each either had its own bathroom or shared one with the room next door. Scattered among them, they found half as many sitting areas. At the end of the hall, a door opened to reveal a spiral staircase.

"It probably goes to the turret," Erin said. "Want to check it out?"

Michelle slowly backed away from the cobwebs that stretched across the doorway. "Mmmm. I'll stay here. I want to get a better idea of what's salvageable and what isn't." Dust drifted in thick layers across the sheets that protected furniture that, for the most part, came from high-end makers. The window treatments and linens, however, were another matter entirely.

"Don't go far," Erin said, brushing cobwebs down as she gingerly climbed the stairs.

"I won't," she promised.

Erin emerged twenty minutes later, grimy but otherwise none the worse for her climb. "It's a neat room. Big enough for a bedroom but, as far as I can tell, it was only used for storage.

I saw a couple of broken chairs, a desk missing a leg. And—surprise—there's an access from the turret into the attic. I just took a quick look around, but I didn't spot any damage. I think the roof is in pretty good shape."

"Well, that's good news." Michelle mopped sweat from her forehead with the back of her hand. "I'm about ready to get out of this heat. How about you?"

"I could use some water." Erin plucked a long strand of cobweb from her T-shirt. "We need to find Nina. And Reggie ought to be back soon."

Had it been an hour already? The time had flown by.

Downstairs, they meandered through the parlors, giggling when a wrong turn took them to the master bedroom instead of the kitchen. Backtracking, they found Nina sitting on a countertop in a spacious kitchen that—judging from the appliances—must have been renovated shortly before Nancy Simmons's passing.

"What do you think?" Erin asked, eyeing granite countertops.

"Sweet," Nina pronounced. "Nancy either had an eye or she hired a professional chef to design the kitchen. Everything is laid out with both functionality and aesthetics in mind. I'll save the rest till we meet up with Reggie, but this you've got to see." She led them to a butcher's pantry. Here, a lowered countertop and extra-wide knee well made the perfect spot for someone in a wheelchair to make a sandwich or assemble a snack. "And look at these." She pulled on the handle of a deep drawer. Inside, dishes, cups and utensils stood within easy reach of someone who might not be able to access an over-the-counter cabinet. "She must have had full-time help, but I think it speaks to her character that she maintained her independence." She tugged on her ponytail. "How's the rest of the house?"

"Great," Erin said, grinning while she fanned herself. "But I've been climbing around in the attic, and I really need to get out of here. What say we grab Reggie and head down to the beach?"

"Works for me," Michelle said.

"I'm game."

Reggie sat on the back steps, picking beggar's-lice off the socks that peeked out above her boots. "Hey! You all finished in there? I was about to launch a search party to find you." She tossed a handful of tiny oval seeds into the dirt.

"Perfect timing," Michelle said. "We were just heading to the beach for lunch and to fill everyone in. Okay with you?"

315

"Awesome. Wait till you hear what I found out there. This place is nothing short of amazing."

They made quick work of grabbing the cooler, along with a blanket and the stack of towels they'd borrowed from the hotel. A short walk down a path through the tall sea grass and palmettos opened onto a secluded spot on the beach where they discarded their footwear.

Michelle curled her toes in the sparkling sand. She bent to scoop a handful and let it dribble back onto the beach. "I guess we know where the area got its name," she said, brushing the last of the sugary sand from her fingers.

She and Erin spread the blanket, which Nina anchored with their shoes. With hardly any discussion at all, they stripped down to the bathing suits they'd worn beneath shorts and T's. Then, laughing, they raced toward the water, where they splashed in the gentle Gulf waves. After a refreshing fifteen-minute swim, they plopped down on the blanket. Easy to burn, Michelle slipped her shirt back on while Nina handed out paper plates. Reggie unloaded boxes of chicken and the prepared salads they'd picked up at a Stop and Shop they passed this morning.

While they ate, Michelle and Erin took turns filling everyone in on the house's remarkable condition. Nina waxed nearly poetic about an Aga gas range and Sub-Zero refrigerators and freezers. "Someone who knew what they were doing prepped the units before unplugging them, which was good 'cause those babies aren't cheap. I counted six different sets of dishes and every pot and pan you could ever want. That kitchen would be a dream to work in."

"You'll never guess what I found out back," Reggie said when the ball landed in her court. "Nearly an acre of the backyard had been a vegetable garden once. Of course, it's all completely overgrown now, but I found a few tomato plants among the weeds. Blackberries grow along a fence. Wild strawberries, too. That all tells me soil's fantastic. Oh, and there's a small lake on the far corner of the property." She nudged Nina. "Are you thinking farm-to-table? 'Cause, from what I saw, that's doable here."

"Well, yeah. I'd—"

"Hold up. Hold up." When her friends turned toward her wearing identical quizzical expressions, Michelle pressed her hands together. "Look. I get that we're all excited about this. I am, too. Still, it may not be feasible. Granted, the house is in remarkable shape, considering it's been sitting vacant for five years. But to turn it into an inn would take

LEIGH DUNCAN

an incredible amount of work. Every inch of the place would have to be scrubbed down, repainted, re-carpeted, reupholstered. We'd need all new linens and bedding. That lien would have to be satisfied first. Then, there's all the legal stuff..." She took a breath.

"But we could do this," Erin insisted. "Reggie could take care of the landscaping and the garden. Nina, the restaurant. I'd take charge of entertainment—bike and kayak tours, give snorkeling lessons and whatever else people want to do. You could handle the books and reservations. I bet we could get Aaron to create a website for us. It'd be awesome."

For one brief second, Michelle let herself get drawn into the dream. Erin was right. Living and working with her friends would be awesome. But there was still one problem, and it was a biggie. "I think we should wait until we find out if I'm even Nancy Simmons's daughter before we go any further."

"Don't look now, but I think the answer to that question might be closer than you think." Reggie stared over her shoulder.

Turning, Michelle spotted a tall, lean figure dressed in jeans and a light green polo emerge from the last line of sea grass. Dave Rollins waved, his short sleeves revealing the kind of natural tan people up north paid hundreds of dollars to achieve. Slipping off his shoes, he strode across the sand to the spot where they'd spread their blanket.

"What's he doing here?" Michelle whispered, though her hammering heart told her she knew the answer.

Erin's hand on her shoulder soothed her. "No matter what you find out, it's going to be all right."

"Yeah. I just hope..." What did she hope? Less than a week ago, she'd been perfectly content to live out the rest of her life without ever learning the identity of her birth mother. After all, she'd reasoned, what would it change? She'd still be a widow with two children who spent more time bickering than supporting her. She'd still have to sell her house and find someplace less expensive to live. She'd still be entering the work force as an inexperienced forty-five-year-old.

But she'd been wrong. Learning she was Nancy Simmons's daughter would change her life in ways she hadn't anticipated. Or not. She gulped as she scrambled to her feet.

"Mr. Rollins, I didn't expect to see you here," she said, the words tumbling through her lips. "How'd you find us?"

"Dave, please. We're not in the office, and it's Friday." His warm smile only made her heart beat faster. "As for how I found you, I mentioned that the manager of your hotel was a friend of mine. When I couldn't reach you, I asked if he knew where you were headed this morning. He said you'd stopped by the office to borrow towels and a blanket and that he'd seen one of you putting a bag of flashlights in the car. From there, it was pretty easy to figure out where you were going."

"Remind me not to plan anything nefarious while I'm in Destin," she said, pretending to be shocked. "As fast as word gets around here, I'd be arrested before I pulled out of the driveway."

Dave's pleasant-sounding laugh filled the air. "It's hard to keep a secret in a town where everyone knows everybody."

Michelle took a steadying breath. "So, what brings you out here?"

Her heart rate shifted into overdrive when Dave pulled a sealed envelope from the thin portfolio he carried. He eyed the three women who stared up from the blanket with unabashed curiosity. "Do you mind if we take a little walk?"

Michelle didn't object when Dave's fingers found her elbow. Together, they walked down the beach to a spot that was closer to the water and out of her friends' hearing. "I thought you'd want these lab results as soon as possible, and I know I'd want a moment to myself if I were in your shoes," he explained.

"No shoes." Michelle kicked one bare foot out in front of her. "But you're right. No matter how this all plays out, I might need a minute."

"I'll be right over here when you want to talk," Dave said when he judged they'd gone far enough. After handing her the envelope, he took a few steps away.

She eyed the envelope. This was it, the moment of truth. She managed to get one fingernail under the flap despite her shaking hands. Gently, she pried the envelope open. A single sheet of folded paper lay inside. Withdrawing it, she held it open. Long columns of numbers that looked like so much gibberish filled the page. Frustration churned in her stomach until she came to a box near the bottom.

Probability of Maternity	99%

Her knees buckled, and she sank into a sitting position. Tears filled her eyes. Her breath shuddered. "Dave?" she called, pitching her voice just loud enough to be heard over the waves that lapped the shoreline.

"Yes?" He took one look at the tears streaming down her cheeks, and sorrow filled his face. In a kind and gentle voice, he asked, "You aren't Nancy's daughter, then?"

"No—I mean, yes. I am. At least, I think I am." With so much riding on the answer, she had to know for sure. "How accurate are these tests?"

"Do you mind if I see the results?" He held out a hand.

She shrugged. "That's why we're here, isn't it? To verify whether or not I was the child Nancy Simmons gave birth to?"

"Point taken." He plucked the document from her outstretched hand and studied it carefully. Squatting down beside her, he anchored the paper on his thigh while he pointed to the box that had drawn Michelle's attention. "See there?" he asked. "According to the test results, you and Nancy Simmons share enough of the same DNA markers that there's a ninety-nine percent certainty she was your birth mother. That's as good as it gets. These results would stand up in a court of law." A slow smile crept across his face. "This means congratulations are in order."

Rising, he extended a hand. Struck by the warmth and solidity of his grip, she gratefully accepted his help in getting to her feet. When she once more stood before him, Dave said, "I imagine you have a lot to think about now. Decisions you'll have to make. Do you think you could come into the office on Monday? We can talk about what you want to do next. I'll have some papers for you to sign, as well."

Could she? She gave her head a sad shake. She'd promised to have Nina and Reggie home in time for work on Monday.

"I'll—I'll need to talk to my friends. We, um, well, I guess I didn't really think this through. We'd planned to head back tomorrow. Let me see if they can stay or…" She started toward the blanket where Erin, Nina and Reggie pretended to show far more interest in their sodas than the shiny aluminum cans deserved. They'd be thrilled with the news, but she needed answers to the many questions that churned in her head. She turned to Dave. "Is there anything else I need to know right away?"

"I don't want to rush you." The good-looking attorney stuck his hands in the pockets of his jeans. "But I do need to remind you that if you intend to hold on to the property, you'll have to satisfy the tax lien before the end of the month."

"About that…" She snuck another quick glance at her friends and crossed her fingers.

Taking a big breath, she posed a question that might very well spell the end or the beginning of all their dreams. "I assume this land was originally zoned for a single-family residence. But you said Orson hoped to subdivide the property, maybe even open some businesses on it. Has the zoning been changed? Or is it still single-family?"

Dave's eyebrows dipped toward his nose. He cleared his throat. "Well, as a matter of fact, Orson has appeared before the zoning commission a couple of times. He couldn't ask for a change—only the legal owner can do that—but the commission voiced no objections to his plans to convert at least part of the property to commercial use."

"Hmmm." She absorbed this bit of information. "To the best of your knowledge, then, you don't think anyone would object if my friends and I wanted to, say, turn the house into an inn?"

Concern eased from Dave's face, and his eyebrows smoothed. "You'd need a business license, of course. But no. I wouldn't foresee any problems. I—I'd be happy to help you with the applications if it's something you want to do."

Not ready to commit, she backtracked. "It's something I'm thinking about, but I'd appreciate it if this just stayed between you and me for now."

"Nancy Simmons was a long-time client of our firm," Dave said, his expression as solemn as a judge's. "As her daughter, anything you tell me falls under that same blanket of attorney-client privilege. I won't breathe a word." He grinned. "But I sure wouldn't mind seeing the look on Orson's face when he finds out." He took a breath. "There is one more thing."

"Good news or bad?" she asked.

"I guess that'll be up to you."

"Um, that's kind of random, Dave," she said, fighting off an uneasy feeling.

He slipped a hand into his portfolio and withdrew a pale gray envelope embossed with the letters N and S. "Nancy asked me to personally deliver this to her daughter, if we found her, and, well, that's you."

A letter?

She sucked in a shocked breath. A note from her birth mother was more than she'd ever hoped for. "Thank you," she said, giving Dave a quick glance. As kind as he'd been, as much as he'd done for her, reading Nancy's letter was something she had to do in private. She slipped the unopened envelope into the pocket of her shorts to savor when she had more than a minute or two alone.

"I'm sure your friends are anxious to hear the news," he said, once more offering his hand. When Michelle shook it, he added, "Let me know about Monday. I hope you'll stay for a while, but if you can't, we'll take care of everything through the mail. It'll just take a little longer." Rather than walking back to the spot where her friends waited, he cut a diagonal across the beach, picked up his shoes and headed back through the grass.

She stood where she was until Dave reached the top of the hill, where he waved a final goodbye before disappearing down the other side. The man certainly was nice to look at, she admitted. If things panned out and she ended up moving to Florida, she hoped they'd be friends one day. As for anything more than that, she had too many irons in the fire to give Dave—or any man—more than a passing thought. Patting her pocket, she tucked the letter from Nancy Simmons a little deeper. Then, her footsteps far more steady than she thought they'd be, she headed for the blanket where her friends sat waiting.

"Whoo! I didn't see that coming," she said, lowering herself onto one corner.

After a quick peek to make sure Dave was out of sight, Reggie tossed her empty soda can on the blanket. "Don't keep us in suspense," she cried.

"I won't," she promised. Stretching forward, she grasped Erin and Nina's hands while Reggie crowded closer. "Nancy Simmons was my biological mother."

Wonder, shock and glee played across the faces of her three friends. Erin, the first to regain her composure, asked, "Are you certain?"

"It's true. According to the test results, there's no doubt about it whatsoever. Dave— Mr. Rollins—asked me to come into the office on Monday and sign some papers to get the property transferred into my name." Saving the best for last, she paused to let the news soak in.

They exchanged hugs amid a chorus of congratulations. When the excitement died down a bit, she shared the news she'd saved for last. "I asked Dave about the possibility of turning the property into an inn. He said he was pretty sure the town council would be in favor of it. And he offered to help us with the business licenses and zoning applications."

"That's…" Erin began.

"Fantastic!" Nina declared.

"I can't believe it. Really?" Hope sparkled in Reggie's eyes.

"So it's real then?" Erin asked. "We're really going to do this?"

We're going to try.

Michelle stopped herself before the words formed on her lips. This wasn't the time for doubt or hope. For trying or dreaming. They were either doing this or not. She studied the eager faces surrounding her. The time had come to commit. Her expression serious, she put the question to them. "Are you all in on this?"

Joy flared in her midsection and spread its warmth through her as one by one, Erin, Nina and Reggie voiced their commitment. When they'd finished, Michelle took one final look at their close circle. The air seeped out of her lungs. The hope that had flickered in her chest for the last couple of days spread.

"Okay, gang," she said when she'd caught her breath again. "Huddle up." She stuck out one hand. In team-like fashion, they each added their hands on top of hers. "Here's to our soon-to-be-opened inn."

"Wait, wait," Reggie called. "We can't just call it 'the inn.' We need a name."

"How about the Sugar Sand Inn?" Nina asked.

"I like it!" Erin declared.

"It has a nice ring to it," Michelle agreed.

"All right then," Reggie said, nodding. "Here's to the soon-to-be-opened Sugar Sand Inn!"

Excitement buzzing, they began throwing out ideas and making plans for a grand opening at the start of the snowbird season. Later, when Reggie, Nina and Erin suggested taking a long walk along the beach, Michelle begged off. She needed some time to think. Her arms wrapped around her legs, her chin resting on her knees, she sat on the blanket and stared out over the Gulf.

Questions raced through her mind. She and her friends would need to accomplish a staggering amount of work if they were going to welcome their first guests in mid-October. Could they really pull it off? What if they didn't have enough money to cover the renovations and repairs? What if Reggie and her husband reconciled? What if Aaron and Ashley swore she'd gone crazy and never spoke to her again? What if the people buying her house backed out of the deal?

One by one, she drove the questions back. The sale of her house in Fairfax would go through and, between the equity she'd pull out of that house and the savings Nina and Reggie had committed, they'd have more than enough to finish the job. As for Reggie's relationship with Sam, that was a bridge they'd all cross when—and if—the time came. That just left the little matter of what to do about the twins. She sighed. At twenty-one, it was time to untie the apron strings. Within a year, Aaron and Ashley would graduate from college, land jobs and start living their own lives. They'd always be her babies, but they certainly didn't need her to baby them anymore.

She'd spent her first forty-five years doing what everyone else expected her to do. And what had it gotten her? She was a widow with two grown children who had their own lives to lead. For her, though, it was time for a fresh start, a new adventure. Right now, that meant setting her doubts and fears aside. She wasn't fooling herself. The road ahead was neither straight or smooth. In places, it curved out of sight. She was sure she'd encounter a few bumps along the way, too. But with the help of her friends, she knew they could all make their dreams a reality.

She rose and dusted the sugary sand off her legs. When she brushed her shorts, her fingers touched the edges of the envelope Dave had given her. She hesitated, but only for a moment. In the end, she tucked the letter from her birth mother deeper into her pocket. She'd save it to read when she had time to sit and absorb every word. For now, though, a bright new future beckoned, and she couldn't wait to get started.

When Reggie, Nina and Erin returned a short time later carrying shells they'd gathered on their walk and bubbling with excitement for the inn, they took a minute to give the beach a final look. Then, one-by-one, they stepped onto the path that led to a fresh start at the Sugar Sand Inn.

Thank you for reading
The Gift At Sugar Sand Inn!

If you loved this book and want to help the series continue,
take a moment to leave a review!

Want to know what happens next in Sugar Sand Beach?

Sign up for Leigh's newsletter to get the latest news
about upcoming releases, excerpts, and more!
https://leighduncan.com/newsletter/

Books by Leigh Duncan

EMERALD BAY SERIES

Treasure Coast Homecoming
Treasure Coast Promise
Treasure Coast Christmas
Treasure Coast Revival
Treasure Coast Discovery
Treasure Coast Legacy

SUGAR SAND BEACH SERIES

The Gift at Sugar Sand Inn
The Secret at Sugar Sand Inn
The Cafe at Sugar Sand Inn
The Reunion at Sugar Sand Inn
Christmas at Sugar Sand Inn

HEART'S LANDING SERIES

A Simple Wedding
A Cottage Wedding
A Waterfront Wedding

ORANGE BLOSSOM SERIES

Butterfly Kisses
Sweet Dreams

LEIGH DUNCAN

HOMETOWN HEROES SERIES

Luke

Brett

Dan

Travis

Colt

Garrett

The Hometown Heroes Collection

SINGLE TITLE BOOKS

A Country Wedding

Journey Back to Christmas

The Growing Season

Pattern of Deceit

Rodeo Daughter

His Favorite Cowgirl

NOVELLAS

The Billionaire's Convenient Secret

A Reason to Remember

Find all Leigh's books at:

leighduncan.com/books/

Want the inside scoop on Leigh's next book?

Join her mailing list for release news,

fun giveaways and more!

leighduncan.com/newsletter/

Acknowledgements

Every book takes a team effort.
I want to give special thanks to those who made
The Gift at Sugar Sand Inn possible.

Cover design
Chris Kridler at
Sky Diary Productions

House photo used in cover illustration
Taken by Jerrye and Roy Klotz via Wikipedia,
licensed under Creative Commons
(link: https://creativecommons.org/licenses/by-
sa/4.0/deed.en)

Editing Services
Chris Kridler at
Sky Diary Productions

Interior formatting
Amy Atwell and Team
Author E.M.S.

About the Author

Leigh Duncan is the award-winning author of more than two dozen novels, novellas and short stories. Though she started writing fiction at the tender age of six, she didn't get serious about writing a novel until her 40th birthday, and she offers all would-be authors this piece of advice: Don't wait so long!

Leigh sold her first, full-length novel in 2010. In 2017, she was thrilled when Hallmark Publishing chose her as the lead author for their new line of romances and cozy mysteries. A National Readers' Choice Award winner, an Amazon best-selling author and recently named a National Best-Selling author by Publisher's Weekly, Leigh lives on Florida's East Coast where she writes women's fiction and sweet, contemporary romance with a dash of Southern sass.

Want to get in touch with Leigh? She loves to hear from readers and fans. Visit leighduncan.com to send her a note. Join Leigh on Facebook, and don't forget to sign up for her newsletter so you get the latest news about fun giveaways, special offers or her next book!

About the Cover

The minute I came up with the idea of writing about four best friends who open a beach-side inn, I knew exactly which house I wanted to put on the covers of these books. With its gingerbread trim and Queen Anne-style architecture, the Wood/Spann house is easily one of the most beautiful homes I've ever seen. Built in 1895 by F.S. Wood, the house is a part of Troy, Alabama's College Street Historical District and is listed in the National Registry of Historic Places. Best of all, it belongs to a member of my very own family!

Aunt Betty, thank you so much for letting me feature your incredible home on the covers of the books in the Sugar Sand Beach series!